# The Last Day of Emily Lindsey

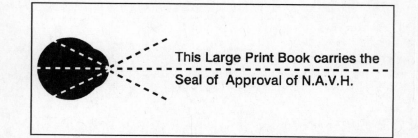

This Large Print Book carries the
Seal of Approval of N.A.V.H.

# THE LAST DAY OF EMILY LINDSEY

## NIC JOSEPH

**THORNDIKE PRESS**
A part of Gale, a Cengage Company

Farmington Hills, Mich • San Francisco • New York • Waterville, Maine
Meriden, Conn • Mason, Ohio • Chicago

Copyright © 2017 by Nic Joseph.
Thorndike Press, a part of Gale, a Cengage Company.

**ALL RIGHTS RESERVED**
The characters and events portrayed in this book are fictitious and are used fictitiously. Any similarity to real persons, living or dead, is coincidental and not intended by the author.
Thorndike Press® Large Print Mystery.
The text of this Large Print edition is unabridged.
Other aspects of the book may vary from the original edition.
Set in 16 pt. Plantin.

---

**LIBRARY OF CONGRESS CIP DATA ON FILE.**
**CATALOGUING IN PUBLICATION FOR THIS BOOK**
**IS AVAILABLE FROM THE LIBRARY OF CONGRESS**

---

ISBN-13: 978-1-4328-4670-1 (hardcover)
ISBN-10: 1-4328-4670-1 (hardcover)

Published in 2018 by arrangement with Sourcebooks, Inc.

Printed in the United States of America
1 2 3 4 5 6 7 22 21 20 19 18

*To Damian, for the morning commute
brainstorming sessions.*

# CHAPTER ONE

*Then*

Here's how the adults tried to protect them:

- locked rooms the size of large closets, on either side of a dim hallway;
- a thick layer of sand on the floor that alerted those in charge to their every step;
- not one but two sets of imposing steel gates, which could only be opened with a single key that was guarded at all times;
- and maybe most important of all — the constant feeling that they were being watched by the tiny, black cameras in the sky, which tracked them while they slept, while they ate, and even while they brushed their teeth.

It wasn't really the sky. They all knew it, even the youngest ones, since no amount of light-blue paint or strategically placed lighting could come close to the real thing, and they'd all seen the real thing at least once or twice in their young lives. When Frank first decided that the ceiling of the children's wing should be painted to look like the sky — so they could "safely and securely experience the beauty of nature" — he'd received overwhelming support from the other adults. But through the years, the dingy clouds that covered the low ceiling served only to mock the children, a reminder of the world they'd never be a part of.

On most days, the locks and gates and cameras truly did feel like protection, and the children played safely and happily within confines they could not quite understand. The rules were the rules, and temptation to break them required an understanding that there could be any other way. The older children occasionally *bent* them — staying awake past bedtime or leaving footprints in the perfectly swept sand as they visited one another secretly in the night. Most days, these small indiscretions were met with nothing more than a slap on the wrist, if there was any punishment at all. The mothers were known to sweep up the footprints of their favorites.

June 2 was not most days.

On this one day every year, the measures didn't feel like protection at all, but rather closer to what they really were: a complex system of rules, procedures, and securities designed to keep the children in their wing, away from the events that took place on the eighth floor. It became essential that the rules, so casually regarded the other 364 days of the year, be treated as law — the mothers turned into different people overnight, it seemed, inflicting the strictest of punishments for the smallest offenses.

Most of the children were careful to heed the rules on June 2. There was no reason not to, since one day was a small price to pay for their relative freedom the rest of the year. They combed their hair neatly and filtered into line when necessary; they were in their rooms when the lights went out, and they spoke in hushed voices. Mothers liked to make examples of troublemakers during this important day, and no one wanted that.

Besides, even if the children did try to break the rules to find out what was going on upstairs, they weren't likely to get very far. Here's what it would take:

First, they would have to find a way to get out of their rooms without being noticed. They would have to take care not to leave footprints as they did this — the mothers would be looking for disruptions in the sand. After tiptoeing to the first of the steel gates, the children would need to open it with a key they didn't have; the gate key swung from the neck of the mother on duty.

Another sand-covered hallway would separate them from the second gate, which would open with the same key. This gate was similar to the first in almost every way, except for one critical difference — the hinges were old and worn, and rust lurked inside every crevice, causing the gate to squeal loudly whenever it opened or closed.

If the children were to get through the second gate unobserved, a moment of celebration would be in order, but not for long. They'd be in a small hallway that offered three ways to get upstairs: the main elevator, the movements of which were constantly watched by security cameras; the stairwell, which required a key for reentry at every floor; and a door that led to a freight elevator, which was typically — conveniently — out of service every June 2.

Regardless of how they entered the eighth floor, the children would have to pass through the heavily guarded main atrium where the evening's events were being held. There were no cameras on the eighth floor, but a guard sat at a desk near the center of the floor, with a view in every direction, for it was critical — absolutely critical — that what took place in the small auditorium at the far end of the hall not be interrupted. If the children did, miraculously, make it by the guards, they'd have to slip into the back of the room without being noticed.

And then, of course — they'd have to find their way back.

Getting caught on the way down would be as bad as getting caught on the way up, maybe worse. Rumor had it that only one child had ever made it all the way up, but he was caught in the stairwell on the way back. He was whipped repeatedly — four lashes on his back for each of the three rules he broke (curfew, stealing a key, and lying) — and the children had been able to hear his cries through the vents in the wall. He'd never returned to the wing, and no one was brave enough to ask why.

Was it worth it? Not for most kids.

But then, just like June 2 wasn't like most days, Jack wasn't like most kids.

It wasn't just that he was quieter and less playful than the other twelve-year-olds. It wasn't just that he was one of the few who hadn't been born there; his mother had brought him to Frank's when he was two, the oldest age children were allowed to come in from the outside.

No, what made Jack different was his careful study of those around him. He noticed things — not just what people said but the *way* they said them, and the way people responded. He noticed the different patterns that each mother swept in the sand and how the second gate didn't squeak as much when you lifted up a little as you pushed. He noticed how at least once a week, Mother Deena sobbed quietly by herself in the back of the cafeteria when she thought no one was watching.

What made Jack different was that he knew that whatever happened upstairs every year on June 2 was the reason that his mother — his *real* mother, not the glassy-eyed women who smiled and called him *Son* — had disappeared two years earlier. What made him different was that despite all of the reasons that he couldn't, and shouldn't, try to get upstairs to find out what happened to her, he knew that he could, and that he would.

Was it worth it?

Of course it was.

# CHAPTER TWO

*Now*

Before Emily Lindsey, I would have said that the line between a person who murders and one who does not should be heavy. Thick, defined, and resolute. That the deliberate act of taking another person's life should separate you, quite firmly, from all the rest.

Before Emily, I might have said that people's dreams and nightmares were theirs and theirs alone — that no matter how terrible or terrifying, ridiculous or absurd, dangerous or inappropriately erotic, dreams were, at the very least, private. Personal.

I may even have said that people can surprise you only as much as you let them and that you can know almost everything you need to know about a person if you get one good, solid look into their eyes.

But again, that was before Emily Lindsey.

Before Emily, I would have said a lot

of things.

I've never told anyone about what happens in the prison nightmare.

It's simply not the kind of dream you talk about in detail. You might tell someone about the dream where you die during sex, or lose all your teeth, or piss in a cup on the subway and leave it beneath the seat. Dreams are ridiculous and weird, but for the most part, they're allowed.

That can't be said for the prison dream.

It's not so much the fact that I kill somebody in the dream or that I don't know who I've killed or why I've done it. It's the fact that I do it *so often.* I've had the dream at least a couple of times a week for as long as I can remember. I'm trapped in a small, gated room, the smell of mildew and standing water so strong, it curdles my insides. I want to get out, but really, all I can think about is that smell and how it's so much more than water damage. It's something rotting, someone dead or dying, and I know that if I look hard enough, I'll find out exactly who it is.

Sometimes I do try to figure it out. Not by looking around, because I couldn't bear to see what was surely rotting flesh, but by stretching my foot out to one side or the

14

other. I grip the bars in front of me and search around with my toes, preparing for the moment when they connect with something soft or sticky. I never find anything, and somehow, that's worse.

I'm always a child in the dream, maybe three or four, but my mind is older, keenly aware of the hell I'm in. I stand there, holding the bars, breathing in particles of someone's lost life, and I stare at a small symbol scratched into the metal gate. It's there every night, etched with a key or some other sharp object: a tightly coiled, tornado-like spiral overtaking a small cross. I drag my thumb across it, the rest of my fingers still wrapped around the bars, and the panic rises, because I know that I'm trapped in there, lifelong cell mates with this dead body that I can't see.

But the biggest problem of all is that, deep down, I know I'm not really in jail. This place in my dream is no prison — it's home. As I trail my finger against the final curve of the spiraled symbol and stare out into the dark space, I pray for death so it can all be over and I can begin to rot, too.

Nowadays, I just pray for morning.

I've become better at managing the dreams, but it was a lot harder when I was

15

a kid. As a boy, I spent hours constructing elaborate lies and explanations for why I'd wake up screaming in the middle of the night.

The first time I had the prison dream after moving in with my parents, Nell said I screamed so loudly that she felt her chest rattle, a whole room away.

She'd grabbed the first thing she could find — the rabbit ears antenna from the box TV in their room — and held it up like a weapon as she charged into my room. Mike, her husband, was just a couple of steps behind her and weaponless, but at six foot two, ex-military, and filled with what would easily be recognized today as a shit-ton of seventies tough-guy swag, he didn't really need one.

"What's wrong?" Nell asked breathlessly as she flipped on the light and raced closer to the bed, her eyes alert, even though sleep lines covered her face. She scanned the room and then looked down at me. "Steven? Are you okay?"

It took a few moments for me to leave the dusty prison floor and make my way back to the room Nell and Mike had put together for me in their small, two-bedroom bungalow in southern Wisconsin.

"I'm sorry," I said, the horror of what had

16

happened sinking in, and I remember thinking that I was stupid for upsetting them this early in our relationship. I was nine years old, and it was my third stop in the Douglas County Foster System. I was old enough to know that forever wasn't a guarantee and young enough to keep trying anyway. "I had a bad dream. I'm really sorry I woke you up. You can go back to bed now."

I remember the look of confusion on Nell's face as she put the antenna down and sat on the side of the bed. She grabbed a tissue off my nightstand and dabbed at my forehead before touching the sheets around my belly.

"You're soaking wet," she said, looking back at Mike, who was still walking slowly around the room, his shoulders tense and jaw clenched. He was wearing bright-red flannel pajamas that Nell had bought him for Valentine's Day, but he still didn't look like someone you should mess with. He walked over to the closet and opened it, peering inside.

"You don't have to apologize for having a bad dream," Nell said.

I pushed myself up in the bed so that I was leaning against the headrest. "I know, but you have to go to work in the morning," I said. "I feel really bad for waking you up."

Nell bit her lip, and I think she was trying not to cry. She leaned forward and kissed me on my sweaty forehead.

"We're going to get up and get you something else to wear and change your sheets," she said. "But first, I need you to make a promise to me. I need you to promise that you'll never apologize to me again for something like having a bad dream. I know we're getting to know each other, and it's going to take us some time, but we have a whole lifetime for that. Forget about what I have to do tomorrow. My most important job is taking care of you, and it's a job I'd give up almost anything for. Sleep included."

I didn't say anything, and she stuck out her hand.

"Promise?" she asked.

I reached out from beneath the covers and grabbed it, my small, damp hand engulfed by hers. I nodded.

When Rose, my foster care coordinator, first took me to meet Nell and Mike, I was torn between wanting to keep my expectations low and hoping that maybe, just maybe, I'd made it home. When I first saw Nell, sobbing like a madwoman because she was so happy to meet me, I'd let myself think it was possible, just a little.

The next time I had the dream, they were both there again — Nell, petite and sleepy with her hair wrapped up under the bandana she wore at night, and Mike, huge and stocky, wearing both his bright-red pajamas and his determined scowl. They were there the third time and the fourth time and the fifth time, too.

There wasn't a hint of annoyance, no shared looks, no "what the fuck did we do" under their breath. Nell no longer brought a weapon, but she still looked concerned, and Mike still checked the closet every time, though I think he did that mostly for my benefit.

About a month after I moved in, an entire week went by without any nightmares.

I knew it was a fluke — gaps like that had happened in the past, but the dreams always came back. Nell and Mike didn't know that, though. I heard them talking about it in hushed, excited tones that Saturday morning.

"They're getting better," Nell said, and I stood just outside of the kitchen door, straining forward to hear them. "He hasn't woken up all week."

"That's right," Mike said as he crunched through some cereal. " 'Bout time the poor boy got to enjoy the feeling of a good night's sleep."

"I bet this is a real turning point," Nell said. "In fact, I know it is. I can feel it."

As I scurried back to my room, I felt the panic rising in me. I so wanted to prove her right — *I had to.* I'd only been with Nell and Mike for a short time, but already, I knew it was different. It wasn't just how they handled the dreams. They laughed at my jokes and asked me what I felt like doing on the weekends. Mike watched *Fat Albert* with me, and Nell packed surprises in my lunch. Nell and Mike didn't just love me like parents should; they *liked* me, and that made all the difference in the world. It didn't matter that we didn't look like any family I'd ever seen — Nell slim, five foot one, and African American; Mike massive and Irish by way of Charlotte, North Carolina; and me, a scrawny kid with pale skin, dark hair, and dark eyes who quite obviously hadn't been borne from either of their loins. We were a family, and I wasn't going to let the dreams come and mess that up.

So I got good at hiding them. Really, *really* good.

As soon as I opened my eyes, I'd roll over and bury my face in my pillow and scream silently until the fear subsided. I'd lie there, my face tucked into the fabric that was wet from sweat, tears, and spit, and I would just cry until the images went away. It hurt more than just screaming out loud, but it was worth it. It wasn't a perfect plan by any means — I'd slip and let the screams escape every other week or so — but Nell and Mike thought I was getting better, and that was all that mattered.

Nell asked me about them occasionally. "You haven't had the dreams as much anymore," she'd say. "Only a couple of times a month. That's great."

"Yeah, it is," I'd say and then quickly change the subject, because I hated lying to her.

It wasn't that I didn't trust them or that I didn't believe they wanted to treat me like their own child. But the fact was, I wasn't, and previous experience had taught me that there was only so much they'd put up with. My last foster mother, Belinda, would hover near my bedroom door until the screams subsided, as if she were afraid to get too close to me.

"Are you all right?" she'd ask, one hand on the doorknob, one foot still in the hall-way.

"Yes, sorry," I'd say, and then she'd be gone. That lasted eighteen months.

Before that, it was Billy and Brie, a nice enough couple who "tried to make it work but had to do what was best for everyone involved," or something like that. And before that, well, it's mostly a blur — just visits from Rose at the sterile but nice enough group home.

Nell and Mike were different.

I had to make it work.

Nell tried a few times to get me to tell her what the dreams were about.

"Oh, they're all different," I lied, certain that it couldn't be a good thing that I dreamed about the same dusty prison and the same dead body so often.

Then, right before high school, things got a lot harder.

I was thirteen the first time that the nightmares — or *visions*, rather — happened during the day. I'd be in the middle of a conversation with someone, or just at home watching TV, when suddenly, I'd start to see flashes of distorted objects or people. The visions were rarely about the prison, but I always experienced the same dry mouth and racing heartbeat that I felt in the dreams.

I was at school taking a test the first time it happened. Suddenly, all of the numbers on the paper jumbled together and sat in the middle of the page in a big, curvy heap. I remember staring at the paper for a few moments, sure I'd fallen asleep or that it would go away in a second. When it didn't, I started to panic, and I stood up from my desk, my pencil still in my hand.

"Steven, what's wrong?" my teacher asked.

I pointed at the paper, unable to form words.

Nell had to leave work early to pick me up that day, but she didn't seem annoyed, just concerned about whether I was okay.

"Just a stomachache," I lied as we rode home in the car. "I thought it was going to go away, but it didn't."

"We'll get you home so you can lie down," she said, reaching over and touching my hair.

Later that afternoon, I heard her on the phone with her boss at the clinic, arguing about when she could make up her hours. I made up my mind that day that I would figure out a way to hide the visions, just like I'd done with the nightmares.

It didn't matter what it took. I wasn't going to give them any reason to send me back.

The worst of the dreams happened later that year, when my uncle Baxter was visiting us from Canada. At twenty-nine, Bax was Mike's youngest brother and a real shit, but I was thirteen, and I desperately wanted him to like me.

He didn't share the sentiment.

Bax was sleeping on the living room couch, just outside of my bedroom. On his last night with us, I wasn't able to stifle the screaming in time, and the next thing I knew, I was clutching the wet sheets to my chest and staring at him, Nell, and Mike as they stood at the foot of my bed.

After I changed and they all went back out into the living room, I crept up to the door where I could hear my uncle still talking to my father.

"How often does that happen?" Bax asked.

"It's really quieted down," Mike said. "It used to happen a lot, but now it's every other week or so."

"Every other *week*?" my uncle asked. "Did you try therapy or something?"

"We tried, but I don't think it was helpful," Mike said. I could tell from his tone that he was trying to end the conversation. "I'm going to head to be —"

"I wonder what kind of trauma he went through before he got here," Uncle Bax said, not wanting to let it go. "Do you ever think about that? Did you ever call the adoption agency or whatever?"

"What for?"

"Well, to tell them what's going on."

"Why would we call them?" Mike asked. "Like I said, we tried the therapists, the doctors, and they all said to give it time. The only other option is medication, and I'm not going to put him on anything now. He's too young."

"Well, you should still call them," Bax said. "I'm sure they knew."

There was a long pause, and I wasn't sure if Mike was still there.

"Knew what?"

My uncle lowered his voice, but not enough.

"That they gave you a lemon," Bax said with a chuckle, and I felt my stomach lurch. "No, I'm just kidding. But I mean, that kind of thing doesn't go unnoticed. All I'm saying is that they should have told you what you were getting into. They definitely knew something was up with him."

"Yeah, well —" Mike started.

"But I guess you guys have sort of exceeded the return period."

I remember crawling back into my bed and staring at the ceiling for the rest of the night.

The next morning, Uncle Bax was gone.

Nell asked what happened to him, and Mike looked over at me before answering.

"Nothing," he said. "He just had to leave early for his flight."

"Aww, I didn't get to say goodbye."

I saw them talking later on that day in hushed tones, and I knew Mike was telling Nell about the conversation I'd overheard the previous night.

I didn't hear anything else about it for about a week, but one afternoon, Nell was vacuuming the living room when she stopped and leaned over to pick something up. She held a small, white object in her hand and raised it up above her head, squinting at it against the backdrop of the light in the ceiling fan.

"Mike!" she called out, still staring at the object.

Mike walked into the room. "Yeah?"

"Do you know what this is?"

Mike looked up at the object in her hand for just a moment and then shrugged in his very Mike way. "Yeah," he said. "It's a piece of Bax's tooth."

I saw my mother blink, and her expression went from confusion to surprise to understanding. "Oh," she said simply. And then, as if he'd told her it was nothing but a crumpled, old gum wrapper: "I'll throw it out."

# CHAPTER THREE

Nell's great-grandmother was born in Haiti. Over the years, Nell would toss out various phrases she'd heard her father say when she was growing up — phrases that he'd no doubt interpreted in his own way after hearing his mother or grandmother say them. Nell had visited Haiti only once, when she was six, but she let the butchered proverbs flow from her lips as if she'd made them up herself.

*"Levisy tay-glees,"* she'd say with a shrug whenever Mike or I faced a problem that couldn't be solved. I looked it up one day during college. She was trying to say *"lavi se te glise,"* which translated to something like "life is a slippery land." When I first told them that I wanted to be a police detective, Mike's jaw had locked, and I could see the concern in his eyes. But Nell had just placed a hand on her husband's shoulder and nodded.

"All we ask is that you're careful," she'd said softly. "*Levisy tay-glees.* We don't know what's going to happen, but if that's your dream, then we support you."

The broken proverb was one of the first things she said three months ago, when I called to tell her about the shooting at Glenwood Bank. Actually, that was *all* she managed to say.

I talked her through the critical details.

One, there'd been an attempted armed robbery at a bank in the quaint suburb of Glenwood, about twenty minutes from where we lived. I'd been inside at the ATM when the robber walked in.

Two, I was okay.

Three, he'd shot one woman in the back, but no one had been killed.

And four, the assailant was dead because —

Five, I'd shot him.

That should've been it. That should've been the whole story — tragic certainly, but final.

Instead, I had to tell her the rest, because it wasn't over. In fact, it was just beginning.

"I had one of my episodes."

"What?" Nell choked out. "When? You mean, during . . ."

"Right after I shot him," I said, and I

29

could barely keep my voice from cracking. "Right there in the bank. In front of everybody."

"Oh, Steve . . ." was all she could say.

Life was, indeed, a slippery fucking slope.

I'd spent my entire life hiding the nightmares and the visions, screaming into pillows at night, ducking around corners, and hiding in my car. My parents had found out about the visions near the end of high school, but they'd accepted them just as they did the nightmares. We did therapy, tried medication for a while, and then we all sort of silently decided that this was my lot in life, my big hurdle, my burden to bear.

I'd even developed a simple, three-part test for the visions. Whenever they started, I'd ask myself a series of questions. If any of them could be answered with a yes, it told me that what I was seeing was real; if I got to the end, and all three were nos, chances were it was a figment of my imagination.

One: Can anyone else see it?
Two: Can you touch it?
Three: Does it interact with you?

The nightmares and visions were a part of my life that I kept close, so close, only my parents, my partner, and my ex-wife, Lara, knew about them. And even then, none of them really understood the true extent of it.

Until Glenwood Bank.

After the shooting, *everybody* knew.

They didn't know about the visions, per se. They called it a blackout, a momentary lapse in consciousness.

"He just got really still," I heard one of the bystanders telling a cop on the scene, as if she were describing a wild animal. "He was still holding his gun, but he wasn't saying anything, wasn't looking at anybody. It's like he blacked out or something."

Her words had stuck. I'd been fine a few minutes later, but it didn't matter.

After months of ongoing evaluation, I was down to only six more weeks.

Six weeks of mandatory sessions with the department therapist.

Six weeks of the Douglas County Police Department pumping my partner, Detective Gayla Ocasio, for information about me and my "mental state."

Gayla has known about the nightmares for a few years but not the visions. She's had to wake me from the dream a handful of times, most recently about a month ago, when I fell asleep on her couch after we wrapped up a case. "That is *not* normal," she said, handing me a glass of water and

31

perching on the armrest while I pushed the sweat from my forehead with the palm of my hand. "I tried to wake you up for at least a full minute."

I took a sip of the water and struggled to catch my breath. The sounds, the smell — in the immediate seconds after I woke from the dream, they stayed with me, making it difficult for me to separate the real world from the imagined.

"You're still not going to tell me what it's about?" she asked. "Your infamous recurring nightmare? Not even with everything that's going on?"

I shook my head, pressing the glass to my forehead. "I don't want to talk about it."

"Steve, you said you've had the same dream for the past thirty *years,*" she said, and she cleared her throat, looking uncomfortable. "Not to mention what happened in Glenwood. You're going to have to talk about it at some point. Maybe not with me, but with someone."

"I'm fine," I said, but my hand was still trembling.

"You sure it had nothing to do with the case?" Gayla asked. She was searching for an explanation, anything at all. We'd just wrapped up a double homicide — a seeming gang-related shooting that had actually been a domestic dispute gone bad. Or gone worse, since they're always bad. The jealous husband had murdered his wife and her boyfriend before tagging the house with the symbol of a local gang to remove himself from suspicion. "Seems like the dreams get more frequent when we're in the middle of the case, right?"

It wasn't that. Gayla and I saw each other more when we were on a case, sometimes around the clock, but the dreams were there all the rest of the time, too.

They wouldn't go away.

They'd been there throughout all four years of my marriage. Early in the relationship, Lara had been there with a glass of water, too, her eyes showing both concern and love. But she got tired, as people do. Her career was taking off, and she had a beautiful six-year-old son — she should've been happy. But at least once a week, I woke up beside her, choking on my own screams.

The nightmares were harder to hide when someone was in the bed with you.

I think it was those moments when I hovered between the dreams and real life that had been the hardest on her. When I was fully awake, I could fix things. I could say something to make her laugh, to diffuse the situation. To remind her that it wasn't so bad after all. They were just bad dreams — it could be worse, right? I could have cancer. I could get into some terrible accident and need her to feed me and clean me three times a day. I was her husband, and during the day, when I was fully awake, I could convince her that *people fucking stayed* for things like bad dreams.

But in those shaky moments just after I woke up, I couldn't do any of that. I could see her face. I could hear her voice, sad, tired, and full of the creeping doubt that she couldn't do this for the rest of her days, couldn't mop the sweat from my forehead and pray that my screams didn't wake up Kit, just a room away.

I couldn't stop her from spinning, couldn't slow her down.

"What about Kit?" I'd choked out when Lara made the final decision to leave, the look on her face that of someone who'd made up her mind but felt guilty about it nonetheless. *What about him?* He was her son, not ours, a distinction that meant everything and nothing at the same time. We'd started dating when Kit was fourteen months old, and he was six when we separated.

Maybe I could have done something more than nothing at all, but probably not.

■ ■ ■ ■

As I sat in Gayla's living room sipping from the glass of water, she stared at me as if I were a science experiment. Since the shooting, she'd been trying to link what happened in Glenwood with my nightmares, but I'd convinced her that what happened at the bank was a one-time thing. She seemed to believe it.

For now.

"What do you dream about?" I asked her, desperate to change the subject. "I can't imagine what goes on in your head when you're sleeping."

She frowned, leaning back against the wall. Gayla is thirty-nine years old, five foot six, lean and muscular, with biceps for days and calves that look like half-moons. She'd been a dancer all the way through high school, a fact she rarely talked about but was evident in the graceful, powerful way she moved. I'd seen her take down men twice her size, men who underestimated the strength and coordination packed into her small frame. Her husband, Kevin, is tall and massive, but I'd rather be in a ring with him any day over Gayla.

"What do I dream about?" she muttered,

35

running her hand through her short, curly, reddish-brown hair. Her eyes had lit up, and she leaned forward. "Oh! Buffets."

"What?"

She shrugged and repeated herself. "Buffets. I hate that dream. I'm in this long line, filling up my plate at this party, and it's just overflowing with food. Ham and corn on the cob and meat pies, and my grandmother's *arroz con gandules,* which I haven't had in years. And there's just so much food, and it looks so freakin' good, and right before I sit down to eat it —"

"You wake up."

"Yes!" she said. "You have it, too?"

"No, it was pretty clear where that was going —"

"Shut up," she said, grabbing a pillow off the couch and slinging it at me. She placed a finger on my forehead. "Whatever. I'm guessing that's not as bad as whatever you've got going on up here."

We were both quiet for a moment.

"You sure you don't want to talk about it?" she asked.

"Yeah, I'm sure."

She drew her finger slowly away from me.

*Damn it, Gayla. Don't do it.*

"But . . ."

*Here it comes.*

"I mean . . ."

*Come on. Just say it.*

"At some point, you're going to have to talk about it," she said. "I haven't told them anything about the nightmares, I promise. But if it's in any way related to what happened —"

"It isn't," I said, the lie slipping easily from my lips.

She sighed and sunk down on the couch beside me. "I'm going to have to tell them something."

It was the massive, glittery, top-hat-wearing elephant in the room. It was the perverted uncle or grandma's drinking problem. Completely obvious, incredibly embarrassing, and something we both wanted to avoid for as long as possible.

But Gayla was right.

She *was* going to have to tell them something.

"I know," I said. "But . . . maybe another time."

She sighed deeply and nodded. "Okay," she said. "Another time."

Six weeks.

Only six weeks, or forty-two days, or one thousand hours were left in the ridiculous, ass-backward investigation surrounding whether I was fit for my job.

Six weeks of everyone wondering if it was going to happen again. Six weeks of me having to be more vigilant than ever to make sure that no one knew how bad it was. Six weeks of Gayla asking me to promise I'd tell her about it "another time."

I'd honestly thought I could do it.

Just like the day I heard Nell and Mike whispering about me in the kitchen, I was determined to prove to everyone that I was okay.

Hell, I'd been managing the dreams and visions my whole life. What was six more weeks?

That's what I thought at first.

But it didn't last long.

Because then, on a cool summer night, I walked into a hospital room and met Emily Lindsey.

And just like that, everything — *absolutely everything* — went to shit.

# CHAPTER FOUR

"I know you have as much interest in pop culture as you do in bird feed," Gayla said as we got out of the car. It was a breezy night, and we both hunched our shoulders as we crossed the four-lane street in front of the hospital. "But how in the hell do you not know what *Carmen Street* is? Seriously, that blows my mind."

I opened my mouth to respond, but she cut me off quickly. "And you can save your lame joke about how Carmen Street is a *street* south of Lake," she said in what I guess was a nasal mimicry of me. She shook her head as we headed into McKinney Memorial Hospital. "To think, Emily of *Carmen Street* had *your* name in her pocket. I'm not going to lie: I'm a little bit jealous."

"And deranged, given the circumstances," I said.

The call had come in half an hour ago. Caucasian female, late thirties.

Found alert but unresponsive in her home.

Covered head to toe in blood, holding a wood-handled, clip point hunting knife in her hands.

And if all that wasn't enough, the responding officers had found two names on a Post-it Note shoved in her pocket.

Max Smith.

And Detective Steven Paul, Douglas County PD.

*Me.*

"Emily's blog has been featured on everything from CNN to the *Herald*," Gayla said. "She's sort of amazing."

"I didn't say I hadn't heard of *Carmen Street Confessions*," I said. "I said I don't *read* it."

"Well, you should. You know she's the one who broke the whole Kempton Food Pantry thing. The guys who were trading canned food for hand jobs. They are in *jail* because of Emily."

"Why is it called *Carmen Street*?" I asked. "I mean, given that she lives up in Whitewater. That's nowhere near Carmen."

"That's the thing. Nobody knew where she lived, not until tonight." Gayla's eyes sparkled as we stepped through the sliding doors of the ER. Gayla is an accomplished and successful detective, but she lives for things like gossip blogs, *The Bachelorette* (*not The Bachelor,* for reasons she once described in excruciating detail), and magazines with exclamation points in every headline. "Everyone speculated that she lived somewhere on Carmen, but of course, that could mean anything from Franklin to the lake. Now we know that it wasn't Carmen at all. Hell, until today, nobody actually knew if there really was someone named Emily who worked for the site. Every post was signed by an Emily, sure, but that could've been a team of teenage boys for all we knew."

"Teenage boys writing about neighborhood affairs, corruption, politics, and scandal?"

"You know what I mean. It could've been anyone."

I stared at the bustling ER waiting room as we stepped inside. As we walked up to the front desk, the two attendants looked up.

"Can I help you?" the woman closest to us asked.

"Yeah, I'm Detective Gayla Ocasio, and this is Detective Steve Paul," Gayla said as we flashed our badges. "We're here to see Emily Lindsey."

The woman nodded and stood, walking

around the counter. She led us through the double doors and back into the emergency room, past the triage area. The smell of the ER stung my nostrils; it was the strong scent of a disinfectant or some other chemical mixed with the tangy smell of something decidedly human that it was failing to hide.

The woman led us through a maze of small rooms closed off only by thick curtains that ended three or four feet above the floor. It was warm in the back of the hospital, and I tugged at the collar of my long-sleeved shirt.

Gayla saw me and frowned. "Aren't you hot in that thing?" she asked.

I shrugged her off. "I'm fine."

She slowed in front of one of the private rooms. A doctor stood outside of it, typing on a small computer on wheels. She looked up as we approached. "You're with the police," she said. "I'm Dr. Erica Suda."

We introduced ourselves. "What happened?" Gayla asked, nodding her thanks to the woman who'd led us back.

"They brought her in about thirty minutes ago. Covered in blood. I've actually never seen anything like it. I could barely see her face," the doctor said. "But we cleaned her up, and the crazy thing is that there wasn't a scratch on her."

"Nothing?"

"Nope. Not even a paper cut, as far as we can tell. We're running some tests to see what could be going on internally, but from the looks of things, physically, she's fine."

As she spoke, I turned to look through the small gap between the curtain and the wall. I could make out a mere whisper of woman, sitting straight up on a small cot, facing us. She was older than me — according to the paperwork, a few months shy of her fortieth birthday — but she was so small and frail that she looked much younger. Her eyes were open but unfocused. A thin, white sheet was pulled up to her waist.

We were only ten feet away from her, with just the small curtain in between us, and I wondered if she could hear what we were saying.

"Her husband is the one who found her. He's around here somewhere," Dr. Suda said. "He said he called her aunt in Tampa. No other known relatives — her parents died in a car crash when she was younger."

"What about the blood?" Gayla asked. "You think it belongs to someone else?"

"Well, it's definitely not all hers, if any at all is," Dr. Suda said. "We've sent it away for testing."

"Can we go in?" I asked.

Dr. Suda seemed to expect the question, but she watched us carefully as she responded. "Yes, but just for a few minutes. She's still in shock from whatever happened to her. I doubt you're going to get much right now. You may do better coming back later."

Gayla and I both nodded as she gently pulled back the curtain.

We stepped forward, and suddenly Emily Lindsey of *Carmen Street Confessions* was real, sitting motionless on the bed in front of us. She stared past us into the emergency room, not acknowledging either of us as we walked in. The doctor drew the curtain closed behind us, giving us just a scrap of privacy.

I stared at the woman in the bed. Except for the fact that her eyes were open and her chest was rising and falling from her breath, she might have been *dead.* Her skin was splotchy, her complexion was pale, and her brown hair hung around her shoulders in a dirty, tangled mess. Her eyes were dark, almost black, the skin around them tight and gray. Her mouth hung open, just slightly, as the loud, shallow breaths escaped her. There wasn't a trace of blood left on her, but in the harsh hospital lights, I could almost see the residue, as if it had tinted her skin and seeped its way deep into her pores.

*What happened to you?* I thought, and I almost asked the question aloud. *Why did you have my name in your pocket?*

Emily was wearing a simple hospital gown, the sheet still covering half of her body. I watched as Gayla took a few steps closer to the bed before stopping to look back at me. I nodded, understanding, and hung back near the curtain.

"Emily, I'm Detective Ocasio," she said. "And this is my partner Detective Paul. Can you hear me?"

Silence.

Gayla took another step closer. "Emily? I just need to know if you can hear me. Can you nod your head?"

Still no response. Emily continued to breathe loudly, and her unfocused gaze landed squarely between us at the slit in the curtain that separated her from the rest of the world.

"Emily?" I said from my position near the corner. "I'm Detective Steven Paul. Were you looking for me?"

Emily began wringing her hands together beneath the sheet, and she shook one foot fervently, but she didn't say anything as Gayla approached. The shaking got worse with every step Gayla took, and I thought about what Dr. Suda had said.

"Maybe we should go to the house first and come back," I said.

Gayla turned to me and nodded. "Yeah, I don't think we're going to get anything right now. What the hell happened to her?"

Gayla asked this in a stage whisper, and though Emily didn't say anything, the fidgeting seemed to get worse. Gayla and I both watched her for a moment. Emily knew we were there — she was responding to us — just not in the way we needed.

Gayla tried a final time. "Emily, did someone hurt you?"

But still, nothing.

Gayla sighed and walked back to my side. "Later," she said before opening the curtain and stepping out.

I nodded and turned to follow her, taking one more look over my shoulder.

But I stopped when I saw something on the sheet.

It was a small, dark-brown spot, no larger than a dime.

The small stain had appeared on the sheet above Emily's hands, where she continued to fidget.

On its own, the spot itself wouldn't have been too worrisome. It could have been anything.

The problem was that it hadn't been there before.

*And* it was growing before my eyes.

"What the —" I said, moving back into the room.

Gayla whipped around. "Hey!" she exclaimed.

We quickly covered the steps between the curtain and the bed. I tore back the sheet to expose Emily's hands, and my stomach lurched when I saw what had caused the stain.

Emily's fingernails weren't that long, but they were long enough. She'd use the nails on her right hand to dig a small, jagged hole — not a scratch, but an actual *hole* — into her left palm. Blood pulsed from it, covering her hands, the gown, and the sheets. Her breath was coming out in loud pants now, but she still didn't say a word.

"Shit!" Gayla exclaimed, running out of the small room to get help while I grabbed a tissue from the table beside Emily. I reached for her hand, and she swung it away, droplets of blood coating the air, and she made the first noise she'd made since we arrived: a loud, guttural moan that flooded out of her body as swiftly as the blood flowed from her palm.

47

# CHAPTER FIVE

I was all but dragged out of the room as two nurses rushed in, followed seconds later by Dr. Suda. Gayla walked up behind them and stood next to me at the edge of the curtain, and we watched as the team sprang into action. One of the nurses grabbed Emily's wrist and pressed a large piece of gauze on the wound to stop the bleeding. The other stood at the bedside, one hand on each of Emily's shoulders.

"Mrs. Lindsey, I need you to calm down," the nurse said quietly but firmly.

Emily didn't respond, and she continued to moan, the loud, painful sound exploding from her parted lips.

"What's going on?"

The question came from behind us, and Gayla and I spun around to find a tall man standing there, peering over our heads.

His face was filled with concern. "What happened to her?" He took a step forward, past the curtain, causing the medical team to look up.

"I need you all *out,*" Dr. Suda said firmly.

Emily continued to moan, a deep, haunting sound that seemed as much a protest as it was a warning. Gayla and I took a couple of steps back, but the man persisted, moving even closer to the bed.

"Mr. Lindsey," the doctor said, straightening as he approached. "Please. We'll let you know the moment it's okay to come back in."

The man said something quietly and urgently to Dr. Suda before turning and joining us out in the corridor. One of the nurses stepped forward and yanked the curtain closed behind him.

Emily's husband zeroed in on us. He had jet-black hair that hung low over his forehead, pale skin, and piercing gray eyes, and he was wearing a simple cotton T-shirt under a worn, tan jacket. He was holding a small, red handbag in his hands. He looked back and forth between Gayla and I. "What happened to my wife?"

"Mr. Lindsey —" Gayla started, but he cut her off.

"I went around the corner to make a call. I was only gone for a minute." He sounded frantic. "Who are you?"

"Detective Ocasio and Detective Paul," Gayla said. She reached out her hand, and the man hesitated a moment before shaking it. "We just wanted to speak with her —"

"Who said you could do that?" he asked.

I saw Gayla's jaw clench. "Her doctor," she said. "Not to mention the fact that she's an adult who doesn't need your permission to be spoken to."

His eyes darted to me, and he took a deep breath. His entire expression changed, and his shoulders slumped forward. "I'm sorry," he said, his voice softening. "I just — is she okay?" He turned and tried to peer through the curtain where the moaning continued.

"She scratched herself pretty badly," I said. "But to be honest, we know far less than you right now, Mr. Lindsey."

"It's Dan," he said.

"Can you tell us what happened tonight?" I asked.

Dan blinked and shook his head, his shoulders slumping a little. "I really don't know," he said. "A few hours ago, I was at work. And now, I'm" — he waved his hand around him, the other hand clutching the red handbag — "I don't *know* what."

"At work?" I asked.

"Yeah. I own an HVAC service and repair company. Most of the jobs are at night and on the weekends, so sometimes I have to fill in at off times. I got home around eight. Emily wasn't even supposed to be home yet."

"Home from where?"

He swallowed. "She was on her way back from Madison," he said. "She was up there on assignment. Since Friday."

"What was she doing up there?"

He shrugged slightly. "I have no idea. Everybody keeps asking me that, because they think it might make a difference, but I don't know. Emily doesn't talk about her stories very much, and I'm okay with that. It's what she wants."

Gayla nodded for him to continue. "What happened when you got home?" she asked.

He swallowed again, and I got the sense that he was thinking hard about the words he was saying. He looked down at the ground. "I didn't know anything was wrong at first," he said before looking back up. "I was actually calling her when I walked inside, just to tell her I was home and to see how close she was. But it was on the second or third ring when I got to the door and saw that it was open."

"Completely open?"

"No, well, it was pushed," he said slowly, his eyes shifting back and forth between

Gayla and myself. "But not closed. That's when I started to panic. Part of me knew I should call the police, but I thought maybe I'd left it that way or something, you know, when I left in the morning. It was possible, and I guess I didn't want to believe that someone had broken in. But none of that mattered anymore when I saw the blood."

"You saw the blood before you saw Emily?"

"Yes," he said. "I turned on the lamp in the front hallway, and I saw it on the wall. A big smudge in the middle of the white paint. I didn't know it was blood at first, but I knew that whatever it was, it hadn't been there when I left this morning. I'd made up my mind to call the cops, but by then, I was in the living room, and I saw her —" He broke off.

"And what?" Gayla asked, stepping forward. "What'd you see?"

"She was just sitting there," he said softly, and it was evident that his wife wasn't the only one still in shock. "Not doing anything, not saying anything, but just sitting there on the couch. And the blood was *all over her.*"

"What about the knife?" I asked. "Did you see that?"

"Not at first," he said. "I ran over to her

to see if she was okay, and that's when I saw it in her hands."

"Had you ever seen the knife before?"

"No," he said firmly, shaking his head. "It's not ours. Someone must have broken in with it."

"Mr. Lindsey, is that your wife's purse?" I asked, pointing to the handbag that was still in his hands.

He nodded. "I grabbed it on the way out the door because I knew I would need her ID and insurance information," he said. "Do you need it —"

He stopped as Emily suddenly stopped moaning.

We all turned back to the room, and Dan reached up to pull the curtain back. One of the nurses was taking off her gloves, and she walked out of the room, moving quickly past us. We all stepped forward, peeking in as Dr. Suda and the other nurse leaned over Emily.

She was calmer now, staring straight ahead, using her hand to cradle her bandaged palm. Her chest still rose and fell with every breath, but she was silent.

Dr. Suda looked up and saw us watching them. She said something to the remaining nurse before walking over to us.

"We gave her a sedative, so she should fall

asleep soon. But I think the interview is done for the day," she said.

Gayla and I both nodded.

"What happened?" Dan asked her.

The doctor began to describe Emily's heightened blood pressure and racing heartbeat in hushed tones.

As she spoke, my eyes went back to Emily, who stared past us all, lost in her own thoughts.

*What happened to you?*

*Whose blood was that, and where did you get the knife?*

*Emily?*

*What did you do?*

And then suddenly, as if she could hear my questions, she moved.

It wasn't much, just the quick, slight dart of her eyes toward mine, and in a second, the foggy expression cleared. She stared at me, and in that moment, it seemed that she was incredibly lucid, perfectly aware, and that even if she couldn't hear us, she could see us.

She could see *me.*

"Did you see that?" I interrupted the doctor, stepping forward past the curtain. The nurse by the bedside looked up. I took a couple of steps closer to the bed, Emily's eyes never leaving mine. "Can you hear me?" I asked her. "Emily, can you hear me?"

"Detective Paul!" Dr. Suda said, joining me, and Gayla and Dan followed behind her. "I said the interview is over!"

"I know you can hear me, Emily," I said, stepping closer. "Please, you have to tell us what happened."

She continued to stare at me, but her gaze suddenly became less focused. And then, as if the moment of clarity never happened, she stared right through me again.

"*Out,* Detective," Dr. Suda said sternly.

I watched Emily carefully for a few beats before straightening and backing out of the room.

We all stepped behind the curtain, and Gayla raised an eyebrow but didn't say anything.

The other nurse followed us out and turned to Dr. Suda. "I finished checking her vitals, and she's stable for now," he said. He turned to the small computer station and began typing. After a few keystrokes, he looked up and saw me watching him. The nurse reached out and wheeled the screen around slightly, shielding it from my view.

"Seriously, come back tomorrow, Detectives," Dr. Suda said, looking at me pointedly.

"We will," Gayla said, throwing me a look.

I nodded.

Dr. Suda turned and walked down the hall.

Dan Lindsey stared at his wife through the slit in the curtain. "I really think it would be best if I take my wife home," he said. "She doesn't seem like she's getting better with all these people around."

"That's not going to happen, not until they check her out," I said. "Mr. Lindsey, what do you think happened tonight? Do you have any idea why your wife might have had my name in her pocket?"

He looked surprised. "Your name? You mean you're . . ."

"Yes, I'm Detective Steven Paul, and I work for the Douglas County Police Department. They called us in because of what they found on the Post-it."

Dan opened his mouth and then closed it, staring at me with an expression I couldn't quite read. "I have no idea, Detective. I guess she wanted to talk to you about something, but I don't know what." He shook his head and looked back at the curtain. "Someone must have broken in," he said. "There's no other explanation."

I nodded. "Okay, sure. But problem is, with that amount of blood —"

"Yes, I know," he said, cutting me off. "I

know what you're going to ask, and I don't know. I get it — with that amount of blood loss, where did this mystery intruder go? I don't *know*. I'm just glad she's okay."

"Mr. Lindsey, do you know if your wife might have been making any stops on her way home from Madison?" Gayla asked.

"Not that I know of," he said.

"Was it her first trip there?" I asked.

He blinked. "Her second," he said. "She went a few weeks ago. Maybe for the same story, maybe not. She doesn't tell me those things. Although . . ." He trailed off and grimaced, looking back at his wife through the curtains.

"Although what?" I asked.

He looked back at us and blinked again. "I don't know," he said. "Hey, do I have to tell you this stuff? I mean, just because you're cops? I don't want to if I don't have to. I don't want to say anything that gets Emily in any trouble. She didn't do anything bad. Everyone keeps looking at her like she did, I guess because of the knife, but I know my wife. Something bad happened *to* her. I really just want to take her home."

"We're just trying to find out what happened," I said. "This isn't an interrogation, but everything you tell us can help us figure that out. That's the only way we can help her."

He seemed to think about it for a moment and finally nodded.

"I think she might have still been investigating that one case," he said quietly. "The Griggs one."

"Ryan Griggs?" Gayla asked, her eyes widening. "The pharma guy? But he went insane when she ran the first article on him. Said he was going to get a restraining order against her and *Carmen Street*."

"I know," Dan said. "And she'd backed off a bit, or at least that's what she wanted him to think. But I heard her mention his name on the phone about a week ago. I asked her about it, but she closed up."

"Who is Griggs?" I asked.

"A couple of months ago, Emily posted an open letter on her blog to Ryan Griggs, president of Kelium Pharmaceutical Company," Gayla said. "They make Zoanet, a cancer drug that hit the market maybe seven years ago or so. Apparently, Emily came across a few sources — some patients, some family members of patients — who were convinced that the drug had made them sick."

"As in progressed their cancer?"

"No," Gayla said. "A totally unrelated illness. The patients she described all exhibited signs of blood poisoning after taking Zoanet. Extremely high levels of a chemical called benzene."

"Wow," I said. "Did she have proof? I mean, before she published the story on her blog?"

"No, and that's why she wrote the letter," Gayla said. "After the fourth source came forward, Emily reached out to Kelium to find out more about what was going on. Apparently, she had the door slammed in her face at every turn. The letter asked Griggs to answer her questions and do what he could to figure out why those people were getting sick. She made a point to say that nothing definitive could be said about the safety of Zoanet."

"I'm sure that didn't do much to appease Griggs," I said.

"Of course not," Dan said, stepping closer. "A letter like that would piss anybody off, let alone someone with a temper like Griggs. He left a comment on the blog post about how Emily was scum, her blog was trash, and that his company was only obligated to respond to requests from real journalists. He tried to delete the comment a few hours later, but by then, Emily had already taken a screenshot. She posted *that* story the next day. That's what really set him off." Dan shook his head. "That story had the most hits on Emily's blog," he said with a sad smile. "She was so proud of it."

"But you weren't?" I asked.

"Oh, don't get me wrong. I'm proud of Emily. She's an amazing woman, and she does amazing work," he said. "She's not scared of anything. That's one of the things that impressed me the most when we first met. But don't think I didn't realize that what she did was dangerous. Hiding behind the anonymity of the internet. She thought that meant you could say anything, about anyone. I always told her to be careful."

There was something about the way he said that last sentence that bothered me, but I couldn't quite put my finger on why.

"So what happened to Griggs?" I asked.

"He's managed to stay out of the limelight for a few weeks. I think his board of directors gave him a firm talking to," said Gayla. "And if they were responsible in some way for what happened to those people, there's no doubt that, by now, they've buttoned up anything that was left hanging out. But Griggs did post that he'd take action against slander. That seemed to quiet things down on *Carmen Street.*" She turned to Dan. "You say you heard her talking about him recently?"

"Yeah, she was whispering on the phone," he said. "Couldn't have been more than a week ago. I don't know who she was talking to, might have been her webmaster. When I came in, she hung up."

"Who is her webmaster?"

"I forgot his name," he said hesitantly. "You can contact him through the site, I think."

The nurse finished up on the computer and walked over to us. "Dr. Suda has asked me to give you a call tomorrow to let you know when you should come back," he said sternly to Gayla and me, and I could tell he was looking for us to challenge him. "If you give me your number, I'll give you a call."

"Sure, no problem," Gayla said.

The man patted his chest pocket and then spun around, looking at the small table next to the computer. "Where's my pen?" he asked.

A full breath passed before anyone reacted. Gayla moved first, ripping back the curtain to Emily's room. When she did, we all froze in shock.

Emily sat in the same place, perfectly still, but she was looking down at her hands.

In them, she held the nurse's black, ballpoint pen.

"How the hell did she get that!" the nurse exclaimed, racing back toward the bed.

He was reaching to grab the pen from her hand when I stopped him.

"Wait," I said.

I stared at Emily as she sat there quietly in the bed, the pen dangling from the fingers on her bandaged hand. She wasn't smiling exactly, but the corners of her mouth were lifted slightly, and she stared through us as we moved farther into the room.

As I surveyed the scene in front of me, my heart skipped a beat, and I suddenly felt light-headed as I saw what she'd done with the pen.

In the few minutes that she'd been left alone, Emily hadn't been hurting herself — she'd been *drawing*.

Little scribbles on every inch of blank space that surrounded her.

The bandage on her hand.

The fresh white sheet the nurse had placed on her lap.

Even her own pale skin.

Not random scribbles but perfectly uniform drawings of the same shape.

A symbol.

I swallowed, the blood rushing to my face, and I tried to force myself to calm down.

To look around the room.

To remember my questions.

*One: Can anyone else see it?*

I turned to look at Gayla, Dan, and the nurse as they all took another step forward.

"What the hell is that?" Gayla asked.

I blinked, certain I hadn't heard her right.

*They could all see it?*

The minute I'd seen the symbol, I'd actually hoped it was one of the visions. I'd felt the small room begin to close around me, tasted the rotting air in my mouth, felt the steel bars just inches from my face.

Emily had drawn the tornado. Thirty of them or so, to be more precise.

Each wound tightly around a small cross.

The exact symbol I'd seen in my nightmares for years.

And *they could all see it.*

# Chapter Six

"Steve?"

*I think I'm screaming.*

"Steve?" Gayla asked. "Are you okay?"

*What is that noise? Am I screaming?*

I reached up to touch my mouth and breathed a small sigh of relief when I realized that my lips were pressed together.

*If it was me that was screaming, it wasn't out loud.*

"Steve, what's wrong?"

*You need to respond to her.*

"Steve!"

"Yeah," I said. "Sorry."

I blinked and looked over at Gayla. She was standing by the curtain, holding it open, and watching me with a curious expression. It took me a moment to realize that she was waiting for me to follow her.

"You coming?" she asked.

I looked back at Emily. A team of nurses had surrounded her again, one quickly grabbing the pen from her hand. Emily was still staring off into the distance with a slight smile on her face.

"Yeah," I said again and turned to follow Gayla out of the room.

"You all right?" Gayla asked me.

I swallowed, feeling light-headed and hot. "Yeah, I'm fine," I said.

She didn't seem convinced. "Were you having a blackout —"

"No!" I said, and I took a deep breath and shook my head. "Sorry. No, I'm fine. I just don't know how we missed the pen. That could've been dangerous."

My voice sounded choppy and robotic, and I was sweating profusely, but Gayla seemed to accept it, at least for the moment.

"Yeah, it definitely could have been. I'm glad she was just using it to draw. What the hell do you think that drawing was? Some kind of code?"

*Game face, Steve.*

*Do not blink.*

*Did you just blink?*

*Shit.*

"I don't know," I said. "Could've been nothing. Maybe she was just doodling?"

"I got a pretty good look at it. We should get it down." Gayla walked quickly over to the nurse's station and asked for a piece of paper and a pen. I watched over her shoulder as she began to sketch the symbol. It was a decent rendition, and she turned the paper toward me, holding it up.

"Pretty close?" she asked.

It was close, but not quite right. The top of the tornado was too wide, the proportions off on the cross.

But all I said was, "Yes, that's it."

Gayla turned toward Emily's room as if she wanted to go back for another look, and I reached out for the paper.

"We should probably head toward the house," I said, taking it from her. "Let the medical team take care of that and come back later."

Gayla seemed to think it over for a moment. "You're right. That'll do for now," she said, gesturing to the paper in my hands. "Let's go."

Before we left the area, I took one final look back at Emily's room, where the curtain was still slightly parted. But the nurses were crowded around the bed, and I couldn't make out her face.

I turned and followed Gayla back out into the waiting room.

A few minutes later, we were in Gayla's car, heading toward the Lindseys' home. With one hand on the wheel, Gayla gestured fervently with the other as she laid out her concerns about the case. I sat there silently, staring out the passenger window, trying to remind myself to contribute to the conversation every now and then. Gayla gets offended by too much silence.

"Why would two people be in a confined space and not speak to each other?" she once asked after being ignored by a woman in a mall elevator. I overheard her telling the story about the "elevator bitch" to three different people that day. "I asked her how her day was going, and she just smiled and looked down at her phone. I watched her. She wasn't texting or checking her calendar or anything! Just staring at the home screen for the whole elevator ride so she wouldn't have to answer me. Who does that? If you're going to use your phone to ignore somebody, at least have the decency to swipe to the right a few times."

As we sped through the street toward the Lindsey home, I let Gayla carry the conversation, adding an occasional "ummhmm" or other sound of agreement so that I wouldn't become the subject of her story about the "car bitch."

It was times like these that I was thankful to have a talkative partner, since I could barely focus after what had happened at the hospital.

"There's something about him that I don't like," Gayla said, making a turn onto a busy street. "I don't know what it is, but something doesn't sit right."

It took me a minute to realize that she'd stopped talking.

"Who, the husband?"

"Yeah," she said, looking over at me as she braked at a stop sign. "You didn't get a weird vibe? Like he was pissed at us for trying to help her, but trying to cover it up by being helpful?"

"Not really," I muttered, and I couldn't think of anything else to say. The symbol that Emily had drawn on her sheets was dancing in front of my eyes, clouding my vision, and I still struggled to take full breaths. It hadn't been a hallucination, I was fully convinced, and yet there was no other explanation for it. The moment I'd seen it, I'd felt as if I were being dragged back into the dream against my will — in front of an entire room of onlookers.

As I sat there in the passenger seat, I felt the familiar crawling feeling in my limbs, and the urge to scream was overwhelming. I took a deep breath. I needed to get back to the hospital, alone, and find a way to talk to

Emily when her husband wasn't around. That wouldn't be easy, but I'd have to find a way.

Did she dream about it, too?

Was it just the symbol or the prison, too?

What about the smell? Did she dream about that awful smell?

"Don't you think?" Gayla asked.

I sat up straight. I was being the car bitch. I blinked, looking over at her.

"Think what?"

"That he was hiding something from us," she said. "That he was more concerned about getting us to leave than he should have been."

"Maybe he knows more about what happened than he's letting on," I said.

She nodded, glancing at me for a second before turning back to the road.

"Maybe he had more to *do* with what happened than he's letting on," she said.

"Yeah, but the fact of the matter is that there wasn't so much as a scratch on her. So whatever happened, it didn't exactly happen *to* Emily."

"Something happened to that woman," Gayla said. "Whether there's a scratch on her or not."

We turned onto the block of the Lindsey home just after 11:00 p.m. Gayla and I both squinted as we drove toward the barrage of police cars that lit up the night sky, bringing chaos to the otherwise serene suburban street.

The Lindseys lived at the end of a block filled with modest two-story homes. Its position made the home feel rather private, since there was a house on only one side of it. The other side was flanked by large trees and opened into a sprawling park and golf course.

The home was a redbrick structure with a large wraparound porch and red painted door. In the dark and under the glow of the police lights, it seemed that the home was covered in blood, marred by whatever it was that had happened inside earlier that night.

Gayla swerved next to the clustering of police cars and stopped the car.

We both stepped out, and I took a deep drag of the clean, cool air, thankful for its calming effect, however temporary.

*Think, think, think.*

I needed to clear my head and focus on the rest of the case. Maybe the symbol was just an odd coincidence.

But she'd had my name in her pocket . . .

Nothing about this was a coincidence.

And I wasn't going to find out anything if I couldn't get past the first hospital visit.

Gayla and I stepped closer to the home, navigating the police cars and people. The scene was filled with quiet activity — about a dozen or so people moved around, focused on their tasks, not speaking to each other. There were a couple of neighbors milling around, and a few standing on their front porches, but not many. Most people had retreated to their homes, closing their doors — and their minds — to whatever horror was going on next door. They'd read about it in the news later or hear slightly embellished details from a friend, but for now, they crouched behind closed doors, praying that they wouldn't be dragged into it.

Gayla and I walked through the grass toward the front door. A tall man was standing at the top of the steps facing the street, surveying the scene in front of him. We'd ascended the steps and were only a few inches from his face before he blinked and turned to us, as if seeing us for the first time.

"Detective King?" Gayla asked.

"Derrick," he said and nodded. He held out his hand, and we both shook it. He turned to me. "You Detective Steven Paul?"

I nodded. "What else can you tell us about what's going on here?"

He shook his head. "Not too much. We're glad you're here to help us out. When we found the Post-it in her pocket with your name, we knew we had to bring you in. What about Max Smith? The other person she wrote down. You heard of him?"

"No," I said. "I don't think so. Any chance there's another Detective Steven Paul out there somewhere?"

"There are two," he said. "One in Camarillo, California, and another who died three years ago in a shootout. We're looking into both of those, but the fact that you are alive and well and only thirty minutes out of Emily's district seems to say a lot."

"So she was found here, by her husband?" Gayla asked.

"Yep. He got home and found her sitting there. Her laptop is missing from her office. There are old files and articles all over the place but no laptop."

"Is that how you knew she was the *Carmen Street* woman?"

"Yeah, one of the detectives put two and two together, and her husband confirmed it." Derrick shook his head. "Our own little celebrity. I always knew that Emily of *Carmen Street* had to be right here in our own community."

Gayla's eyebrows shot up, and the man shrugged. "What? My wife reads it."

We followed him across the porch and

toward the door.

"Any news from the hospital?" he asked.

"Nothing," I said. "She's not saying a word, and she howls whenever anyone gets close to her. We're going back there in the morning."

Derrick nodded. "Before we go inside, do you see what's missing here?"

Gayla and I both scanned the outside of the house — the driveway, the street in front of the house, and the open garage where two officers were standing, talking to one another.

The *empty* garage.

"No cars," I said. "How did she get home?"

"We don't know," Derrick said. "Mr. Lindsey drove himself to the hospital. That's why his car isn't here. But that still doesn't explain where Emily's car is or how she got home tonight from Madison."

"What does she drive?" I asked.

"Black SUV," he said. "Dent on left side of back bumper, according to the neighbors."

"Nobody saw her get dropped off?" Gayla asked.

"Nobody seems to have seen anything," he said. "Except for the neighbor who came over when Dan found her. We've already taken her statement, but you probably want to go over there."

"What neighbor?" Gayla said.

"Jane Paxton," Derrick said. "Right next door. She stopped by to see Emily and saw what was going on. She was the one who called the police. She was pretty hysterical when we first got here, and I think she's smoked an entire pack of cigarettes in the last hour. I already got her statement, but feel free to drop by if you think it will be helpful."

We nodded and followed Derrick into the house. The first thing I noticed was the smell. The home smelled clean enough, but there was a tinny undertone, a metallic, biting scent that made me wrinkle my nose as we stepped through the threshold and into the narrow foyer.

All of the lights were on in the house, and there were a few police officers and crime scene detectives milling about. The Lindseys were obviously doing pretty well — the home was tastefully decorated, with ivory walls, a plush floor runner, and expensive-looking art on the walls.

It was obvious that, on most days, the Lindseys' home was well kept, well designed, and impressively put together.

Today, the sight was stomach turning.

Everything in the foyer — the rug, the walls, the light switch — was covered in thick swipes of crusty, dark-brown blood.

"Careful," Derrick said as we navigated the evidence.

Gayla didn't get upset easily, but she was dead silent as we walked through the house.

"What the hell happened here?" I muttered. There was a lamp toppled over in front of a broken mirror, and shards of glass were everywhere.

"Something really, really bad," Gayla said quietly, navigating through the hall as we moved toward the living room.

And that's when we learned that the hallway was just the beginning.

We both actually gasped out loud as we turned the corner into the living area. The pale-green couch was covered in the same deep-brown stains, the cushions soaked through with the blood. It was smeared on the armrests and the carpet right in front of the couch.

I let my eyes roam the rest of the room, and it took me a moment to realize what was wrong with it. "There's no more blood," I muttered, looking at the pristine dining room table on the far side of the room. The rest of the space was remarkably clean. Gayla's gaze followed me around the room. "It's all so . . . contained."

"You're right," she said as she breathed out. "There's blood in the foyer, leading up to the couch, and on the couch itself. Does that mean that she walked in and —"

"And went straight for the couch," Derrick said, walking up behind us. "There's no sign of blood anywhere else in the entire house. Given the amount of blood on her when we found her, we'd know if she'd gone somewhere else."

"Why would she come and just sit down?" Gayla asked. "I mean, she had to know that her husband was going to find her like that. Maybe that's what she wanted?"

"Doesn't look like she was doing too much intentionally," I said.

"Putting the on-the-scene report together with what the husband told us, it looks like she got home, stumbled to the couch, knocking a ton of stuff over on the way, and sat there until he got home," Derrick said.

"No clues about where she got the knife from?" Gayla asked.

"None. Husband said he'd never seen it before. Not much reason for either of them to have a clip point, that's for sure."

"What is it for, anyway?" I asked, and I saw Derrick hesitate.

"It's, uh . . ."

"It refers to the edge of the blade," Gayla cut in. "Clip point blades are usually thinner at the end, which makes it easier to stab and remove from game. That's compared to other types of hunting blades that are thicker and made for setting up your camp, cutting wood, and things like that."

We both stared at her, and she shrugged. "What? Kevin and I go camping three times a year."

"I'm going to look around upstairs," I said.

Gayla and Derrick nodded.

As I climbed the steps, I frowned as a familiar sensation flooded over my body.

*Shit.*

*Not here. Not now.*

My vision became blurry, and I wrinkled my nose as the smell — the rotting, decaying smell of my nightmares — washed over me. I paused, my heart speeding up, my hands clenching at my sides.

*That smell.*

I swallowed and kept going.

The walls of the stairwell were lined with art, which lent a certain modern beauty to the house. But it was noticeably absent of any of the things that made a house feel like a home — group photos, shot glasses from vacation, books with a piece of mail stuck in them to save the page. The Lindseys had only lived there a few months, and it showed.

I reached the landing on the second floor and paused, trying to ignore the tightening in my chest and breathing shallowly out of my mouth. The smell seemed stronger now, and even though I knew it was all in my mind, I looked around for the source.

*Ignore it.*

But the symbol was clouding my vision now, the tornado-wrapped cross, plastered all over Emily's skin. I swallowed and walked into the master bedroom and took a look around. It looked as though it hadn't been touched since Dan Lindsey left for work that morning. I stood in front of the bed, examining it.

The dark-green comforter was pulled up to the top of the bed. On one side of the bed, the nightstand held an alarm clock, a half-empty glass of water, and a pair of reading glasses.

On the other side of the bed, there was a matching nightstand, and it held —

A lamp.

And nothing else.

I stepped closer and drew my finger across the base of the lamp, leaving a streak in the dust.

I had an inkling of what it might mean, and I walked quickly over to the master bathroom to test it.

If my theory was correct, there'd only be . . .

One toothbrush.

I picked it up and stared at it for a moment.

It wasn't much, but it was something. I walked quickly out of the bathroom and then out of the master bedroom. There was a spare bedroom across the small hallway, along with an office and another bathroom. I stepped into the bedroom and frowned at the piles of boxes on the bed. It was obviously being used for storage at the moment. I walked back into the hallway and into the office. It contained a desk and chair, along with a couch. I walked over to the couch and looked around.

Bingo.

Sitting on the carpet halfway under the couch was an alarm clock. And it was still plugged in.

Emily and Dan weren't sleeping in the same room.

I walked into the guest bathroom and turned on the light.

I stopped abruptly, the smell suddenly making me queasy. I blinked a few times, the pictures of the cell, the steel bars, hovering in front of my eyes, and I stumbled backward. I took a deep breath and stepped farther into the room. For a house that was relatively clean, the spare bathroom was not — it was obviously the most used. The white porcelain sink was covered in dirt, used makeup wipes, and black smudges that looked like spilled eyeshadow. It was also covered with products — combs, makeup, moisturizers.

And, just like I'd expected, another toothbrush.

The smell was too overpowering, and I stepped out of the bathroom. I turned to head back downstairs. I needed some air. As I reached the bottom of the steps, Gayla and Derrick were talking about something near the patio door. I headed toward them but stopped as I looked over at the living room couch again.

As I stared at the bloodstains that covered it, I felt the telltale dryness in my throat that let me know that something bad was about to happen.

"Do you smell that?" I asked.

They looked at each other and then back at me before responding.

"Smell what?" they asked at the same time.

*Shit.*

*Not here.*

I blinked a few times as the couch began to swell in size. I swallowed.

*Not now.*

Derrick and Gayla were only inches from me, and they were still talking, but slowly, their voices began to fade away.

I kept staring at the couch, and I clenched my hands into fists at my side. The cushions continued to expand, right in front of my eyes.

Puffy and blood-filled, the mattress stretched and distended, and I fought the urge to turn and run out the room.

*Fight it.*

But it was too late. The vision was taking over, and I knew that I was going to have to flee. I took a step back and choked on my breath. Out of the corner of my eye, I could see both Derrick and Gayla looking up at me, expressions of concern on their faces.

"Steve?" Gayla asked.

*Breathe.*

*It's not real.*

But the couch continued to swell, pulsing with each of my heartbeats.

"Steve," she said again. "Are you okay?"

I looked at her and nodded, but the couch was still morphing behind her head. I fumbled in my mind for the checklist.

*One: Can anyone else see it?*

A resounding no. There was a massive, blood-filled couch expanding right behind them, but neither Derrick nor Gayla seemed to notice it.

*Two. Can you touch it?*

Even though I knew they were watching me, I reached a hand out, because I had to be sure. The couch was expanding quickly, and now it was only inches from me. I reached out to touch it but connected with air.

*Of course you can't touch it.*

"Steve?"

I didn't need part three of the test to know that it was time to get out of there. My chest tight and tongue chalky, I looked over at Gayla's and Derrick's worried faces.

"Is everything okay?" Derrick was asking me, stepping forward, now shoulder to shoulder with Gayla.

"Yeah, sure," I said, and my voice didn't sound like my own. "I just need a moment. Got to . . . got to step out and make a call."

They stood there, frozen, as I turned and stumbled back through the hallway and out the front door.

Once I was outside, I gulped in the fresh, clean air. I reached into my pocket and pulled out a tin of mints from my jeans pocket. It was a trick I'd learned a while back — the cool sensation helped to relax me. I popped a couple in my mouth and let them sit there a moment. I stared at the people milling about on the front lawn; none of them were looking at me, but I still felt exposed, bare. I turned around and saw Gayla walking down the front steps alone.

"Hey," she said.

"Hey," I responded, and even though I knew it didn't make any sense, I swallowed the mints quickly. "Sorry about that."

"You want to talk about it?"

"It was nothing, really."

She stared at me for a moment and then pointed to the house next door. "You ready?"

"Yeah." I nodded, not returning her eye contact. "Of course. Let's go."

# CHAPTER SEVEN

As we walked across the lawn toward Emily's neighbor's house, Gayla watched me the way you watch a group of kids playing too close to the street. You drive by slowly, just waiting for the ball to roll out in front of your car and for one of the kids to dart off after it.

"You sure you're all right?" Gayla asked slowly, squinting as if that would help her see inside my head and catch me before I ran into traffic.

I plastered on the most convincing smile I could muster and nodded. The crawling feeling in my arms and legs continued, and I used my right hand to gently rub my left forearm. Sometimes, the tingling was so intense, I could barely focus. "Yeah, I'm fine," I said. "Just needed some air."

"Was it —" She lowered her voice. "Was it one of the blackouts?"

I took a long, slow breath, my jaw

clenched, and shook my head.

*That word.*

"Nope. Just the air thing. That I just mentioned . . ."

Gayla had asked me that question at least two dozen times since the shooting. She asked me on days like this, when there was actually some truth to it, but she also asked on days when I looked tired, or wasn't smiling enough, or took too long to respond to a question.

I'd echoed the word *blackout* only one time, but it had stuck, *hard.* The word fell from my lips during a therapy session two days after the Glenwood Bank shooting. I was sitting across the desk from Dr. Mary Cain during one of our mandated follow-up session.

"You understand that this is just a routine evaluation after what happened on Tuesday," she'd said.

"Yes," I'd responded. "I understand."

"Good." Her hands were crossed on her desk in front of her. There was an open file folder beside them, but she hadn't looked down at it once. "Thanks to your quick action that day, the assailant, Vincent Crane, was killed on the scene, and no innocent lives were lost. The only injury was that of the teller, Patricia. She owes you her life."

I nodded. I was tired of that phrase, too. Pat didn't owe me anything. But all I said was "Yep."

"So how have you been?"

"How have I been?"

"Yes. Since the incident."

I spread both hands in front of me, not sure how to answer. "I've been okay," I said. "Not, you know, amazing. But okay."

She nodded in her slow, deliberate way. "Are you ready yet to tell me about what happened after the shooting?"

"Nothing happened," I said. "It was just, you know, a lot of stress, and I just . . . I needed a moment."

"You were unresponsive," Mary said. "That's what the officers said. Right after you took Crane down, you just stood there."

I'd practiced a hundred answers for her, but in the moment, I just wanted her to stop talking about it. I couldn't tell her that the moment my gun went off, the visions had started — the bullet fragmenting into millions of tiny pieces and hurtling not at the perp but right at me. I'd frozen, raising my hands above my head to shield myself. I still remember rocking back and forth, fumbling through my three-part test as everyone else rushed toward Patricia.

"I was tired, and my adrenaline was high,

and I guess I blacked out a little," I said.

"You blacked out?"

"Not really. I mean —" I took a deep breath. "I'm not sure."

"Does that happen often?"

"No," I said, and it was partially true. I never blacked out, but the visions happened all the time. I could always tell when they were coming, and I knew how to excuse myself, pop a couple of mints, and slow my breathing down.

"We're going to ask Gayla to watch out for any signs of the blackouts and keep us updated, okay?" she said.

I started to protest, but she shook her head.

"This is coming from the chief, so there's no point in arguing it."

The chief of police, Ben "Brick" Peters, was not the kind of boss you questioned — he rarely changed his mind, and he was even less inclined to do so if he felt pressured. Brick was known for his loud, booming voice, his quick temper, and his ability to silence a room just by walking into it. He'd gotten his nickname because someone once said that talking to him was like talking to a brick wall — you could never win an argument with him.

Brick had taken it as a compliment.

Mary was right about one thing — there was no point in arguing it.

Gayla was quiet as we made our way across the property. There were even fewer people milling around now. The handful of neighbors that had been outside when we arrived had all gone back home. There were only two police cars left out front. Even with the scattering of people left, it was remarkably quiet, as if someone had pushed a Mute button on the night and everyone was treading as lightly as possible.

As we stepped onto the neighbor's property, Gayla turned to me. "Whenever you want to talk, you know I'm here for you."

I knew that she was genuinely worried about me, but that didn't make her prying any easier. I nodded and hoped we could put the whole thing to rest, at least for the night.

The Paxtons' home was similar in structure to the Lindseys', and they'd both obviously been built around the same time, maybe by the same developer. We walked up the steps and crossed the porch. I could see that the lights were still on in the home, which wasn't too surprising given all of the activity next door. Gayla and I stood side by side as she pressed the doorbell and waited.

A moment passed, and I heard a noise on the other side of the door.

It swung open a few seconds later, and we stood eye to eye with a petite, nervous-looking woman.

"Yes?" she said. The woman was in her thirties, wearing a long, light-blue bathrobe, and she folded her arms across her chest. There was a cigarette hanging from her fingertips, and it shook slightly, giving away her nervousness. Her long, brown hair was pulled back from her face in a low ponytail.

"Hi, we're with the police," Gayla said, introducing us. "Do you mind if we come in?"

The woman nodded and stepped back so that we could enter. "I saw you when you arrived," she said.

"Are you Jane Paxton?" I asked.

She nodded.

"We know that you already talked to some of the officers on the scene, but we were wondering if we could take just a few more minutes of your time. Sorry to bother you this late."

The woman looked back over her shoulder and nodded again. "How is Emily?" she asked, her arms clinched across her body like a shield. "Is she going to be okay?"

"Emily is at the hospital right now. We just came from there," Gayla said. "She's obviously been through a lot tonight, but it seems like she is going to be okay. We're trying to figure out what happened to her."

"This is so ridiculous," Jane said. "I just . . . I can't believe this is happening."

While she was talking, a man appeared from the rear of the house, wiping his hands on a dish towel. He was tall and thin, and he walked quickly toward us, a mixture of exhaustion and concern on his face. "Hi, Detectives. What can we do for you?" he said.

"Mr. Paxton?"

"Ed," he said.

"We just have a couple more questions about what happened tonight," Gayla said. "Jane, I'm sorry to make you do this again, but you're one of the last people to have seen Emily before she was taken to the hospital. Is there anything else you can think of, that you didn't already tell the officers outside, that might tell us what happened?"

Jane bit on her bottom lip. "Not really," she said. "I mean, I told the other guy, Mr. King? Yeah, I told him everything I knew. I don't know what else I can tell you."

"How close are you and Emily?" Gayla

asked. "Are you two friends?"

Jane seemed to think about this for a moment, and she took a long, slow pull of her cigarette. She dropped her hand to her side and exhaled, the smoke curling its way out of her nose and mouth. "I mean, we're as close as I think she is to anyone else in the neighborhood," she said. "If that means anything. I always try to get her to come out more, to hang out with some of the ladies from the block, but she's very private. I'm okay with that, though." She shrugged.

"What do you mean?" I asked.

"I don't know," she said. "Everyone has their way. I don't think people allow for that enough, you know. You're supposed to be this or that, or outgoing, or funny, or charming, but Emily wasn't like that, and I think it rubbed people the wrong way. She liked being alone a lot more than she liked being with people, which was okay with me. I have a lot of friends. So when she wanted to hang out, she told me, and we did. It wasn't weird for me not to hear from her for a few weeks, too."

"What do you mean, it rubbed people the wrong way?" I asked.

"Oh, nothing serious," she said. "Some of the other ladies in the neighborhood, you know, we have a little girls' club. We get together and go for walks, or watch movies, or whatever. Emily didn't like to do all those things, and I think some of the girls thought she was a little stuck-up. Nothing big, though, just neighborhood chatter."

"Honey," Ed Paxton said wincing. "You're making it sound like —"

"I'm not saying that has anything to do with what happened," she said. "I'm just telling them what the girls thought."

"What do you all think happened to her?" Ed asked Gayla and me. "I mean, you guys have to have some idea, right? Did someone break in? We just got a new alarm system, just in time, I guess. You can never be too careful."

"We're not sure, and we're trying not to make any guesses," Gayla said. "But there was no sign of a break-in. What can you tell us about Emily's husband, Dan? Were either of you close to him?"

"Nah, I never met him," Ed said. "They've only lived there for a couple of months, and the husband's always at work."

"Yeah, he's never home. Emily's always by herself. He seems like a sweet man, though, from what Emily has told me."

Gayla and I glanced at each other. I could think of a lot of words to describe Dan Lindsey after our brief meeting, and *sweet* wasn't one of them.

"She talks about him a lot?"

"I wouldn't say a lot, but she's told me some stories," Jane said. "Since she works from home, sometimes she'll invite me over for a cup of coffee, you know, when she's feeling social. And she'll tell me stories about him, about their honeymoon, things like that."

"Mrs. Paxton, do you know what it is that Emily does for a living?" Gayla asked.

"Uh, she's some kind of consultant, I think," she said, frowning. "Must be nice, because she can work at home on the internet. I've been thinking about looking for some kind of part-time work from home myself."

Gayla looked at me and raised her eyebrows but let it go.

"Do you think they could have gotten into an argument?" I asked. "Have you ever heard or seen the Lindseys fighting?"

"When?" Ed asked. "It's not like they would come and do it on our front yard. We don't know what goes on in people's houses, so we would just be speculating."

"Ed!" Jane said to her husband.

"What?" he asked. "I just . . . Honestly, I really don't think it's our place to get involved."

"They just want our help," she said. She turned back to me. "Look, if what you're asking is whether I think Dan Lindsey could have hurt his wife, the answer is definitely no." She looked at her husband, who rolled his eyes. "You're right, I don't know that," she said to him before turning back to us. "But if you could hear the way she talks about him, the things he does for her . . . Those two are in love."

"Jane, now you're just making things up."

"No, they asked me what I think."

Gayla cut in. "If you don't mind, could you go through what happened tonight once more for us? Every detail matters in a case like this."

Jane nodded and took a brief glance at her husband before responding. "I went over to the house, because Emily borrowed a can opener from me a couple of weeks ago. So I went by to get it back. I didn't know if she was home, but I figured it was worth a try. I went out my kitchen in the back and walked over to her patio door. That's when I saw her."

"What exactly did you see?" I asked.

"I walked up to the patio door, and there was really only one light on in the house. It was dark in there, pretty hard to see." She paused and swallowed as she rearranged her

94

robe and crossed her arms in front of her again. "But then I saw her sitting there. Her husband was standing over her, and she was all covered in something. At first, I just thought it was dirt or something. Just these dark smudges on her face."

"Any reason why you went to the patio door and not the front?" Gayla asked.

Jane shrugged. "I do that sometimes. We both do. My kitchen is in the back of the house, just like hers, and so we usually come in and out that way."

"What was Dan Lindsey doing when you got to the door?"

"Well," she started, biting her bottom lip. "He had both hands on her shoulders, and he was shaking her a little."

"Shaking her?" I asked.

"Not hard, not like that," she said. "Just . . . trying to get her to move. She was like . . . I don't know how to describe it. She kind of flopped around while he was shaking her, as if she wasn't holding her body up, you know? I'm not explaining it right. Point is, I didn't really understand what I was seeing, so I tapped on the glass, and that's when he saw me."

"What did Emily do when you tapped on the glass?" I asked.

"Nothing," she said. "I don't think she

moved at all."

"Then what happened?"

"I waved at him to come over, and when he opened the door, I told him who I was and asked him what was wrong. He looked completely freaked out, which scared me even more. He told me to go and call the police. Said something happened to Emily, and he didn't know what."

"Did you see the knife?"

"Not really?" she said. "When I first saw her through the glass, I could see that she was holding something, but I didn't know what it was. I didn't find out it was a knife until later."

"Did you hear her say anything?"

"Not until he opened the door. She was moaning, like she was in pain. It was horrible."

"So what happened after that?"

"I ran back to my house to call the police. They were here in less than five minutes. By the time they got here, Dan had gotten her halfway into the foyer, but she was fighting him. Screaming. It was horrible. They wouldn't let me get close, but the sound was just . . ." She shook her head. "The cops took over when they got there, and they sent me back home."

"So you didn't interact with her at all?"

Gayla asked.

"No, they told me to stay back. I don't even know if she actually knew I was there," Jane said. "She was so messed up."

"Maybe Emily's not the one who was hurt," Ed said suddenly. "Maybe she did something to her husband. Everyone always assumes the husband had to pull a dick move, but maybe it was her. She's the one with the blood and the knife."

Jane gave her husband a scathing look. "I thought you didn't want to get involved," she said.

He shrugged.

"All right, well, I think that's all for tonight," Gayla said. "We really appreciate your time. If you think of anything else, please give us a call, okay?"

"Yes, of course," Jane said, and she tossed a look at her husband when he didn't respond. "If *either* of us thinks of anything, we'll call you."

Gayla and I stepped back outside and walked slowly back to the Lindsey home. My arm was still tingling, and I rubbed it again. Gayla looked over at me, but she didn't say anything. We'd just reached the Lindseys' front steps when Derrick came walking out quickly, his cell phone to his ear.

"Yeah, I'll let them know," he said before hanging up. "We have to go to the station," he said.

"Why, what's up?" I asked.

"A call came in from a cabdriver. He said he made a drop in this area earlier tonight. Around 8:00 p.m."

"Emily?"

"Yeah, it looks like it. When the cabbie got home and checked his backseat, he found a lot more than loose quarters and lost wallets. He found blood. Lots of it. He's on his way to the station now."

"Let's go," Gayla said.

# CHAPTER EIGHT

*Then*

There were five of them.

There was twelve-year-old Jack, of course, the unlikely leader. When he first told Lill that he wanted to try to get upstairs on June 2, she'd all but laughed in his face.

"Impossible," she'd said. "Sorry, Jack. You're not the first kid to try it, by far. I guarantee, every trick you've come up with has been tried before." Lill was only thirteen, but she added things like "by far" and "I guarantee" to her sentences sometimes, making her sound much older. "Why do you want to get up there so badly anyway?" she asked.

They were sitting side by side in the library, a six-hundred-square-foot room on the compound's third floor. The children were allowed to spend an hour there in the afternoons, after their daily lessons were complete. It wasn't a library in any traditional sense, since it had only a small selection of books that had been carefully chosen by Frank and the mothers and which the children rarely touched. Mostly, they spent their time in the library working on assignments or socializing before dinner.

Lill had been humming softly to herself and working on her warrior project when Jack approached her. The older children had been tasked with defining what it meant to be a female warrior and creating a figure to represent it.

"Our mothers are the strength of our community," Frank had said during assembly one day. "I want you each to create a warrior — modeled after one of our mothers — using tools from the art room. Be creative. We'll display them in the library."

Lill was sketching on a piece of paper when Jack sat down beside her, the soft melody she was humming filling the air. There were a couple of other children in the room, but no one seemed to mind. They were used to Lill singing — she sang in class, in the hallways, in the nursery, and in the children's wing before bed. The mothers all loved her voice and rarely asked her to keep it down.

Jack wasn't sure how to respond to Lill's question about why he wanted to go upstairs. He decided to go with honesty. "Because . . ." he answered, trailing off as he watched Mother Paula, the librarian, approach them. The woman smiled thinly and nodded as she moved past them toward the back of the room. "Because of Mother Breanna."

Lill's expression didn't change, but her eyes softened. She checked behind her to make sure that Mother Paula was out of earshot. "Look, I know how much you cared about Mother Breanna, but she's been gone for two years now. You should try to get to know some of the other mothers. I know it's hard when you build a connection with some of them, but they're really nice, too. Okay? Some people just move on, Jack. You've got to let her go."

Jack nodded, not because he agreed, but because he wasn't the type to argue about things when he knew his mind couldn't be changed. He knew facts, and nothing Lill could say could change them.

Fact one: Mother Breanna wasn't the first mother to disappear. A few years before she left, another woman had disappeared the night of the ceremony.

Fact two: He knew that Mother Breanna was his real mother.

There was an understanding across the

complex that *all* of the adults were parents to *all* of the kids. The mothers knew who their children were, of course, but they weren't allowed to acknowledge it.

"It is our collective responsibility to raise our children in the light," Frank often said at assemblies and gatherings. "That is what a community does. That is how we survive."

Jack had been chastised for referring to Mother Breanna as his real mother, but it was the truth; he knew it. She was the only one who made him feel safe.

Once, when he tripped going up the stairs and banged up his knee, he'd cried for a solid hour for her. The other mothers had tried to console him by pulling him against their warm, suffocating bodies and murmuring soft, rehearsed words.

*You'll be okay.*

*We're here for you.*

"You have to stop, Jack, please," Mother Breanna had said when they finally let him see her. "Frank is already worried about us coming to the family from the outside."

"You mean he's worried about *me* coming from the outside," Jack had screamed. "He wanted you, not me."

"Don't say that!" his mother had said harshly, looking back over her shoulder. "And keep your voice down."

Jack felt bad for making her angry. Aggression wasn't allowed at Frank's — in fact, acting out could be cause for pretty severe punishment, and the children had been taught to tread lightly. Especially the boys.

"You are more likely to suffer from fits of anger and rage," said Frank in one of his frequent assemblies with the boys. "You have to fight your nature. You can't let aggression creep in. You have to work hard to let your strength shine through and to protect the women of our community."

Jack had dropped his head, and immediately, his mother had softened. "I know it's hard, but the others are just here to take care of you, to help me. Frank cares about you just as much as everyone else. I couldn't do it alone, and now we have everything we need, okay?" As she said this, she pulled him close, and he relished in her smell, the familiar feel of her slight frame.

The final fact — the one that kept him going — was that he knew Mother Breanna hadn't just decided to move on two years ago during the June ceremony.

Because if so, she would have said goodbye.

As Jack stood to leave the library, Lill reached out a hand to stop him. "We'll get up there when we're supposed to," she said just before he left. "*If* we're supposed to. I've heard that only some of the adults are invited, so we may never know. But it probably has nothing to do with Mother Breanna, so just let it go, okay?"

Jack looked at her hand on his arm and nodded before turning to walk away. He needed her help — without it, there was no way he'd get upstairs.

Good thing he had a backup plan.

There were eight floors to the building: the basement where the children aged six to seventeen lived; the first floor, which housed the adult quarters and rooms for younger children; the second floor, where there was a large, open cafeteria; the third floor, which was the nursery; the fourth through seventh floors, which contained the library, classrooms, gymnasium, and offices; and, finally, the small auditorium on the top floor.

The gates to the children's wing and elevators remained unlocked for most of the day, only requiring keys and lock codes between 8:00 p.m. and 7:00 a.m.

"We're not animals, for Christ's sake," Jack had overheard Frank saying to one of the new mothers during a tour when she asked him if the gates were locked at all times. "We're just worried about their safety."

Jack took the elevator downstairs to the basement, and with his books in his hand, he opened the first rusty gate and headed toward the bedrooms.

He walked down the sand-covered hallway and paused outside Shy Perry's door, which was partially open. He pushed it farther and stepped inside. Jack watched the boy for a moment without saying anything.

Perry sat at his desk, scribbling on a piece of paper. He was so engrossed in what he was drawing — a platter of fruits — that he didn't notice when Jack walked up behind him and peered over his shoulder.

"Got a sec?"

Shy Perry dropped his pencil and looked up. "Oh, hi, Jack," he said, his eyes wide. "I, uh, I didn't hear you come in. What's up?"

Jack rested one hip against the desk and quietly told the boy what he wanted to do.

When he was done, Shy Perry looked down at his hands and shrugged. "I mean, I'd help you if I could, but I don't think there's much I could do," he said. "What would you need from me?"

Jack smiled, lowering his voice even further. "Well, that's the thing. I'd only need you to do one thing," he said. "All you'd have to do is draw."

Shy Perry frowned. "Really?" he asked. "Draw? That's it?"

"That's it."

Perry looked down at the drawing in front of him. As he did, a slow smile began to spread across his face. "Just draw," he muttered to himself before looking back up at Jack. "I might be able to do that."

Brat and Gumball were next. Jack approached them together, because the twins never did anything alone, and he knew he was going to need Brat's help to get Gumball on board.

"Let's. Do. It." Eleven-year-old Brat had said, closing her eyes and spreading her arms wide as she reclined back in her desk chair. "Yes. Yes. Yes. We are 100 percent in. No doubt about it, green light says go, yes, yes, yes." She looked over at her sister, who was sitting on her bed, watching them while she chewed on a piece of gum. "Right, Gloria?"

Brat was the only person who called her twin sister by her real name. Even the mothers had gotten used to calling her Gumball. The children weren't allowed to eat sweets because of their limited access to dental care on the compound, but sugar-free gum was okay. Once, when the mothers had forgotten to pick some up during one of their weekly grocery runs, Gumball had actually chewed the same piece of gum for six days straight.

"It won't work," Gumball said, finally pausing between smacks to share her reluctance. Gumball was eight minutes older than Brat and genetically predisposed to be the buzzkill. "It's practically impossible to get up there."

"What if I said I figured out a way?" Jack said, looking back and forth between the twins. "A way that I'm sure will work."

"A way to get us upstairs."

"Yes."

"On June 2."

"Yes."

"And back down without getting caught."

"*Yes.*"

Jack had known that question would come up, and he hadn't wanted to lie, so he'd taken the time to figure out a way back downstairs. He wouldn't tell them that he didn't actually care about that part — he just needed to see what was happening up there.

"Come on, Glo," Brat said. "Jack is right. They can't get away with this forever. Don't you want to know what they're doing up there? Why they never let us come up on that one day?"

Gumball shrugged. It was amazing how different and similar the two girls could look at the same time. Gumball's hair was always dirty and matted, her nails clipped short, and her clothing oversize. In contrast, Brat was always neatly dressed, her hair in a long braid. Both girls had the same bright-blue eyes, but the spirits behind them were worlds apart.

"Not really," Gumball said. "There's got to be a reason for the rules, and I'm not interested in getting in trouble. Maybe if you told us what the plan is . . ."

Jack had been waiting — hoping — for that question. He spread both hands out in front of him and shrugged. "I wish I could, but I can only tell people who promise, and I mean really promise, to come on board."

As he expected, Brat practically tumbled out of her seat. "Oh, come on, Jack," she said, rushing to his side and almost knocking him over in the process. "You gotta tell us. What's this plan? How will it work? Have you asked anybody else?"

He pretended to hesitate and looked over at Gumball. "I can't . . ." he said.

Brat followed his gaze and glared at her sister. "Gloria!" she said in a high-pitched squeak, fully earning her nickname.

Gumball looked at both of them and chewed faster on her gum. "I don't know . . ." she said uncomfortably.

"GlooooRiiiiAaaaa!" Brat was nearly screaming now.

Jack hoped none of the mothers were walking by. But he didn't want to interfere now that he'd activated full Brat mode; it just might work.

"But what if we get caugh—"

"Gloria!"

"Ugh! All right, fine!" Gumball said, the gum flying out of her mouth and landing somewhere on the bed. She searched around for it, and when she found it, she reached up and stuck it to the underside of the bunk bed, above her head. She reached into her pocket and pulled out another piece.

"Fine," she repeated as she unwrapped it with shaking fingers. "I'm in. Now, Jack, you better tell us your plan, and quickly, before the poor child explodes."

With Shy Perry, Brat, and Gumball all on board, Jack had to go back to Lill. She was the final piece of the puzzle and the toughest sell. But Jack knew he couldn't do it without her. Brainy, rule-abiding, and well-liked by all of the mothers, Lill was the perfect person to help them avoid suspicion.

Luckily, Jack had one more trick up his sleeve.

And it all depended on Mother Deena.

Jack had been dreaming about getting upstairs for two whole years. But he hadn't thought it was a real possibility until a few months ago, when he had noticed Mother Deena's strange behavior in the cafeteria.

Mother Deena was a quiet and reserved woman. She rarely smiled at the children the way the other mothers did, and she didn't talk to anyone unless she had to. She must've been in her early thirties, but she looked much younger.

Jack had noticed that for the past few weeks, after lunch ended and everyone left, Mother Deena had stayed behind. Even when it wasn't her turn, she volunteered to stay back and clean up the kitchen, sending everyone else away.

Several times, Jack had seen her sobbing, quietly, as she rearranged the chairs at the back of the cafeteria.

He'd trailed behind the other kids, watching her movements, the way she wiped her nose on her sleeve when nobody was looking or rubbed the underside of her growing belly. Jack knew what was going on. He hated to see her upset, but he knew that he could help her — and that she could help them.

On the day that he was to convince Lill to help him, Jack began by asking her to meet him in the back of the cafeteria ten minutes after lunch.

"I can't," Lill said. "I have to go to the library to study before my afternoon classes."

"Please," Jack said. "If you do, I'll stop asking you about the whole June 2 thing."

Lill considered it, packing up her lunch tray. "All right, I'll come by, but just for a moment."

Jack nodded and put his own tray away, moving slowly as he always did so that the room would empty out. He stood by the garbage can, slowly drinking the rest of his milk. He watched as all of the mothers and the other kids headed toward the door. As he threw his carton away, he turned and walked toward the back of the cafeteria.

"Jack?" one of the mothers called out. "Where are you going?"

"My stomach hurts," he said. "I'm just going to ask Mother Deena for some crackers."

The woman frowned, but she nodded. "Hurry up, please," she said before walking out the door.

Jack walked quickly to the kitchen near the back of the room. As he stepped around the corner, he saw Mother Deena leaning over the sink and washing a plate. She was scrubbing it hard, her entire body bent over the sink, and it seemed that it would break in her hands if she washed any harder. After a few moments, she pushed the plate down in the sink and leaned forward, up to her arms in soapy water. She hung her head, and then her entire body shook, and a sob escaped her, quietly at first, then more loudly.

Jack swallowed. This was going to be harder than he thought.

"Mother Deena?"

She gasped and straightened up, turning her head to him. Her eyes were red and puffy, her face covered in tears.

"Jack," she said, sniffling, her arms still in the water. She pulled them out and reached up toward her face, stopping when she realized that they were soaking wet. She paused midair, her hands dripping water onto the floor as tears clung to her chin. "Why aren't you going to class?"

"I wasn't feeling well," Jack said.

Mother Deena cleared her throat, her arms still out in front of her. "Did you go to the nurse?"

112

"Uh, no. I thought maybe I could just get some crackers."

Mother Deena watched him for a moment, and she looked both embarrassed and tired. Finally, she walked over to the other side of the kitchen and grabbed a towel, wiping her hands quickly. She used the towel to wipe her face and then turned back to Jack.

"You should have gone to the nurse," she said, walking over to one of the cabinets. "But okay, let me get you some crackers."

"Thank you," Jack said. He took a step closer. He didn't realize how nervous he would be. "Hey, are you okay?"

Deena turned back to face him, her hand still on the cabinet door. "Yes," she said. "Of course. I'm just not feeling so well today myself."

Jack felt bad for pushing her. But he needed her help. There was no other way.

"Are you sure?" he asked. "Because you were really crying a lot."

Mother Deena's puffy eyes widened. She cleared her throat and dropped her hand to her belly. "I'm just tired, Jack, okay?" she said. "I'm sorry you had to see that. Let me get your crackers so that you can get to class."

"You're not just tired. You've been crying

almost every day for the past couple of months. I've seen you. In the cafeteria, in the hallway. You thought nobody noticed, but I saw you. Almost every day. Something's wrong, and I can help you."

She looked shocked . . . and then mad.

"You're making things up, Jack," she said, her voice angry. "And I don't appreciate that. Thank you for being concerned, but you should not be talking like this."

Jack wasn't ready to back down yet. He knew he should — the only reason he hadn't gotten in trouble yet was because it was so out of character for him.

He had to keep going. He knew he was right. And he knew this would work.

It had to.

"I can help you," he said again.

"What are you talking about?" Mother Deena asked quietly, looking over his shoulder and back into the cafeteria. "Why do you keep saying that?"

"I know why you're crying," Jack said. "You're crying because of Lill."

"What?" she asked sharply.

"And the baby in your stomach."

"What?"

"You're crying because you're worried about them, both of them, and —"

"You don't know what you're talking

about," Mother Deena said, but she'd blanched and reached one hand out to steady herself on the counter. "I'm a mother to every child here, you included —"

"No, your *real* daughter," Jack said. "Everybody knows it. We just can't talk about it. But I've seen the way you look at each other."

She stared at him for a few moments. "So what?" she finally said. "It doesn't matter. I love you all just the same."

"But you're unhappy. I've seen you crying. All the time."

Deena looked down at the ground, and her eyes filled with tears again. "I'm sorry you had to see it," she said. "I've been trying so hard. Really, I have. It's just so hard."

"What is?"

But she wasn't really listening. She stared past Jack. "I just hope he's healthy," she whispered. "If God takes my baby, I understand, but I'm just so scared."

Jack had overheard one of the mothers saying that Deena wasn't sleeping at night, that they could hear her crying through the walls. He knew this was his only chance.

"Lill wants to help you," he said.

Deena's eyes darted back down to him. "She what?"

"She noticed that every time she sings,

you light up. That you seem happier. She wants to help you, to sing for you at night when you're feeling sad. It could help you sleep. It could help you, but . . ."

"But what?" Deena asked, and Jack knew she was interested.

"But of course, if you come down to the wing at night, everyone will see you, and they'll feel like you're giving her special treatment because she's your daughter."

"You're all my —" she started robotically, but she saw Jack's face and stopped. "She's right, you know. I can't come down there. I just can't."

"I told her that maybe you could get her a stairwell key. That way, she could come upstairs and sing for you, and nobody would know. But you know Lill. She said that it was against the rules, and you couldn't do that. She hates to see you so upset."

She shook her head. "You're just a child," she whispered, and the tears welled up in her eyes. "What's wrong with me? I shouldn't be talking to you about this. You're just a child."

The next couple of events happened so perfectly that Jack couldn't believe his luck.

As if on cue, he heard footsteps behind him. The sounds of Lill's humming as she walked along stopped both Jack and Mother Deena in their tracks.

He couldn't stop a smile from coming to his face. He couldn't have planned it better.

The humming stopped, and he heard Lill's voice.

"Jack?"

But by then, the tears were already spilling down Deena's cheeks. As Lill turned the corner, the expression that crossed Deena's face told him everything he needed to know.

He'd done it.

Lill paused as she saw Mother Deena, her forehead scrunching up as she took in her tear-streaked face and puffy eyes. She rushed to Deena's side and grabbed her hand. "Mother Deena," she said. "Are you okay?"

Deena looked up at Jack, who raised his eyebrows.

"Well," he asked. "What do you think?"

As she looked down at the young girl holding her hand, Deena took in a sharp breath and then nodded fiercely, the tears still flowing. "Thank you," she whispered to Lill, who stared at her in confusion. "I'll get you the key for the stairwell if you'll really come sing for me. Nobody will know. Thank you so much." The tears were flowing again

117

as she pulled Lill close. "I haven't slept in weeks. Thank you, thank you, thank you."

As they stood there, Lill stared at Jack over Deena's shoulder, her face filled with confusion and emotion as she hugged her mother back.

# CHAPTER NINE

*Now*

Right before we left for the station, I overheard Gayla telling on me.

Granted, I *had* run out of a crime scene in the middle of an investigation and practically hyperventilated on the front lawn.

Over a couch.

And the tone of Gayla's voice as she whispered into her cellphone was considerably more worried than it was mean-spirited.

*And* we were both fully adults, and at the end of the day, Gayla was just doing her job.

But it sure *felt* like tattling.

Her phone had rung as we were talking to Derrick, and she slipped away with a quick "be right back." I didn't think much of it, since Gayla was constantly taking calls. She hadn't returned by the time I finished up with Derrick, and I headed toward the car to find her.

When I got there, she was standing with her back to me, her shoulders hunched over as she spoke softly into her phone. But not softly enough. I didn't mean to eavesdrop, but her first words stopped me in my tracks.

"You can ask Derrick about it later, too, but I think he had another episode," she said.

I knew instantly that she was talking about me, and I couldn't stop the flood of anger that swept over me. We had just talked about this, and she obviously hadn't believed me. The fact that I had been lying made no difference; she was my partner, and she should *trust* me. I remained silent as I stepped even closer, straining to hear what she was saying.

"No, we were in the middle of a case, and he just got all quiet, turned, and ran out of the house." She paused. "Yes, we're at a crime scene right now. I don't know, Mary. It kind of freaked me out. I thought you should know. I'll call you later, okay?"

There was a conscientious, mature part of me that would have backed away and pretended that I hadn't heard a thing. But the other part of me — defensive, embarrassed, and, above all, hurt that she couldn't have at least waited until she got home — took a sullen step closer.

"Hey," I said, and she whipped around, the phone in her hand, her eyes wide. "Got that out of the way?"

Her shoulders slumped, but she didn't look embarrassed, only concerned. "I'm worried about you," she said as she moved toward the driver's side door. She opened it as I walked around to the other side of the car and got in. She started the car but didn't put it in drive.

"You're not telling me what's going on, and you're lying and saying you're okay," she said. "When I know you're not. I had to do something. Are you ever going to tell me what happened back there?"

"I already did," I said.

She shook her head as she put the car in drive. "I guess the answer is no," she said as she made a U-turn and headed for the main road.

I opened my mouth to protest again, but I knew it wasn't worth it. I closed it and turned to look out the window.

We drove the whole way back to the station in silence.

By the time we pulled into the station's parking lot, I knew that Gayla was *pissed.* She hadn't said another word during the trip, which was completely unlike her. We got out of the car, and there was an apology lingering on my tongue, but I couldn't get it out.

As we walked into the station, the operations officer, Dori, looked up and gestured toward the waiting area with her head.

"Cabdriver is in there, waiting for you," she said. "His name is Freddy Cruise. Fair warning, he is not in a good mood."

I nodded, and Gayla and I walked over to the small waiting area where a man was sitting by himself. He was slumped down in one of the chairs, his stubby legs stretched out in front of him, his eyes on the ground. He was holding a hat in his hands, and his thinning hair was combed over to one side, held by sweat and maybe a little bit of gel, too. He looked up as we walked into the room, and his eyebrows shot up as he stood, still gripping his hat tightly in front of him.

"Mr. Cruise?" Gayla asked.

"Yes," the man said. "Are you the detectives that they asked me to wait for? What's going on with my car?"

"Your car?" I asked.

"Yeah, who's going to pay to have my car cleaned?" he asked. "That's why I waited. I don't have time to be here all night, but I need to know who's going to pay for it."

"Sir, we can get into that later," Gayla said. "We really need to know what happened to the woman you picked up and dropped off in Whitewater."

"We can get into *that* later," he snapped back.

Gayla drew back in surprise. She threw me a quick glance as Cruise continued.

"There's blood all over my backseat. That shit doesn't come out. And you think people are going to want to get into my car when they see that?"

"No —" Gayla started.

But the man continued, cutting her off. "Somebody's going to have to pay for that," he said. "We're already hurting out here, with Uber. You don't know how hard it is to get a ride most nights. I can barely cover my gas. I don't need this, too. Somebody's got to clean my car."

"Look, we'll work out something with you for your car," I said, taking a step forward and lowering my voice. "But we need your help with this investigation. A woman's life might be in danger. Help us, and then we'll talk about the car."

Cruise let out a long, exaggerated sigh. "I'm sorry for her, but that's not my fault," he said. "I didn't do nothing to her. Just picked her up and dropped her off."

"Mind if we step to the back?" I asked, gesturing toward the back of the station.

He paused for just a moment before nodding. He still looked angry, but he followed Gayla and me out of the waiting area and back to a small chair next to my desk.

"You can have a seat here," I said, putting my hand on the back of the chair.

Cruise sat down and placed his hat back in his lap. I sat in my own chair, and Gayla perched on the edge of my desk.

"So what do you mean her life is in danger? Something wrong with her?" he asked. "You think she's the one who is responsible for the blood in my car?"

"Well, you'll have to tell us," Gayla said. "She's currently in the hospital, suffering from some kind of shock. When she was found, she was at home, covered in a lot of blood. Are you telling us that you didn't see any blood on her when she got in the cab? Or when she got out?"

"Naw, I didn't see anything," he said. "I was so happy to get the fare, I didn't really look at her."

He didn't seem to be making it up, which meant one of two things. Either he was completely unobservant and he'd missed the fact that his passenger was covered in blood when he picked her up, or whatever had happened to her occurred while she was in the backseat.

"So you didn't see anything?" I asked. "Nothing that seemed suspicious?"

Cruise crossed his arms and leaned back in his chair. "No, not really," he said. "I mean, they said that she must have been covered in it for there to be that much on my backseat, but I didn't see anything. I know she had a lot of hair or whatever, hanging all in front of her face, and she had a long coat on. And that was it."

"Where did you pick her up?"

"Believe it or not, off the interstate. Near the intersection of 59 and Highway 12. Over by those woods. What is it? Piper . . ."

"Piper Woods," I said. "Near the lake. What were you doing out there?"

"I took a job out there, coming from the airport. I was on the way back, and I was pissed, because that's an empty cab ride back to the city. Do you know how hard it is on us to have an empty ride back to the city? It basically cancels out any profits I make from the entire night. Anyway, I stopped to get gas and then got back on the road, and there she was. Standing by the side of the road, her hand out."

"And you didn't see anything odd about her?"

"Not really, but I just told you, I wasn't looking. All I saw was a figure in the dark, a lot of hair, and a hand out. I pulled over, and she got in."

"What did she say?"

"She gave me the address. The place out in Whitewater. It wasn't back to the city, but it was closer, and I was happy for it. I just told her I needed the cash up front."

"You did?" I asked.

"Yeah. I wasn't about to pick up some hobo out in the middle of nowhere and give a free ride back to the city," he said. "I told her it would be seventy-five dollars, and she handed me a wad. Hundred on the outside. That was all I needed."

"Did she have a purse with her?"

"I think so."

"Is that where she got the money?"

"I don't know!" he said and let out an exasperated sigh. "So many questions. I have no idea. Her purse, her pocket . . . I don't know. She just handed it to me. Like I said, I didn't ask that many questions."

"But she had to give you her address. What did she sound like?" Gayla asked. "I mean, did she sound . . . okay?"

"I guess," he said. "Kinda robotic, like she didn't want any more conversation. Which is normal for me. A lot of people don't really want to talk. Some people want to talk your ear off, or tell you about their day, or ask about yours, as if they really care. I always wonder about those people who act like they want to know my life story. Think it makes them feel good about themselves, like they're talking to the hired help, you know? I don't mind it, though, 'cause they're usually the best tippers —"

"Mr. Cruise?" Gayla said.

"Oh, sorry. So yeah, she didn't say anything else. Just gave me the address and the money, and that was it."

"Did you notice any blood on the money?"

"I noticed that it was dirty, but that's not the kind of thing that bothers me, really. I didn't notice that it was blood until I got home."

"Ok, so when you dropped her off, did she go right inside?"

"Did she go inside?" he asked. "How would I know? She got out of the car, and I left."

"I thought you might have noticed —"

"Nah. I kept working for about another hour or so. I had a bunch more clients. I guess they couldn't see it in the dark, thank God. Probably got all over their clothes, but not my fault. I bet you they're going to call the company and say it was my fault, but it wasn't. I can't do anything about it. Anyway, I never really know what's going on in the back of my car during the night. Sometimes, a smell will hit you, and you know something has happened. But when I get home, I check the car out in the garage, with all the lights on, so I can see what kind of damage there is. Usually I find a bunch of junk that I have to throw away. Gum, cigarette lighters, things like that. Sometimes, wallets and gloves, which I turn in, 'cause you can get in trouble for that. But tonight, I turned on the light, and all I see is all these brown spots that are obviously blood. And that's when I called you guys."

"I'll be right back," I said. "I need to check something."

I stepped away from the desk and headed back to the front of the police station.

Dori was typing on her computer. She looked up as I approached.

"Hey," I said. "Piper Woods, over by Highway 12, where he says he picked up the Lindsey woman —"

"We already have a team out there," she said. "I'll send the exact location to your phone."

"Thanks," I said. "Make sure they contact me right away if they find anything."

She nodded, and I walked back over to

my desk.

Gayla was writing down some information for the cabdriver. "I think that's all we need for now," she said. "Please call me if you remember anything else, and we'll let you know if we have any more questions."

"What about my car?" the man asked. "You said we'd work something out if I told you what I knew."

"And we will," I said. "*After* we take a closer look at it. We're going to need to keep it for a while since it's evidence now."

Cruise balled his fists. "You gotta be kidding me!"

It took another fifteen minutes for us to talk him down, but finally, he stormed to the front of the station and out the door.

"There's no blood anywhere else in that house," Gayla said. "She must have had it on her when she got in the cab. I think she could have had a monkey on her back, but as long as she had the fare, Cruise wouldn't have noticed anything else."

"Yeah, I guess so," I said. "So whatever or whoever that blood came from, it's gotta be out there in Piper Woods."

I had three missed calls from Mary when I got home.

"Steve, Gayla told me you had a rough

129

night," she said on my voicemail. She was one of the few people who actually called my apartment rather than my cell phone. "I'm just calling to check in on you. Give me a call back."

I considered calling her back that night, but I knew she'd just grill me about what happened at the Lindsey house. She'd use the word *blackout* a few times. I'd make something up that she wouldn't believe, just like Gayla.

No, I'd call her tomorrow.

I picked up my phone to make one more call. As I did, I reached over and picked up a small, black-and-white race car off my nightstand. It was Kit's car — he'd loved it as a toddler, especially when I drove it back and forth over his belly and did the "*vroom vroom* thing," as he called it. After Lara and I separated, I'd found the car nestled between the cushions in the backseat of my car.

I balanced it on my palm as I dialed her number. As always, when Lara's name flashed across the screen, I felt a pain in the middle of my stomach. I took a deep breath. As the phone continued to ring, the nerves began to slip away and turn into something else. Disappointment, and a little bit of anger. It was late, true. But being married to her for four years let me know that she always slept with the phone beneath her pillow because she hated missing calls.

She wasn't missing my call.

She was ignoring it.

"Hey," I said, angry at myself for sounding breathy. "It's me. Steve. Sorry." I took a deep breath and tried to push through. "Just calling about seeing when I could stop by. Just . . . yeah, call me back when you have a chance. Thanks."

*He's not your kid.*

*He's not your kid.*

I tried chanting it to myself a few times a day when the divorce was first finalized.

*He's not yours.*

It seemed like it should mean something, like that fact should make a difference, but it didn't. I'd been there for most of the first six years of his life. He sure *felt* like my son.

I hung up the phone and walked into my bathroom, where I grabbed a washcloth, along with the box of tissues from my vanity. Then I walked into my bedroom and sat down on the side of the bed.

*Go somewhere, Steve.*

I knew I should leave. I should grab my keys and wallet and hightail it to the nearest bar or all-night diner or Walgreens or absolutely anywhere else that wasn't home

131

by myself. I should call Mary or go sleep at Nell's.

I should *leave.*

I leaned over and opened the drawer on my nightstand. On top of a small wooden box that Nell and Mike had brought me from their twentieth-anniversary trip to Puerto Rico was a small and recently sharpened razor blade. As I stared at it, the waves of guilt began to wash over me.

The guilt was one of the worst parts.

The throbbing in my arms, the dry mouth, the actual feeling of the blade on my skin — all of that had nothing on the guilt.

And even then, the guilt had *nothing* on the urges.

I lifted my sleeve slowly, averting my eyes from my arm as I reached into the drawer and picked up the blade.

# CHAPTER TEN

Adult males in their late thirties do not cut.

It was widely accepted as fact, and yet here I was, sprawled on my back, my arm neatly bandaged, the razor disinfected and back in my nightstand drawer.

The cutting had started when I was fifteen. The visions had been particularly bad at that time, worse than the nightmares, and I spent my days looking for any and all ways to keep Nell and Mike from finding out. After a close call at Nell's birthday party one Saturday afternoon, I locked myself in my bedroom while the party continued just steps outside my door. Everyone, Nell included, thought I was simply having a temperamental teenager moment; in reality, I'd ducked out of the room just as the vision was starting.

As I sat in my room listening to the laughter out in the living room, I felt helpless. I was angry at myself for jeopardizing my relationship with Nell and Mike. For a reason I still, to this day, have not been able to pin down, I'd grabbed the first thing I could find — the jagged tab of a Coke can — and used one of the edges to make a small cut on my finger. As I watched the blood bubble up and then begin to slide down my finger, I'd felt an immediate sense of relief from the pain inside of my head.

That feeling of release hadn't changed in more than twenty years.

I stared at the ceiling a long time, the symbol that Emily had drawn filling my vision, the guilt of what I'd just done heavy on my chest. I must have dozed off for a couple of hours, because the next thing I knew, there was sunlight on my face, and the alarm clock next my bed said it was six thirty.

I got ready, pulling on a long-sleeved shirt, and headed to the station.

Gayla was already there, and she looked wide awake. In typical Gayla fashion, she got straight to the point. "Hey, sorry about last night," she said. "Mary called me about something else, and then she asked me how things were going, and I thought I should fill her in. But it wasn't the right time, and I should have waited to give her my . . . opinion."

I nodded. "Thanks, and I'm sorry for being a jerk about it."

"I'm sorry, you're sorry, blah blah," she said, and I smiled. "Enough of that. Look, I've been digging around on *Carmen Street,* trying to see if there's anything interesting on there."

"Did you find anything?"

"Sure did," she said, spinning her laptop around so that I could see the screen. "Emily took on a lot of people, but none as bad as Ryan Griggs."

"The pharmaceutical guy."

"Yep," she said. "We need to stop by there today. I'll give them a call."

"Okay, but I have to stop by Pat's first."

Gayla gave me a look, but she nodded. "Okay."

I looked back down at the computer screen. "So what did you find?" I asked, leaning forward to look at the screen.

She'd pulled his personal Twitter account and scrolled down a few weeks back. She hovered the mouse over one post in particular.

2w ago. @CarmenStreet keep talking bitch must be nice to hide behind your computer.

"That's the president of one of the leading pharmaceutical companies in the region?"

"Yep," she said. "Don't know that it's evidence of his involvement in this, but it sure seems like proof that he's got a temper — and that he hated her guts."

I nodded slowly, staring at the screen. "Yeah, but her guts are fully intact. We need to go make sure his still are, too."

Since the shooting at Glenwood Bank, I'd met with the bank teller who'd been shot, Patricia Michaels, eight times. Once a week for almost three months, except the one time I was sick, the time I had to work late, and the time I had to cancel for Nell's birthday. As I drove to Pat's apartment that morning, I thought hard about canceling for the fourth time.

Truth was, I thought about canceling on her almost every week. It wasn't just that I didn't have the time, or that I should probably be working on the case, or that it was out of my way. It was that I knew it would be as awkward and uncomfortable as it had been all other eight times I visited.

But I wouldn't let myself back out. I couldn't let myself. The moment I started canceling, I knew how quickly it would all go to shit. I'd skip this week for some very important reason, and then I'd skip next week because I skipped this week.

All I had left to hang my hat on was my consistency.

My visits went the same way each week. I'd give Pat a call on her landline right before I left my home. She always answered on the first ring and told me she looked forward to seeing me.

"Drive safely," she'd say before hanging up.

I drove the thirty-five minutes or so to her apartment complex. She lived on the second floor of a five-story elevator building in a quiet neighborhood filled mostly with retirees. That evening, I pulled into my usual spot, a few doors down from the apartment building.

I walked up to the front door and pushed the buzzer for 2C. It only took a few seconds for her to buzz me in. It had taken a while for us to get there. The first few times I'd stopped by, she'd grilled me for at least ten minutes to make sure it was really me.

"How do I know you're who you say you are?" she had asked, her voice wobbling through the intercom.

"Because we just spoke about thirty minutes ago. It's me, Detective Paul. I can show you my badge when I get upstairs."

"Yes, but by then, you'll already be inside, won't you?"

I'd actually considered going home that day, as I stood outside talking into the rectangular metal box, wondering what the hell I was doing there. What I thought my visits were going to do. How long I could keep it up. But I had stayed, and finally, she had buzzed the door open.

Secretly, I had been a little bit disappointed that I had missed my opportunity to run away.

I pulled the door open and stepped inside. I headed straight back toward the elevator, unbuttoning my jacket as I walked along. There was something about her building that trapped heat, and today, it was downright oppressive. I already knew what the second story had in store for me. I wasn't sure my weekly visits would have lasted this long if she'd lived on one of the higher floors.

I stepped out of the elevator, and even though her apartment was several feet down, I could hear her unlocking the door. She always timed it just perfectly. I stepped up to the door just as it swung open.

"Hello, Detective Paul," she said, wheeling herself backward in her chair to let me inside.

"Hi," I said. We didn't say anything else for the first couple of moments, which was sort of our pattern. I took off my jacket and hung it up, because Pat was particular about things like that, and I wanted to make her comfortable. I'd learned in the last few months that what made her comfortable was having everything in its proper place.

After I hung up my coat, I followed her into the living room, like I always did, and she wheeled up to the side of the couch. "How are you feeling?" I asked. "How's your week been?"

"Not bad."

Our conversations always started out slowly, and I was still getting used to it. Gayla would have pulled her hair out trying to fill in the silences. The few times we'd talked about my weekly visits, Gayla had tried her best to get to the bottom of my behavior.

"It's some kind of guilt thing, right?" she had asked. "That's got to be it. You feel like you could've done more, moved the gun just a little bit to the right, so she wouldn't be in that chair at all. Right?"

"It's not weird for me to want to go visit someone from a former case," I had said.

139

She'd raised her eyebrows in a no-bullshit kind of way. "You've seen a lot of victims, a lot of hurt folks in your time," she had said. "But you've never been this committed to going to visit them on such a regular basis."

"What about Barry? The teenager who was in the fire at Piermont High School. I went by to visit him."

"Yeah," she had said. "You went to visit him twice? Three times maybe?"

"Look," I had said. "You know this is different."

"Yeah," she had said. "I do. I just don't know how long you can keep it up."

That conversation had occurred around the two-month mark.

And here I was, another month in, still sitting in Pat's living room.

"Do you want some tea today?" she asked.

I knew to say yes. Saying no could change her mood completely. "Sure, that would be great."

She pushed back and wheeled into the kitchen. She reached for a couple of mugs that were already sitting out on the counter and then rolled herself over to the table, where the tea was also already out. I wondered if it had been sitting there since last week.

"I'm sorry, but I only have Earl Grey,"

she said. "I haven't had a chance to get anything else."

It was the same conversation we had every week, but I just went with it. I really didn't need any caffeine, but I'd once offered to pick up something else, and that didn't go over so well either.

She rolled over to the stove and heated up a pot of water before turning back to me.

"How's work going?" she asked. "Any interesting cases?"

She knew that I couldn't tell her about what was going on in any of my cases, but I did try to give her some general information about them, because she always seemed very intrigued. Plus, it gave us something to talk about.

"I'm on a new case, and it's giving me a lot of trouble," I said, sitting down at the kitchen table.

She rolled up to the table and placed a tea bag into each of the mugs. "Why?" she asked. "What's the matter?"

In another lifetime, before she became a bank teller, Patricia had been a teacher at a middle school on the southwest side of the city. She still spoke in a calm, soft way, and I imagined that her voice used to work wonders on the children.

"There's a woman involved, and she won't

speak to me," I said. "She knows a lot about what happened, but she won't say a single word. And I'm not sure how to handle that."

"Maybe *you* should talk to *her,*" she said. "Maybe you're putting too much pressure on her, asking her to speak when she's not ready."

"But she's the one who needs to talk," I said. "She's the one who knows what's going on. It's frustrating, because she's right there, right in front of me. But I can't get to her."

"I understand that," she said. "But try it my way. When you meet with her again, you should just speak to her."

"I don't know what to say," I said.

"The right thing will come to you," she said. "Maybe tell her a little bit about yourself, take some of the pressure off her."

I couldn't explain to her why that plan wouldn't work without giving away too many details of the case. I couldn't tell her that Emily's refusal to speak to me wasn't a deliberate choice; it was like trying to convince a ghost to speak to me.

I nodded and thanked her for the advice. Pat rolled over to the stove and turned it off, lifting the pot of hot water. I resisted the urge to stand up and help her. I knew she would chastise me if I did. I'd made the mistake of trying too hard the first couple of times I'd come to visit. Now, I sat there, my body tense, poised to spring into action if she started having trouble with the pot, which was about halfway filled with water.

Patricia rolled back to the table and slowly, with shaking arms, poured water into each of our cups. I was careful not to let out a sigh of relief when she was done.

"Sugar?" I asked, picking up the sugar and scooping a spoonful into my own cup. That was my contribution.

She nodded, and I added some to hers. With shaking hands, she set the hot pot down on a towel.

Making tea for a guest hadn't been so much trouble for sixty-three-year-old Pat a few months ago. Before the shooting, she'd been active, choosing the stairs over the elevator, doing small fitness tapes in her living room every now and then. Now, as I watched her lift her mug to her lips with shaky hands, I had a hard time imagining the woman she must have been.

We said goodbye about twenty minutes later at her front door, and like always, she looked tired. But happy.

"See you next week," I said.

She nodded. Pat never said it first, maybe because she didn't know if I was actually coming back. But I knew that she was waiting for me to say it. I was her only visitor in the past week, and there would be no one else until I returned.

"See you then," she said. "Drive safely."

As I drove away from Patricia's apartment, Gayla's question struck me.

How long *could* I keep this up?

I don't know if it was learning that Patricia didn't have a single family member to come visit her — she was the only child of two only children, who'd both passed away — or that I'd seen the moment when Crane's bullet struck her in the back that had made me come the first time, but after that, I would have had to make the decision to *stop* coming.

And that was almost impossible.

As I headed to meet Gayla at the Griggses' house, I thought about Patricia's suggestion. Maybe we needed to stop focusing so much on what Emily wouldn't say and focus on what we knew. We knew how she'd gotten home. We knew that about an hour before her husband found her, she'd been cognizant enough to hail a cab, tell Cruise her address, and pay for it.

I needed to use what we knew and find a way to crack her, to get her to talk.

Because that was the only way to find out

what happened to her.

And maybe the only way to find out why we seemed to share the nightmares and what that symbol meant.

# CHAPTER ELEVEN

Ryan and Eleanor Griggs lived in a massive peach-and-ivory house out in the northern suburbs of the city. We were only about twenty-five minutes away from where the Lindseys lived, but we might as well have been on another planet. A planet that included "Big Money" or "Green" in its name, or maybe just dollar signs where there would normally be the letter s. Even the air smelled richer. As I followed Gayla's car through the Griggses' neighborhood, I took in the enormous homes, the perfectly manicured lawns, and the expensive cars in every driveway.

Gayla stopped her car in front of the Griggses' home, and I pulled up behind her. We both stepped out onto the street and, with our doors still open, leaned back to take the house in.

"Dayum," she purred. "If I lived in a house like this, I'd probably be a pretentious asshole, too," she said.

"Possibly dead asshole," I reminded her.

"Yeah, yeah," she said. *"Possibly."*

Gayla had filled me in on Griggs back at the station, and as tough as his brash personality was to swallow, it was hard not to be impressed by his steady and determined climb to the top.

Griggs had started at Kelium fresh out of college at twenty-three and was a manager by the time he was twenty-seven. In a magazine interview about thirty rising stars under thirty, he was quoted as saying that the best business advice he could give was to find out who the people who mattered were and make those people like you.

"Make them *really* like you," he had said. "It only takes one person to open each door. When you're up against an obstacle, find the person who can break it down for you, and make them like you. It's not about impressing them with your educational background or résumé or this or that. Just get them on your team, whatever that takes. For most people, that means figuring out one of their obstacles and solving it for them. It's not as hard as you might think."

Griggs became the youngest CEO of the company at thirty-nine, and now, ten years later, with his shoulder-length hair and in-your-face personality, he'd established a solid reputation for always getting what he wanted.

"I called his office, and they said he's not in today," Gayla said. "According to his assistant, it's not unusual for him to work from home. Hasn't been in for about a week. She hasn't heard from him during that time, but that's apparently not that weird either. I called the house earlier — nobody answered."

"Looks like somebody's home," I said, pointing to the shiny black sports car in the driveway. We walked up to the front door, and I pressed the buzzer. From inside, I could hear the melodic chimes as they floated through the house.

Nothing happened for a few moments, and I reached over to press it again.

After another beat, the large door opened slowly, and a short, balding man peered out.

"Yes, hello," he said, standing rigidly at the door. "How can I help you?"

"We're here to see Ryan Griggs," I said.

He squinted. "Yes, sir," he said. "And who are you?"

We introduced ourselves and pulled out our badges. He reached for them both and looked at them carefully before handing them back. He stepped back and let us inside, closing the door behind us. I took my hat off and held it in my hands.

"If you'll be kind enough to wait here," he said. He walked away toward the back of the house.

When he was out of sight, Gayla spun around and faced me, her eyes open wide, an expression of astonishment on her face. She placed her fingertips at her temple and made an exploding motion as her jaw dropped down.

"A butler?" she said with a hiss. "You have got to be kidding me."

I smirked. "Maybe he's their . . . cousin?"

"He asked us to 'be so kind as to wait here,' " she said. "That man is their butler. I didn't know that was actually a thing."

I choked on nothing, and a chortle escaped me. "Wait, so let me be clear. You're saying that you thought butlers were, what, fictional characters?"

She frowned, and I think she was giving it real thought. "Yes," she said after a moment. "I guess I did. I mean, I get that some people much more fortunate than me have maids and au pairs and regular cleaning services. Hell, I can have any of that with Groupon. But an actual 'be so kind as to wait here' butler? Who *butles*? That's ridiculous."

"Hello. How can I help you?" a voice said.

We both looked up at a woman who was walking toward us from the direction where the man had gone. She was a tall woman, with big, exaggerated features and a severely cut bob that framed her face. She was wearing an apron, and she had oven mitts on both hands.

She walked up to us and took off the mitts, one after the other, before extending a perfectly manicured hand to Gayla. "I'm Eleanor Griggs," she said. "My assistant told me that you're with the police?"

I glanced over at Gayla and saw that her cheeks were bright red.

"Oh, your assistant . . ." she started. She cleared her throat. "I'm Detective Gayla Ocasio, and this is my partner Steven Paul. We're here about a matter concerning your husband. Is he home?"

"No, he's not," Eleanor said, frowning, still holding both of the oven mitts in her hands. "My husband is in Philadelphia."

"Philadelphia?" Gayla asked, stealing a glance at me.

"Yes, on business. He's been there the entire week, working out of that office. What's going on? Is something wrong?"

"We just need to talk to him about an important matter. We spoke to his assistant earlier today, and she thought he was working from home. Any reason why she wouldn't know that he was in Philadelphia?"

"She knows where he is," she said. "Sam can be a bit protective of Ryan and his time. A bit too protective."

"When is the last time you spoke with him?"

"This morning," she said. "Why, is something wrong? You can't keep asking me these questions without giving me some clue as to what this is about."

"Nothing is wrong. We just wanted to touch base with him," Gayla said. "Would it be possible to give him a call now?"

I saw something flicker in the woman's eyes, but she covered it quickly. "When he's on business, it's very hard to get ahold of him. I'm happy to try, but I happen to know that he's in meetings all day."

"Do you have a way we can get in touch with him?" I asked.

"Sure," she said hesitantly. "I can give you his cell phone number. He'll be back today, though, so you could just talk to him when he gets home."

"What time are you expecting him?"

"Late. I'll ask him to call you, but it might not be until tomorrow."

Gayla nodded, and she handed the woman

her card.

Eleanor took it and looked at it for a moment. "You have to tell me what's going on," she said. "Something has to be wrong. Otherwise, you wouldn't be here."

Gayla and I looked at each other again, and she finally nodded.

"We want to talk to him about his correspondence with a woman named Emily Lindsey," I said. "From the website *Carmen Street Confessions.*"

Her eyes narrowed, and she shook her head. "I should have known," she said. "Is that woman at it again? Ryan told her that he would sue if she continued to post such libelous information about him or the company. My husband works very hard at his business, and safety is one of his top concerns. Everyone who works with him would say that."

"She hasn't written a new article," I said. "She was attacked last night."

The woman's eyes widened, and she took a step back, the mitts dropping from her hand.

"Attacked?" she said, bending down to pick them up. "Where?" The perfectly polished woman disappeared for a second, and I could see real concern in her eyes.

"We're not positive," I said. "But she was

found in her home."

She stood there for a moment, her mouth slightly open, her eyes wide. After a pause, she blinked. "Oh, my cake," she said. "It's —" She turned and walked quickly toward the kitchen, pausing to look over her shoulder. "Please, come," she said.

We followed her toward the back of the house. We stepped into the huge, modern kitchen, which was filled with granite and stainless steel in places it wasn't needed and a large island in the middle of the room with a built-in wine cabinet. I stepped closer to the island and put my hat down. Eleanor walked over to the oven and put on her mitts before opening it and pulling out a cake. I noticed that the cake wasn't burnt at all — it was barely done — and I had a feeling she'd really just needed a moment to compose herself.

"It's for a fund-raiser that I'm going to tonight," she said, spinning the pan and placing it back in the oven. "I mean, that I was going to. I don't know . . . So what happened to her? You don't have any idea who attacked her?"

"No, that's what we're trying to figure out," Gayla said.

"You mean, you think Ryan had something to do with it?" she asked. "I hope

153

that's not why you're here."

"We don't think anything at the moment," Gayla said. "We're here to learn more about what happened, and we're trying to talk to anyone and everyone who has had interaction with Emily in the last couple of months."

"You mean bad interactions, right?" She sighed. "Look, I'll admit that my husband didn't handle himself in the best way during that whole ordeal, but it wasn't all his fault. If you read the story, you'd see that she was jeopardizing his entire livelihood because of a few rumors," she said. "And to make it worse, she published his post the next day, but she removed everything she'd said in their back and forth. Yes, he got carried away, but she did, too. She didn't post her comments, only his."

"Which threatened to find her and make it impossible for her to type another word about him," Gayla said.

Eleanor cringed. "I told you, he didn't handle that well. But my husband isn't the type of person to break into a woman's home and *attack her*," she said. "Not even close to it."

"What are your thoughts about her accusations?"

"You mean the horrible, defamatory article she wrote about my husband's business, which he has put blood and sweat into for more than twenty-five years?" she said. "You're really asking me what I think about that?" She shook her head. "I think it's a great way to get views."

"So you don't think there's any truth to the Zoanet safety concerns?"

"Look, Detectives, is this why you're here?" she asked. "To probe into that? Because believe me, we have every regulatory agency you can think to make up an acronym for knocking on our door, and we'll be dealing with this for a long time. We don't need you doing that, too."

"No, we're here to find out what happened to Emily Lindsey," Gayla said. "And your husband was known to have a problem with her. So we're just asking the questions we have to ask. I hope you can appreciate that."

Eleanor sighed and nodded. "Yes, of course. Look, I don't know what else I can tell you. I'd be lying if I said that anyone in my family, or with Kelium, was a big fan of *Carmen Street,* the infamous Emily, or any of her fans. I'm not going to pretend that's the case. But we had nothing to do with whatever it was that happened to Emily last night. I'm sorry I can't be any more help to you."

"Okay, well, thanks for your time," Gayla said.

Eleanor let us out though the patio door off the kitchen, and we walked along the side of the house, back toward the street.

"Philadelphia, huh?" I asked, looking back at Gayla over my shoulder.

"Yeah. Still find it odd that his assistant didn't know that," she said. "I'll call her when we get back to the station."

We walked across the driveway back to our cars. Gayla stopped at hers before she got in. "Part of me thinks we're barking up the wrong tree, and we need to get out to Piper Lake soon," she said. "Griggs may have been the worst of them, but there were a lot of other people who could have been upset about what Emily was posting on *Carmen Street*. What if we have the wrong one?"

"Yeah, it's possible," I said as she opened her car door. "I'll see you back at the station."

Gayla got in her car and drove off. I followed suit and made a U-turn on the Griggses' street to head back to the highway.

I'd only gotten about two blocks when I looked down on the seat beside me and realized I'd forgotten my hat back at the

156

Griggses' home.

"Shit," I said out loud, making another U-turn and heading back.

I stopped the car in the same place and opened the door. I stepped out and jogged back up the driveway, moving back around the side of the house.

I reached the screen door of the kitchen and peered inside. Eleanor had left the glass door partially open, and I could still smell the scent of the vanilla in her cake as it drifted outside.

I'd raised my hand to knock on the glass when I saw movement in front of me.

Eleanor Griggs was walking back into the room, her cell phone up to her ear, and she was looking down at a piece of paper in her hands.

"Ryan!" she said angrily, and I froze, my hand inches from the glass. "You have to call me back. I don't know what the hell is going on, but the cops were just here. Something happened to that *Carmen Street* bitch, and I haven't been able to get in touch with you in *three* days. Call me back the minute you get this."

As she finished speaking, she looked up and saw me standing on the other side of the screen door, watching her with my arm still poised to knock.

"Oh shit . . ." she said on a breath, her face covered in shock and her eyes wide as she pitched the cell phone directly at my face.

# CHAPTER TWELVE

The cell phone bounced off the screen and hurtled back toward her before clattering noisily on her kitchen floor. Eleanor stared at me, her mouth forming a perfect O, and I slowly lowered my arm down to my side.

*Well, damn.*

Even with the screen door and distance between us, I could practically see her racking her brain for a way to spin what I'd just heard.

I put one hand on the glass and leaned my face close to the screen. "Sorry to sneak up on you," I said. I cleared my throat and pointed to the edge of the island. "I forgot my hat?"

"Your what?" she asked, her gaze not moving from mine.

"My hat," I repeated, still pointing. She finally turned to look at it, but she didn't move closer to it or say anything.

A few moments passed, and she finally

spoke again. "Why didn't you come back through the front door?"

"Because I just came out this way, and I knew you were back here," I said. "I didn't know you were on the phone."

She still didn't move, and I think she was trying to figure out what to say to get me to go away. She blinked a few times and then opened her mouth, but nothing came out. Finally, she walked over to the patio door and pressed her own face close to the screen.

"You should probably let me back in," I said.

"Do I have to?" she whispered.

"What?"

"Do I have to let you back in?"

I sighed. "No, you don't have to, but trust me, it's better for us to talk about this now, okay?"

Her bottom lip was shaking, and she nodded. She reached forward and unlocked the screen door, pushing it open so that I could step back into her kitchen.

I'd just been there, moments earlier, but everything felt different now. Eleanor Griggs had been so in control, practically kicking us out of her house, promising us that there was no way her husband could be involved in what happened to Emily.

Now, her entire body was shaking, and she looked down at the floor. The truth was out. She'd lied to our faces, and there was no going back.

I watched as she swallowed nervously. I walked over to the island to pick up my hat and then took a few steps behind the island and bent down to pick up her cell phone. Walking back, I handed it to her. She stared at it as if she'd never seen it before.

"Mrs. Griggs?" I said.

She blinked before reaching out to take it. "Thanks," she said.

"You know, you shouldn't throw things at people," I said, hoping to calm her down a little bit. Her face scrunched up as if she were about to cry. "Hey, sorry," I said. "Look, why don't you just tell me what's going on?"

"I don't know what you're —" she started.

I raised my hand to stop her. "I heard every word," I said. "So let's not go through that. Let's start with the fact that you haven't heard from your husband in three days, and just a little while ago, you told me that you talked to him this morning."

Eleanor walked back over to the island and put both hands on it, leaning forward. I could almost see all the resolve flowing out of her, and she sighed deeply, her shoulders sagging.

"If you heard everything, then I don't know what else I can tell you. I've been calling him nonstop since Thursday," she said. "He won't pick up or text me back or email or anything. It's so frustrating. And then you guys showed up here this morning, and I didn't know what to do."

"So you decided to lie?" I asked.

"I didn't know what you wanted, and I didn't want to admit that I hadn't heard from him," she said, shaking her head. "He's a good husband. He really is. Sometimes, he's just sort of absentminded, you know. He knows I'm okay, and he doesn't have to check on me all the time. It can just be a little difficult sometimes."

I didn't feel the need to point out that she seemed to be trying to convince herself more than she was trying to convince me.

"Are you sure he made it to Philadelphia?" I asked.

"He called me Wednesday night when he got in, so I think so," she said.

"Is it normal for him not to call you back?"

"Sometimes he gets really busy." She looked down at the phone.

I could tell there was something else she was hiding. "If there's something else, you need to tell me, Mrs. Griggs," I said. "You should do so now. Please."

Her bottom lip wavered. "He just wanted to go talk to them," she said quietly. "I promise, that's all it was."

"Talk to whom?"

"The patients in the *Carmen Street* article."

"What?"

"There are four of them, one in Philadelphia. That's why he went there."

"He went to visit them?" I asked. "I thought you said he was traveling on business."

"Well, it is business, of sorts," she said. "He was supposed to leave Philly on Thursday and head to Indianapolis to meet another. Then one in Chicago and finally one back here."

"Why was he going to visit them?" I asked.

"Just to talk to them," she said. "That's it. He wanted to see how they were doing, learn more about what they're going through, without the media or any thoughts of that *Carmen Street* woman —" She covered her mouth and stared at me. "I shouldn't talk bad about her, I'm sorry. But he didn't do anything to her. I promise you, my husband's not like that."

"But you just admitted to me that you don't know where he is. Truth is, you don't know if he actually made it to Philly and whether he ever moved on to Indianapolis."

"Yes, I don't know that for sure, but I know what type of man my husband is," she said. "And like I told you before, he's not a lunatic. He didn't break into her house and attack her. He could never do that, Detective. You have to believe me."

"Okay," I said. "But maybe I should explain this a little better. Emily Lindsey was attacked last night, but she is fine. Yes, she's shaken up, but she's okay. Not a single scratch on her."

"Wait, what?" Eleanor asked, her face turning white.

"Not a scratch," I said again. "But there was a gallon of blood found on her body and in her home. Blood that did not come from Emily Lindsey. So we need to hear from your husband, and we need to hear from him soon — he might be the one who's hurt."

She stared at me, her whole body shaking, and I could tell I'd gotten through to her.

"Now," I said. "Will you call me the moment you hear from him?"

"Yes," she whispered. "I will."

I met Gayla back at the station about half an hour later. She was typing on her computer as I walked in, and she looked up with a frown on her face.

"What took you so long?" she asked. "I thought you were right behind me, then you disappeared."

"I went back to the house because I left my hat in the kitchen," I said. "And you'll never guess what happened." I filled Gayla in on the cell phone incident.

She stood up abruptly. "She lied to us. What the hell is wrong with her?" she asked.

"I think she thought she was protecting her husband," I said. "But I brought her up to speed."

"Do you think it's possible?" she asked. "That such a small woman as Emily could overtake a guy like Ryan Griggs?"

"Yeah, I think anything is possible when someone has enough rage in them," I said.

Gayla walked over to her chair and picked up her coat. "I got a call from the hospital," she said. "They want us to come by."

"She's ready to talk?" I asked, my heart pounding.

"No. Apparently, word's gotten out that the owner of *Carmen Street Confessions* is there," she said. "And the response has been, let's say . . . mixed. You ready?"

I thought back to the last time we'd been there and the symbol that Emily had drawn all over her body.

*No, I'm not ready.*
*Not even close.*
"Yeah, sure," I said. "Let's go."

We walked through the doors of McKinney Memorial Hospital less than twenty-four hours after our first visit, but we were armed with a lot more knowledge than the first time around. A lot more information, but a lot more questions, too.

First, we knew that Emily had taken a cab from the side of the road and that she'd left blood all over the backseat of it. But we didn't know how she'd gotten to that point or what had happened to her car.

Second, we knew that Ryan Griggs had made several threats against Emily and that he hadn't returned home the night before. But he was supposedly miles away on a trip in Philadelphia. So why wasn't he returning his wife's phone calls?

And third, maybe the oddest part of it all, somehow, she'd gotten my name and scribbled it on a note found in her pocket. But why? Was she planning on contacting me? Or maybe the Steve Paul in California? Who was the other person whose name she'd written — Max Smith? And what did we have to do with the symbol she'd drawn?

As we walked through the hospital, I

166

thought back to the hole that Emily had dug into her hand. For a woman who never showed any signs of being depressed, she definitely seemed to be reaching breaking point. Given the Paxtons' interview, it seemed completely out of character, but I'd seen crazier things in my years on the job.

Overnight, Emily had been moved out of her small, curtained room in the McKinney emergency department and upstairs to a quiet unit on the third floor of the hospital. Gayla and I moved around the nurses' station and spoke to a woman who nodded before standing to lead us back to Emily's room.

The feel of the unit was much different from the hustle of the ER. Paper cutouts from cards drawn by the kids at the school nearby lined the walls, along with large nature scenes and other "uplifting" imagery. The nurse stopped in front of a room and knocked quietly on the door, stepping in before anyone answered.

As we walked in behind her, Gayla and I both stopped in shock at the sight of the room.

It was covered in flowers.

Not just a handful of bouquets from friends and family members — every single surface of the room was covered in flowers of all shapes and sizes.

*Get well.*

*You are missed.*

Dan Lindsey looked tired and annoyed, but he stood up as we walked into the room.

"What happened?" I asked. "Who are these from?"

"It's gotten around the blogosphere that Emily is in the hospital," he said. "They've been coming all day. Don't get me wrong, it's nice, but I wish the hospital would just stop delivering them. It's out of control."

"How the hell did they find out?" Gayla asked.

"It had to be someone from inside the hospital," he said. "Someone posted it in a comment on the site. Along with our address."

"Wow," Gayla said. "But why?"

"People have been clamoring for Emily to reveal herself for years," Dan said. "For most people, that was part of the fun of it. That she was this anonymous voice but a real person in their town who could talk freely about what was going on, with no fear of retribution. But there were always people, both fans and not, who felt that she was hiding behind the internet, using it as a shield to say things she shouldn't say. Whoever leaked it must have decided that it was time for Emily's true identity to be known."

"I see they've increased the security presence on this floor," I said. "That's because they want to make sure that nobody sneaks in and takes a selfie with the famous blogger?"

"No, I wish," Dan said. "I wish it were just that. It's because of these."

He took a deep breath and walked over to the other side of Emily's bed. He lifted a small trash can and held it up to us. It was filled, almost to the top, with cards, paper, and other gift wrapping.

"What's that?" I asked.

"This is all the stuff that's arrived that's not flowers," he said. "Far from it. Take a look."

He held out the basket, and I picked up a card off the top. Opening it, I felt my stomach sink as I saw the words scribbled inside. In messy handwriting, someone had written quite eloquently:

Finally, the bitch gets what she deserves.

I picked up another card and turned it over in my hands. It was a simple postcard, with no return address. I turned it over and read the text on the other side.

Emily of Carmen Street ruined my life and my marriage. She published an article about one small incident in my restaurant where a handful of people got ill (and in reality, it wasn't my fault, but a supplier's, but that's a different story). The week after her article ran, we had our lowest profit margins in our history. It was a downward spiral after that. We couldn't keep the business afloat. My wife left me. To the person that did this to her — thank you!

I held the card up to Dan Lindsey. "Is this true?" I asked.

He was staring at me, but he looked distracted, and he blinked a few times before responding. "I don't —" he started. "I guess the truth of the matter is I don't really know. Emily and I don't talk about her work that much. That was our agreement."

"But did she write a story about a restaurant that closed down soon afterward?"

He shrugged slightly. "She wrote a lot of things she probably shouldn't have," he said softly, and I got the sense that he was avoiding telling us something. "I tried to tell her that she needed to be safer, that she had to be careful. She just wouldn't listen."

His last words were punctuated with

anger, and he stared at the ground. It was a different side of him, and I took a step closer.

"Mr. Lindsey, you sound as if you're talking about something in particular. Are you sure you don't know anything else about where your wife was this weekend?"

He whipped his head up, and his expression changed immediately, the anger that was there just moments earlier disappearing. "No, sorry, I don't," he said. "I'm sorry. If I did, I would tell you."

There were several more messages of hate, filled with expressions of joy that she was in the hospital. The words all varied, but the message was the same: that Emily had it coming given the types of things she wrote about in her blog.

Stuffed into the bottom of the trash can was a heap of dead flowers. I pulled them out and held them up to Dan Lindsey.

"Were these . . ."

"Yeah, they arrived like that," he said.

"How do you even buy dead flowers?"

"I wondered the same thing," he said. "I found a few sites online."

"You're kidding," Gayla said.

"I wish I were."

"If someone will buy it, someone will make it," I said.

171

"Some of it is ridiculous, but some of it is pretty serious," Dan said. "There are death threats in there," he said. "It's unbelievable how many people took the time to send things like this." He put the trash can back down and sighed. "I don't know what to do. I know it's safer here, I guess, but she needs to be home. In her own bed. *We* need to be home."

I frowned.

Something didn't add up, and it took me a moment to realize what it was.

"In her bed?" I asked. "Mr. Lindsey, forgive me, but when we stopped by your house yesterday, I saw that there was an alarm clock beneath the couch in your office. And a toothbrush in the second bathroom. Were you and your wife sleeping apart?"

Dan Lindsey froze.

"No, we were not," he said tersely. "That clock is there because every now and then, I have to get up early for a job, and I'll sleep in the office so I don't have to wake Emily up. Why would you ask me that?"

Before I could respond, Emily shifted in the bed, and we all turned to look. Her eyelids fluttered, and she drifted more soundly to sleep. She looked peaceful, a sharp contrast to the last time we'd seen

172

her, fidgeting, the ink covering her skin. It was gone now, and I wondered how she'd handled the nurses washing it from her skin. I shuddered at the thought and tried to keep my mind focused on the present and what was really happening in the room. I couldn't afford to have another episode right now, not in front of Dan Lindsey, and especially not in front of Gayla. I turned back to Dan, and he was still frowning, waiting for me to respond.

"It's my job to ask those questions," I said.

He grunted and looked away.

Gayla and I exchanged a glance, and she cut in. "How long has she been sleeping?"

"A few hours," Dan said. "She'll wake up soon. They gave her something to get her to rest. She was awake all through the night."

"Has she said anything?"

He shook his head. "Not a peep. I just wish they'd let us go home," he said again. "They have guards all around the hospital, which is ridiculous. I mean, I get it since . . ." He gestured to the trash can. "I get it. But it's not like anyone is actually going to try to hurt her. It's all show."

"You do realize that there's a good chance someone *did* try to hurt Emily," I said. "Which is why she's here."

"No, I get that," Dan said. "It's just that I

think there's more to why they have all the guards out there."

"What do you mean?" I asked.

"They're trying to make it seem like it's just about the threats. Like it's for *her* protection. But you all have also made it clear that she's the one under investigation. Or maybe me, given the questions you have to ask to *do your job,* Detective. You think one of us did something bad. The guards are there to keep us from leaving as much as they're there to keep any threats out, right?"

"No, Mr. Lindsey," I said. "They can't keep her here unless there's a serious threat to her health. In the condition that she's in, it's best for her to stay here."

"You sound just like them," he said. "And I'm getting tired of everyone acting like I'm an idiot. The reason you want her to stay is because of the knife. But it doesn't mean anything."

"You're sure you have no idea where that knife could have come from?"

"No," he said. "I don't know how many times I'll have to tell you all that. It's not ours."

"The blood belonged to someone," I said. "You do know that. It had to come from someone. We tested it. It wasn't Emily's but definitely all human. So we just want to find out what happened."

"I want the same thing," he said. "But I also want to take her home. I don't see why that's so hard for everyone to understand. My wife shouldn't be here, among all this."

"But you do realize that your address has been published online. The hospital may be the safest place for her right now," Gayla said.

"Yeah, sure," Dan muttered, but it was clear that he hadn't internalized a single word she just said. "Look, just let me know when we can go, okay?"

# CHAPTER THIRTEEN

Mary, the department therapist, and I met every Monday afternoon at three.

As I walked into her office that day, I checked my watch. I was desperate to get back to the case, but these meetings were a necessary evil. I had to convince her that I was in tip-top shape, so she could, in turn, convince my supervisors.

"She's ready for you," her assistant said.

I thanked her before walking back down the narrow hallway to Mary's office. I could usually get in and out within forty-five minutes, depending on how much Mary wanted to probe. I felt a familiar sense of frustration rush over me — there was too much to do, too much at stake for me to stop and have a chat.

But there was no point in dwelling on it.

*In and out.*

"Hi, Steven," Mary said as I walked into her office. She worked in a two-story building about ten minutes away from the station. Her office was sterile and cold, with only a desk and a couple of metal chairs in it.

I sat down across from her and leaned forward, placing my hands on the desk. "Hey," I said back. "What a morning."

"Yeah?" she asked with a half smile, and I could tell she was trying to read me right off the bat. "How so?"

"Just a lot going on with this case," I said. "When I leave here, I'll go right back to the scene."

Mary smiled and also leaned forward in her chair, placing her hands on the desk just like mine. "Is that your way of telling me that you can't wait to get out of here?"

"No, I was just . . . telling you what I have planned for the rest of the day," I said.

She shook her head. "Well, let's just go ahead and get it all out there, so you can get back to what you need to do," she said. "Fair enough?"

"Yeah, of course," I said.

"So how have you been?" she asked me, her hands now clasped in front of her on her desk.

When they first told me I was going to have to start seeing the department therapist, I'd pictured a long lounge chair, as she sat next to me in an armless chair. I was pleased that she always remained behind her desk and that the sessions felt more like business meetings than they did meetings with a shrink.

"Fine," I said. "Look, I know that Gayla called you."

She nodded. "I asked her to."

"I know, but do you think that's the best idea? Given how closely we work together?"

"Yes," she said. "It's a good idea *because* of how closely you work together."

"But it's affecting our relationship."

"It shouldn't," she said. "She's just worried about you and wants to do what she can to help. It only affects your relationship if you have something to hide."

"That's bullshit," I said, and she sat back in her chair. "Sorry. But it feels like she's spying on me," I said. "She's my partner. I should be able to trust her."

"I've never asked Gayla to tell me anything about your personal life, and I think we both know that she wouldn't cross that boundary. But for me to determine if you're . . . in the right mental state for this work, right now, I need all the information I can get." She paused. "Look, why don't you tell me what happened at the Lindsey house. Just be honest. It's not a guarantee

178

either way that . . ."

"That what?" I asked. "That you're going to recommend me for a suspension?"

"That's not what I was going to say. It's not a guarantee of anything, okay?" she said. "Just tell me."

I sighed. "I just started overheating, and I needed to step outside for some fresh air."

"You weren't having a blackout?" she asked.

I tensed. That damned word.

"No."

"Do you need to step out for fresh air often?"

"No, just here and there," I said. "And it's never happened under pressure. So I don't see why it's such a big deal."

"Gayla said that you wouldn't stop staring at the couch. Like you saw something there."

"Of course I did," I said, and I swallowed, because the image of the couch started to return, and I felt the familiar tingle beneath my skin. I sat up straight and gently rubbed my arm, making sure my bandages stayed in place beneath my sleeve. "I saw a couch covered in blood. Everything I do doesn't have to be overanalyzed," I said.

"That's exactly the point," she said. "Don't you get that? We're overanalyzing

179

things right now, and we need to know that, even with that, you're okay." Mary scooted her chair closer to her desk and leaned forward, peering at me. "Let's talk about something else. How are your parents?"

"They're fine," I said. "Not much to report. They spend most of their time in the garden. Mike has been having some back problems, but he's going to get it checked out next week. Nothing too serious."

She nodded, and if she knew that I was being dismissive, she didn't say anything. "And Kit? Any progress with him or your ex-wife?"

I shrugged. "Not really," I said. She didn't say anything, and I knew she was doing the thing where she went all silent to get me to say something. I tried to resist and finally shrugged again. "Seriously, there's not much to tell. I haven't even talked to Kit since last week. Lara is . . ."

"She's what?"

But I didn't know how to finish the sentence.

*Lara is avoiding me, even though she said she wouldn't.*

*Lara is sleeping with the potato-shaped man she left me for, and he's probably telling her not to let me see Kit.*

*Lara is not there to help me through the*

180

*nightmares, and they're getting worse.*

"Can we change the subject?" I asked.

"Okay," she said slowly. "Do you want to talk about your probation period instead? You only have six weeks left. You can handle that, right?"

"I can handle it, and it's actually five weeks and four days," I said. "But to answer your first question, no, I don't want to talk about that instead."

On my way to the station, I decided to make a detour and stop by the site where Cruise said he'd picked up Emily.

I got off the highway and drove in the direction of the spot that Dori had texted me.

It took another fifteen minutes for me to reach the search area, and when I did, I pulled off on the side of the road. I didn't see any members of the search crew out there; they'd likely be back in a few hours. I got out of the car and shut the door, looking around for any signs that they'd found something — a strip of yellow tape, a cone, anything.

*What were you doing out here, Emily?*

*Why were you out here alone?*

*How'd you get here, and where's your car?*

I tried to imagine what was going on in

181

her head as she walked along the side of the road, covered in blood. She'd been lucky that Cruise was driving by. If he hadn't, it would have taken her a couple of hours to get anywhere that she could be helped. And then what?

Where was she coming from, and where was she going? And what did the symbol that she'd drawn mean?

I walked farther into the woods, looking around for any signs or clues that would explain what had happened. It would take days to search the area, if not weeks. The dense forest all looked the same, and there seemed to be layers upon layers where even the smallest clue could hide.

I kept walking, looking for anything out of the ordinary.

I couldn't shake the feeling that Dan Lindsey was hiding something, that behind his kind eyes, there was something more. When he'd let his guard down, just a bit, I'd seen something else, a deep anger with the way his wife was living her life. And he seemed to be upset about something in particular.

But what would he have to hide?

And there was still no indication about how she could've known about me. Or who the other man was whose name she'd scribbled next to mine.

The breeze billowed through the trees, pushing hot air around my face, and I straightened, my eyes scanning the land-scape for any clue about how and why Emily had gotten there.

And then, I heard a noise.

I spun around, my gaze searching the trees for what had made the crackling sound. It was the sound of someone, or something, stepping on dry foliage. Deer were known to roam Piper Woods, but it seemed unlikely that one would get so close to me.

I kept walking, my body alert, sweat form-ing beneath my arms and above my lip.

*It's probably nothing.*

*It's probably just the trees.*

But then I saw him.

A man, whose face I couldn't make out, wearing a tan suit and standing next to a tree about forty feet away from me.

From the distance, he seemed to blend in with the background, and I almost missed him.

"Hey," I said, not loud enough for him to hear, as I started off in his direction.

His gaze trained on mine, the man took a single step to one side, and then he was hid-den, blocked by the tree.

I picked up my pace and tore through the

woods toward him, my chest tight, and when I reached the tree, I stopped and spun in every direction.

He was gone. There was nothing. No one. No sign that he'd actually been there, that I wasn't crazy, that I hadn't made it all up.

Nothing.

I leaned back against the tree and reached into my pocket to fish out my Altoids case. Opening it with shaking hands, I popped a mint into my mouth and waited for my breathing to slow.

# CHAPTER FOURTEEN

*Then*

Shy Perry didn't know exactly when he'd gotten his nickname, but he remembered the day that it stuck. It was when Mother Samantha added "shy" to his name one day in class and then giggled with the rest of the students as she corrected herself.

"I'm sorry, *Perry,*" she said, as if it was a strain on her to say his name correctly. "It's just that's what everyone calls you, and I've gotten used to it." She seemed embarrassed about the mistake, but she laughed it off with everyone else so that *he* ended being the one that was embarrassed.

Perry was shy; he knew it. It was hard for him to forget it. He didn't know why he was shy or what he could do to get over it. He wished he could, but shyness wasn't one of those things you could just will away.

He'd tried.

He'd finally decided that it was easier to

just live with it; he avoided people as much as possible and stumbled when he had to read aloud in class, only because he couldn't think when anyone was watching him.

Shy Perry was one of the last people the mothers would expect to try to break the rules on June 2. He just wasn't the type. He tended to do what was asked of him, which wasn't too dangerous, since he was rarely asked to do anything out of order.

Maybe that's why he'd said yes. Jack could have asked anybody, and he had asked him. Perry was pretty good at drawing, but he wasn't the best by any means.

It was April, and the whole team was sitting in the library. Jack, Lill, the twins, and Perry. They hadn't met that many times, because it was hard to get all of them in the same place at the same time. But Jack had been adamant that they needed to spend time together, to get the mothers used to seeing them as a group, so that nothing would seem out of the ordinary. They were going to have to work together a lot over the next couple of months, and it would help if the mothers just thought it was a natural friendship that they'd seen develop before their eyes.

As they sat in the library, Perry nervously twirled a pen in his hands. Jack had told him that he had an important job for him and that all he would have to do was draw. Today was the day he'd learn what that meant. Perry might be shy, but he wasn't silly; he knew it wasn't going to be as simple as the drawings he did every day during and after class.

No, Jack needed something in particular, and Perry just hoped that he'd be able to pull it off.

Perry continued to tap his pen against the paper in front of him. Brat was talking a mile a minute about all the things they still had to do in the next couple of months. Perry hoped she would leave time for Jack to talk about the drawing he needed.

"We need a broom," Brat said, smacking her gum. "That's the only way we can sweep the sand up after we walk through it."

"A broom?" Gumball said slowly, smacking her gum. "Nobody said there were going to be chores involved."

"Well, what else would we do?" Gumball asked. "Float? We have to sweep it up. Right, Jack?"

"Don't worry about the broom," Jack said with a small smile. "That will be the easy part. What we need to work on is the gate key."

"Yeah, how in the world do you propose

we do that?" Lill asked. She took two fingers from each hand and rubbed her temples in slow circles. She did this whenever she was stressed. "I mean, assuming we have the stairwell key . . ." She trailed off, and Perry watched as Jack and Lill exchanged a look. He didn't know what they'd done, but they said they had the stairwell key covered.

Perry wasn't sure what Jack meant when he said that getting the broom would be the easy part — but he believed him.

Lill bit her lip nervously, still rubbing her head. "Seriously, what's your plan, Jack?" she asked. "It's impossible. Whoever is on duty will have the gate key with her at all times. And we don't even know who that's going to be. We won't know that until it's too late."

"That's why we're going to get the spare that Mother Beth keeps."

There was a collective gasp at the table, and Perry looked over to see if any of the mothers had noticed.

Perry trusted Jack, but this was too much.

Mother Beth was the writing teacher. She had a spare key, everyone knew, but it wasn't one that came out often. Only once did she have to use her key, when one of the mothers dropped the key in the space between the elevator and the floor. It had taken them fifteen minutes to find Mother Beth and for her to bring her key down. The children had gathered near the first gate, waiting for someone to come relieve them.

It had been terrifying, but Jack had locked the information away.

"You want to get Mother Beth's key?" Lill exclaimed, and they all shushed her and looked around the library. "That's crazy. She'd kill us if she ever found out. We don't even know where she keeps it."

Perry watched as Jack turned to him. "Right. Which is where we need your help, Perry."

Perry swallowed. "Okay," he muttered. "Wha— what can I do?"

"We need you to make some drawings of Mother Beth's office."

"Some . . . drawings?"

"Yeah, sort of like a floor plan."

"How should I do that?"

"Every day, you walk by it, right?"

"Yeah."

"We need you to look inside, remember as much as you can, and draw it."

"But there's no way I can get it all," Perry said. "I walk by the room so quickly."

"I've seen what you can do," Jack said. "You have to have faith in yourself. I know you can do it. Just do a little at a time."

"That's crazy," Lill said. "We walk by that office all the time, but he'd have to be inside to get a good look."

"You just have to take your time," Jack said again. "You won't get it all at once, and it may take a couple of weeks, but that's okay."

Perry wanted to protest, but he squared his shoulders and nodded. "Okay, I'll try," he said.

"There's no way that's going to work," Brat said, crossing her arms.

The next day, Perry stood in the elevator on his way to class. As the elevator doors opened and he stepped out onto the floor, he took a huge breath. He filed into line behind the other students and walked toward the end of the hall where his classroom was located.

As he walked past Mother Beth's office, he slowed down as much as he could and turned to take a quick peek inside. He only got about two seconds — anything else would have been suspicious. It wasn't enough. He walked sullenly to class and sat there staring at a blank piece of paper.

The next day, he tried again, and he was able to sketch out one chair on the side of the room. And the next day, he did it again, and then the next day.

A few weeks later, the group met in the library, and Perry pulled out his drawing. He laid it out on the table in front of them.

A loud laugh escaped Brat's lips. "You're kidding!" she said. Perry had drawn one corner of the room, the corner where the bookshelves met, and nothing else. "There's nothing there," she said.

Perry frowned and looked down at the table. He'd only been able to get a little at a time, and he wanted to make sure he wasn't missing any details. But Brat was right. It had already been weeks, and the picture didn't look like much.

"Wow," Jack said, and Perry looked up. "That's amazing."

"It . . . it is?" Perry asked.

"It's perfect. The level of detail is right on," Jack said. "This is just what we need. Keep going."

Perry smiled and placed the paper back in his folder.

The next day, Perry peeked again, getting another side of the room, and then another. Another week went by, and Perry had one complete corner and large blocks to sketch out the rest of the room. He'd drawn squares for everything — the desk, the bookshelf behind it, the fake tree on the side of the room — but every square was perfectly placed on the page. Now, he would just have to go back and fill in details for all of the items, and he would be done.

Perry was in class tracing over the square that represented the vase on Mother Beth's desk when he felt a presence behind him. He felt his breath catch as he turned and saw Mother Beth herself peering over his shoulder.

"What's that?" Mother Beth asked.

Perry froze, the pen between his fingers, his heart racing.

He knew there wasn't time to cover it up — *she'd already seen it!* — and he couldn't think of a single response that would make any sense. So he sat there as Mother Beth reached over his shoulder and picked up the sheet of paper with the drawing of her own office, staring at it silently in front of the entire class.

Perry felt his heart sink into his shoes. He turned and looked at Jack, who was staring back at him with an expression of horror.

Mother Beth looked at the picture. She even turned it over in her hands. She seemed to do this in slow motion, spinning the picture around, upside down, turning it over and then back again. Then she just stared at it, as if it were moving, or as if she were waiting for it to do something. Perry thought he'd fall out of his chair, he was so nervous.

"Perry, you really have to stop scribbling and pay attention," she said. "And if you're going to doodle in my class, you have to realize that everything that happens here gets judged. Since this is your work for the class, I'm going to have to give you a grade." She took the cap off the red pen she wore on a rope around her neck and scribbled something on it. "If you don't mind, I'll take this up to the front of the room with the rest of the projects."

She walked through the desks with the piece of paper in her hands. It seemed like the slowest walk in history. The entire room leaned forward, their gazes on the paper, practically salivating, waiting to see just what it was that Perry had drawn.

Mother Beth reached above her head and used a pushpin to secure Perry's drawing above the chalkboard. She'd written "−5 pts."

Perry sat there, mortified, waiting for someone to say something or for Mother Beth to look more closely at the curves on the page and recognize what it was.

But it never happened.

Someone giggled, and someone else muttered something that sounded like "just a bunch of squares," and then that was it. Mother Beth was back to her lesson, and Perry was still frozen in the exact same place, the same expression on his face.

When he could finally breathe again, he turned to look at Jack. But the other boy was looking down at his book in front of him coolly, as if nothing had happened.

Perry took a deep breath and tried to follow suit.

*Too close.*

# CHAPTER FIFTEEN

*Now*

When I woke up the next morning, my arm had fresh bandages on it, and my razor was clean and put away. I rolled over and stared at Kit's race car on the nightstand for a few moments before pulling the duvet up and over my head.

Who was the man at the lake, and why the hell was he following me?

What did he want?

Did he know something about Emily? The symbol?

And most important of all: *Had he even really been there?*

I'd called it in as I left Piper Woods, but I didn't have much to tell them.

"That's it, a man wearing all tan who ran away from you in the woods," said Dori.

"That's it."

About an hour after I woke up, I finally sat up and reached for my phone on my

195

nightstand. I had a missed call from Gayla. She was taking her niece to the doctor that morning and would meet me later.

I texted Gayla back and told her I'd go to see Emily's webmaster and that I would fill her in later. She'd simply written back *K.* I finished getting ready and left the apartment.

We'd found Todd Rugel using the "contact the webmaster" link on Emily's page. It took two requests, but he finally responded with his name and phone number. I pulled up to his home, a modern, five-story apartment building near the river. It was a beautiful building, with polished brick everywhere. I parked in an alley on the side of the building. I got out of the car and walked up to the buzzer, searching for his name.

I rang his doorbell a little past ten, and he spoke a couple of seconds later.

"Yeah?"

"Todd, it's Detective Paul. You spoke with my partner about *Carmen Street*? Wanted to ask you a few questions."

"Yeah," he said again. "She said you'd be coming by. Come on up, third floor."

He buzzed the door, and I pushed it open and stepped inside the tastefully decorated, blue-and-tan lobby. I took the elevator up to the third floor and headed toward his apartment. I knocked, and the door swung open just a few seconds later.

"Todd?" I asked the man standing in front of me.

He tilted his head to the side. He was about five foot eight, with brown skin, curly black hair, glasses, sharp eyes, and a nervous energy that made me think he spent more of his time behind a computer than in front of people.

"Yes," he said. "Please, come in. You know, you could have parked out front in the permit area."

I frowned as I stepped inside. "How do you know I didn't?"

"I've been watching you since you parked," he said, pointing at his open balcony door. "That overlooks the alley. You didn't have to park there."

I didn't ask him why he'd been out there in the first place. "It's okay," I said. "It often helps keep things quiet around the building. People see a cop car parked out front, and their minds go all sorts of places."

"That's logical," he said. We stopped walking at the edge of the living room, and he turned to me. "So, what can I tell you?"

"I'm here to learn a little more about you and Emily — your relationship, how you met, how you work together," I said. His eyebrows shot up, and I added, "Your business relationship."

"Oh, okay," he said, putting a hand out for me to sit down. "Well, I do all of her web stuff — infrastructure, site architecture, maintenance, analytics. Whatever she needs. But you knew that already."

"Does she have a team of writers?"

"No, I don't think so," he said. "I think it's just her."

"And how was it that you came to start working together?" I asked.

"I got in touch with her," he said. "That's how I've gotten about 35 percent of my clients." He stood up and walked over to a computer, moving the mouse. He clicked a few times, pulling up a basic, two-column blog. "You know what this is?"

I leaned closer and looked at the screen. "No. What is it?"

"It's *Carmen Street,* back when Emily first started it," he said. "I got in touch with her when I kept seeing mentions of it. That's what I do. I asked her what her metrics were. She didn't even know how to track them, really. I couldn't believe it when she finally found it and told me that her private blog had upward of three thousand visitors per month. That's fantastic. I told her that with my help, she could double it, and we started working together for a fee. The site grew, my role grew, and here we are today."

I looked at the old site — it did look much different than the site Gayla and I had pulled up at the station the other night. This one looked like a basic template for a website that you could get on a free site.

"So you do that often? I mean, approaching people and offering your services."

"Yes," he said. "I send out notes at least a few times a week. It's difficult to get new business, but once you get a client, it's a pretty steady revenue stream for what can often be minimal work."

"So you approach Emily, she agrees to give you a try, and you succeed," I said.

"Exactly."

"Tell me about how often you and Emily met, how you worked together," I said.

He spun in his chair and looped his arms behind his head. "We only met in person maybe once a month. Other than that, we texted, emailed, talked on the phone."

"What was she like to work with?"

"Emily is really . . . introverted, I guess," he said. "She's an amazing writer, and she has a lot to say but not actually *say*," he said. "I hope that's not out of line. I just never got the sense that she liked interacting with people."

"Nothing's out of line in an investigation like this," I said. "Not if it's the truth."

He nodded.

"Her doctor told us that her parents died when she was younger?" I said.

"Yeah, in a car accident."

"Do you know who raised her?" I asked.

"I don't know all of that," he said. "I mean, we just worked together. I only knew about her parents because she wore that locket around her neck with their pictures in it."

"Locket?"

"Yeah," he said. "That thing was a beauty. Had to be worth a small fortune. My father was in the jewelry business, and the minute I saw it, I knew it was something special. When you grow up around jewelry — I mean, real jewelry — you notice little things," he said.

"What do you mean?"

"Like the way someone responds when you compliment them on a piece. It's usually pretty easy to tell when it's something that means a lot to them or if it's something they picked up randomly at the mall. This locket, it was something different, that's for sure."

"What did this locket look like?" I asked.

"Gold with teal stones flanking each side

in the shape of a heart. She had a picture of each of her parents on either side." He paused. "Wait, she's not wearing it?"

I shook my head.

"That's weird," he said. "She was wearing it each time we met, and I finally asked her about it. She told me that she never took it off."

"Do you think she could have just been exaggerating?"

"No," he said. "The way she said it, I could tell it was really important to her. She had it on the few times I met her, and she always toyed with it. Like a nervous habit, you know?"

I made a note about the locket. It didn't make any sense — where could the locket have gone? Did she lose it on the way home? Or worse, did she lose it in some kind of struggle? Had it been stolen?

And why hadn't Dan Lindsey said anything about it? If it was so important, wouldn't he have noticed?

"So you think someone attacked Emily for her locket?" he asked. "I guess crazier things have happened."

That hadn't been what I was thinking, but I didn't feel the need to correct him.

"How does Emily interact with her blog readers?" I asked, switching angles.

He paused, and I couldn't tell if he was trying to figure out what the answer was to the question or how to answer it.

"Depends on the type of reader," he said, measuring his words. "She spends hours on the site, answering reader comments, starting discussion threads. Sometimes it wasn't so pleasant, but it's the nature of what she does. But she never shied away from it. She didn't like interacting with people in person, but she's a whole different person online," he said. He shrugged. "Online, she *was Carmen Street.*"

"When you say it wasn't pleasant sometimes, you mean the readers? Or Emily?"

He sighed and lifted one hand to rub the back of his neck. "I guess I mean both?" he said. "Emily . . . let's just say she could shoot fire from her fingertips, just as much as her internet trolls could."

"Would Ryan Griggs be one of those trolls?"

He rolled his eyes. "That asshole. Not much to tell that you don't already know, I'll bet. He's definitely hiding something when it comes to his drugs. I'll bet he knew what was in 'em and thought he could get away with it."

"Ever had any interaction with him? In person?"

He shook his head.

"One more question," I said. "Did you ever meet Emily's husband? Dan Lindsey?"

Todd nodded. "Yeah, a couple of times. Like once, I had to go by their house to drop off a report for Emily, and he was home."

"Now I need you to be completely candid with me. What was he like?"

"Dan? He was great," he said. He narrowed his eyes. "Oh, you don't think he could have had anything to do with this, do you? They were a perfect couple."

"How can you say that?" I asked. "You said you only met him a couple of times, and you worked with Emily mostly online anyway."

"Yeah, but Emily talked about him all the time. I mean *all* the time. About how wonderful he was. And when I went to the house, they seemed great, happy. He was doting and loving. Couldn't keep his hands off of her. It was kind of gross, actually. You know those couples. Honey baby this, and baby honey that."

If their sleeping situation was any indication, there was a lot more to it than that. It was the second time someone had described them as being extremely happy and in love — Emily's neighbor had said the same thing. Emily seemed to go out of her way to tell anyone who would listen about her wonderful marriage, even her business acquaintances.

Perfect couple, or a cover for something else going on?

And "doting" husband could easily be a misread for possessive.

"Well, thanks for your time," I said, standing and heading toward the door. I pulled a card from my pocket and handed it to him. "If you think of anything else that seems important —"

"Yeah, sure," he said. "I'll call you."

I left and headed toward the station. The missing locket was one of those small details that could be nothing at all.

When I got back to the station, Gayla was sitting behind her desk, typing furiously.

"Hey," she said. "How'd it go?"

I filled her in on everything that happened with the webmaster.

"That is weird," she said. "We'll have to search the house again for the locket. It's hard to believe that all of this could have been about a theft, but I've seen crazier things."

"Yeah, I guess so," I said.

As I walked to my desk, I heard a man's voice behind me.

"Excuse me?"

I spun around. Standing in front of me was Eleanor, Ryan Griggs's wife, and a man I'd never seen before. They both looked nervous as they stared at Gayla and myself. We walked over to them.

"Mrs. Griggs," I said. "How can we help you?"

She looked at the man standing beside her. Her eyes were puffy and wide, and I could see something else in them, besides the nervousness.

Determination.

She looked at the man and waited for him to say something.

The man spread his arms, and they communicated with each other silently.

"I don't . . ." the man started.

She shook her head. "You have to tell them," she said. "He could be hurt."

The man sighed and turned back to us. "My name is Philip Jameson," he said. "I work for Kelium Pharmaceuticals. I'm on the executive committee."

"Okay," Gayla said. "What can we do for you, Mr. Jameson?"

He hesitated again, and I saw something that looked like frustration on Eleanor Griggs's face.

"If you don't tell them, I will," she said,

and she sighed, softening her voice. "Please, Philip. You're going to have to let them know sooner or later."

"Let us know what?" Gayla asked, stepping forward. She didn't do well with things like this, and I knew that if one of them didn't speak soon, she was going to find a way to pull it out of them.

Jameson sighed again and shrugged. "She wanted me to come and tell you this, even though I'm not really sure that it's relevant right now. But I guess it could be, even though he'd kill me for coming here."

"What is it?" I asked. "Anything you can tell us, any information you have, might be beneficial and help us in finding Ryan and figuring out what happened. You have to tell us."

"Okay, okay," he said. "Look, I don't know what he was doing exactly. Ryan could be a hothead. That's his biggest problem. He's not really a bad person, but he just couldn't let things go sometimes, even with all of us telling him he had to."

"Couldn't let what go?" Gayla asked.

"The whole thing with the *Carmen Street* woman. He called me the other night," he said, trailing off again.

"And?"

"He told me that he was meeting up with her."

"Wait, when was this?" I asked, feeling my heart rate increase.

"Uh, like Thursday, I think?"

"He was meeting her where?" I asked.

"I don't know," he said. "He said that first, he went to see one of those patients, Enid Greene, and then —"

"Wait, one of the patients that Emily interviewed?" Gayla asked. "But isn't Enid Greene the one who lives here? I thought he went to Philadelphia first."

"I thought so, too," Eleanor said, her eyes watery. She looked over at Jameson. "Tell them the rest."

"Well, yeah, he said he went to see Enid and then that he was on his way to meet Emily. I think they talked sometimes. Not a lot, but I know they had each other's cell phone numbers, because I caught him talking to her one day at work. I told him he should quit, that he didn't need to keep talking with her, pleading with her, threatening her."

"Wait, he threatened her?"

"Well, I mean online. I never heard him threaten her on the phone. Actually, when I overheard their conversation, it sounded pretty cordial."

"What were they talking about?" I asked.

"I think they were arranging some kind of meeting."

"How long ago was this?"

"A few weeks ago," he said. "And then I didn't hear anything else until he called me a couple of days ago."

"What exactly did he say?" I asked. "His exact words."

"Just that they agreed to meet up to settle some things," he said. "To sort of . . . squash it."

Eleanor Griggs was staring at the man, her entire body shaking, and when he finished speaking, she turned back to me. "So what are you going to do?" she asked. "You have to find my husband. I know she did something to him. I just know it. Please, tell me you'll do absolutely everything you can to find him."

# CHAPTER SIXTEEN

*Then*

Lill sat on her bed with her legs crossed beneath her. She looked down at the key in her hands.

*You can do it.*

Mother Deena had given her the key just one week after she'd sobbed in her arms in the kitchen, but Lill hadn't used it yet. As Deena's belly grew, she seemed sadder and more tired, and Lill had made up her mind that she was going to go visit her tonight.

At first, she'd been mad at Jack for tricking her.

"There's no way I'm doing this," she said. "We could get in so much trouble."

But Jack had stared at her, his jaw set, and he'd spoken so softly that it broke her heart.

"I can't make you do it," he said. "But please, you have to. I need to know what happened to Mother Breanna. It's killing me. And Mother Deena —"

"Don't even try it," she snapped, and she felt bad, but she knew she was right. "This isn't about helping her. You're using her to get what you want."

"You're right," he said, slumping, and he looked up at her. "I didn't have any other choice. You could give me the key, say you lost it, and I'll never tell anybody, I promise. But we have to find a way to get upstairs."

She'd thought about it. And in the end, it had been Mother Deena, the way she looked in the hallways, that had made up Lill's mind. It was getting worse. Now, it seemed like she was crying every day, her eyes puffy, her stride slow. And every time she saw Lill, she'd smile and raise her eyebrows.

Lill had seen her earlier that day in the cafeteria, and Mother Deena had taken her aside. "Maybe you could use the key I gave you," she said softly, sniffling and wiping at the corners of her eyes, and Lill had nodded furiously.

But as she sat in her room, she was scared. She didn't want to get in trouble, and she didn't want to get Mother Deena in trouble either. But if she didn't start using it, Mother Deena would just ask for it back, and then Jack would be upset. Lill bit her lip. She still wasn't sure that she'd help Jack, but she had to help Deena.

Steeling herself, she hopped off the bed and walked out into the hallway.

It would be so much easier if Mother Deena could just come downstairs. Sometimes, when the babies and toddlers in the third-floor nursery had fits, the mothers would bring them downstairs to Lill's room, where she'd sing them to sleep. Or the mothers would let her spend the night up in the nursery. Lill loved curling up in the bed with the sweet-smelling babies and singing until their eyes got droopy. One of the babies, who they'd nicknamed "Hiccup" due to the strange hiccupping sound he made when he laughed, giggled merrily every time Lill did so much as hum a single note.

"You have the voice of an angel," Mother Deena had said once while standing in the doorway to Lill's room as she sang Hiccup to sleep.

The gates would be locked in about an hour, so she didn't have much time. Mother Deena would be in her room reading or studying before bed. Lill crept through the gates and toward the stairwell. The mothers walked around occasionally, but they weren't that vigilant until bedtime. Without a key, the kids were stuck on the floor unless they used the elevator, which would alert the guards to their movements immediately. Lill took one look over her shoulder and then moved quickly into the stairwell.

She took a deep breath as she rounded the stairs to the first floor. The adults rarely used the stairs when they could use the elevators instead, and as she peered through the small glass in the door, she was happy to see that the floor appeared empty. Everyone was unwinding before bedtime, and they all thought the kids were safely downstairs. Lill used her key to unlock the stairwell door and stepped inside, letting it close gently behind her.

She walked down the hall slowly, being careful to stay close to the wall in case anyone came around the corner. The hallway was narrow, and there weren't that many items in it, which didn't give her anywhere to hide. She moved toward Mother Deena's room. She'd been there a couple of times before, but what if things had changed? What if she'd moved somewhere else? They hadn't talked this through well enough, hadn't figured out all the details, and now Lill was nervous.

She walked up to the door that she thought was Mother Deena's and took a deep breath before lightly knocking on it. She stepped quickly to the side, hoping she could duck out of sight if it was the wrong room. But a moment later, the door cracked open, and she leaned forward to see Mother Deena standing there, her face covered in tears.

"Lill!" she said softly and then stepped back so the girl could enter.

Lill walked inside and fought the urge to hug her. Mother Deena had always been so kind to her, and while she knew it was wrong to think of her as her mother, there was no denying their special connection.

"I just came to see if you were okay," Lill said nervously. "I know I shouldn't be up here."

"It's okay," Deena said, but she nodded, and it was clear that she was also nervous about Lill being upstairs. "I haven't been able to sleep in three days. I just lie here."

"What's . . . what's wrong?" Lill asked. "I mean, I know you're nervous about having another baby. But you're also happy, right?"

"Of course I'm happy," Deena said with a sad chuckle. "I'm happy, but I'm also worried about what's going to happen to my baby."

"What do you mean?" Lill asked.

"Three out of the last seven mothers who

have given birth have lost their babies," Deena said softly. "Almost half. Don't get me wrong. I trust Frank, and he says that if it's God's will, it's God's will and to never doubt it. And I don't. It's just . . ."

Lill waited, watching her carefully.

"It's just I don't want that to happen to me."

Lill nodded and sat down on the bed next to her.

Deena stared past her. It was unlike her, and Lill wasn't sure how she was supposed to respond. Deena seemed more like a child than one of the adults. Lill hesitated before reaching out and grabbing Deena's hand.

Deena blinked a few times and looked down at their hands, and the tears began to spill over her cheeks.

"I'm sorry," Lill said, pulling her hand back.

Deena shook her head. "No, it's okay," she said. But the tears wouldn't stop.

Without realizing what she was doing, Lill began to hum. It was a soft, gentle sound, because she felt uncomfortable and also because she couldn't take the risk that any of the other mothers on the floor would hear her. But the sound — a hymn she sometimes sang in assembly on Sundays — began to flow from her, softly filling the room. Deena stopped crying immediately, her eyes going to the young girl's face, and they stared at each other as Lill continued to hum.

Then Lill opened her mouth and began to sing. It was still incredibly low, so soft she could barely hear herself as she whispered the words across the bed. But it was effective. Deena grasped her hands tighter, and a soft, peaceful expression took over her face. She slid down lower on the bed until she was lying down fully. With her free hand, Lill took the book that was sitting beside her and placed it on Mother Deena's nightstand, then helped arrange the covers over the woman's body. It felt wrong, tucking her in this way. They both knew it, and yet Lill could see the effect she was having on Deena and knew that she couldn't stop. She kept going, letting the melodic sounds fill the room, as Deena settled peacefully into bed.

When her eyes drooped, Lill knew that she was going to fall asleep, and she launched into another verse. She trailed off as she saw that her mother was finally asleep.

She stood up, dropping Deena's hand before turning the light out beside her. She was surprised to find that her own cheeks were damp with tears. She turned and walked back to the door, opening it slowly and scanning the hallways. There was nobody there. Jack was right — the kids definitely would have noticed Mother Deena downstairs — but it wasn't too hard for her to go unnoticed up here. She slipped back into the stairwell and headed downstairs. She didn't know how long she could keep this up, but she felt happy, as if she'd done the right thing.

She reached the ground floor and peered into the children's wing. That door was always unlocked from the stairwell, and she quickly let herself inside. As she stepped through toward the first set of steel gates, she heard a noise behind her.

She whipped around and saw one of the other boys, Ellis, standing there, his eyes glued on her face.

"Hey," she said, her heart pounding.

"Hey," he said, stepping closer, a slight frown on his face. "Where were you?"

"Hmm?" she asked.

"Where were you?"

"Nowhere. I'm just going to bed."

"You just came from the stairwell."

"Oh, yeah, Mother Deena needed me to tell her about something from class. She just let me back in."

He frowned. "Why did you all use the

stairwell?" he asked. "That's weird."

Lill shrugged. "No reason."

"It's against the rules," he said.

"I —" Lill stopped herself and squared her shoulders. "Are you gonna tell?"

Her heart was beating fast, but she knew she could handle this. Ellis was a quiet boy, one year older than her, and he always followed the rules.

But Lill had also seen him staring at her sometimes.

Lill stepped forward and reached out one hand to him. "Tell me you won't say anything," she said. "Please?"

Ellis blinked a few times, and a soft smile crossed his face. He reached out, took her hand in his, and nodded, his cheeks turning red.

"Okay," he said. "I won't tell. I promise."

# CHAPTER SEVENTEEN

*Now*

Lara and her new husband lived in our house. The not-too-big, not-too-small one with the modern appliances and vintage charm. The one where we were going to raise Kit and maybe another kid, too, if the birth control gods said it was to be.

It would have been in a good neighborhood, our house, but not *too* good, not *too* sheltered, because we weren't *those* people whose kids grew up like *that.*

We'd lie in bed in our one-bedroom apartment, wrapped up in our sweat and body heat and adoration for each other, and talk about the house we'd never see. The one she'd be living in with him just a few years later. The one I'd drive by when I felt lonely or ached for a glimpse of her and Kit.

"We should look for something just outside of the city," Lara had said one time, the sheets tangled around our bodies, her nose pressed into my neck. "So that we can have enough space for a yard, but also be just a quick drive to the train. I don't want to be one of those couples who moves out to the suburbs and then gets defined by it. Like Sam and Tina in Rosemont. Or Jim and his wife."

"Jim?"

"The ones who live in Greta."

"Oh yeah."

As I pulled up in front of their house, I couldn't help but think back to one of our first dates. I'd taken her to a Vietnamese restaurant in her neighborhood, and halfway through it, I'd had the sudden urge to tell her about the nightmares, just to get it out of the way.

"What's the one thing that you haven't told me yet that you think I should know about you?" I asked.

She put her fork down and cleared her throat. "Okay, here it comes, huh?" she asked. "You're married?"

"What?" I cried out, choking on the forkful I'd just stuck in my mouth.

"Are you married?"

"No —"

"Okay then, is it toe fungus?"

"What?" Louder this time.

She leaned forward in her seat and, with a

completely level voice asked, "Do you have toe fungus?"

"I don't, no —"

"Because 'tell me one thing I should know about you' is the kind of thing you say when you're itching to get something off your chest, which means you have something you want to tell me that you think I'm not going to like." The couple at the table next to us looked over and then back at each other, barely pretending that they weren't listening. "Just so you know, those are two things that I really, really wouldn't like. For really different reasons."

"Okay," I said. "Well, no, I'm not married, and I don't . . . Wait, why toe fungus? That's very specific —"

"Excuse me."

We both turned and looked at the table beside us.

"Could you please stop saying 'fungus'? We're trying to eat."

I apologized and turned back to Lara, whose face was bright red.

She stifled a giggle as she picked up her fork again. "Sorry, it is specific, but it's just a thing I have. Everybody has their things." She said this last sentence softly, pointedly, and I knew she was giving me my opening.

"You're right," I said. "There is something

I wanted to tell you. I . . ."

And then it seemed stupid, and I played around with the words in my mouth before letting them spill out.

"All my life . . . I've had these . . . or I've suffered from . . ."

"What, Steve?"

"Chronic nightmares."

I waited for her to laugh or to look uncomfortable, but she didn't move. She just sat there, her fork in her hand, waiting for me to continue.

When I didn't say anything, she finally spoke.

"Is that a thing? Aren't nightmares by nature . . . chronic?"

She wasn't trying to be funny, and I could see that she was genuinely trying to understand. And at that moment, I realized that I'd never — not once — had the conversation I was about to have with her with anyone else.

I told her about the dreams, the nightmares, the stifling, the waking up, right then and there over a bowl of pho on our third date. I whispered because of the eavesdroppers next to us, and she leaned in closely as I told her things I'd never said out loud to Nell or Mike or anyone else. She listened and asked questions, and as much as I could

221

tell, she cared.

I'd been burned in the past, and then there she was, so clearly and beautifully the one. Lara was smart, and not just in the book-smart way. And best of all was that with her, I was smart, too. I didn't have to *try* to be — my natural thoughts, my responses, my inclinations were always right with her. I was funnier, more compassionate. I was awesome with Lara. I knew it, and she knew it, and by date number three, I knew I wanted to spend the rest of my life with her.

As I sat in my car outside their house, I struggled with my desire to drive away and the deep pull to go and bang on the door and demand that she let me see Kit.

I'd called her again that morning, and she'd picked up on the last ring.

"Steve . . ." she'd started.

"Look, if I can't see him, just say it," I'd said. It was mean, I knew it. I should just let it go. Put her out of her misery. Lara would never say no. "Just tell me that you have no obligation to let me see him, that you won't let me, and I'll leave you alone."

She hadn't said anything for a while, and not for the first time, I had marveled at how different our relationship was from what it had been only a short time ago.

"Lara?" I had said, and then I had been whiny. "You're the one who said it would be okay for me to see him once in a while, and it's been four months."

"Come over tonight," she had said suddenly. "I'll tell Kit that you're coming. Just for an hour or so."

"Are you sure?" I had started, but it was halfhearted, and we both knew it.

I had heard her sigh deeply. "Text me when you're on your way."

I'd texted her, but she hadn't texted back.

I got out of my car and walked up to the door. The front stoop was lined with plants and flowers of every variety. My leg brushed against a pot of roses as I climbed the steps, and I rolled my eyes.

When I first learned that she was remarrying just seven months after our divorce was finalized, I hadn't been able to focus on anything except the guy's job.

"He's a what . . . horticulturalist?"

"No, Steve, he's a dentist. Who has a green thumb."

As I navigated the plants that led up to their front door, it was clear that it was much more than just a hobby.

I rang the doorbell and waited, my heart pounding against my rib cage.

The door flew open, and I sucked in a breath when I saw who it was.

Greg, the dentist with the green thumb.

I shouldn't have been surprised to see him — it was his house, after all — but I'd been preparing myself to see Lara. I figured he'd avoid me or at most walk by to make sure I knew how unhappy he was about me coming over.

But to answer the door?

"Hi," I said slowly. "Is Lara —"

"She's not here," he said.

I froze. "She isn't?"

"No, she had to make some stops after work. She told me you were coming over." He stepped back and opened the door wider to let me inside.

What the hell?

"Should I come back later?" I asked.

"Why?" he asked levelly. "Kit's here."

We glared at each other, and I finally nodded. "Yeah, of course."

As I stepped into the house, I was overwhelmed with the smell of nature and the sight of greenery everywhere. Plants and flowers, of all shapes and sizes, lined the floors, the windows, the entire house.

Greg led me to the living room and told me to take a seat. I was surprised that he seemed as uncomfortable as I did. As I sat there, I felt an overwhelming feeling of self-doubt, and I wondered what the hell I was doing there.

How had it come to this?

I should just leave.

I was that guy, and I desperately, painfully, needed to *stop being him.*

For the sake of Lara and her husband, and, arguably, for Kit.

I was standing to leave when I heard a noise behind me. I spun around, and there he was.

And every bit of the awkward mess I was creating made sense.

Kit stared at me, his eyes round, one hand in Greg's. And then he flew across the room and buried himself in my arms. As he did, I felt like the unthinkable was going to happen, that I would start to cry right there in the living room, without Lara there, just me and Greg and our kid. I felt the tears rush to the surface, and I stood up quickly, lifting him up into the air.

"Hey, buddy," I croaked out.

"Hi," he said shyly.

We spent an hour together. He told me about the turtles they were taking care of at school, his friend Robby, and the play that Greg and Lara were making him participate in.

225

"Everyone has to do it, but I could've just been in the choir," he said softly. "They told Mrs. Lewis to give me a bigger role, so now I have the second biggest part."

I felt a wave of anger at Lara for pushing him too far out of his comfort zone. Kit had been an incredibly shy toddler, and she'd acted as if it was the end of the world, as if it were a sign of the kind of life he'd face.

"We have to push him out of it," she'd said. "I read that this is the most important age for socialization."

"Four?" I'd said. "That's what's most important for him at *four*? How about we just let him grow out of it naturally?"

I leaned over and ruffled Kit's hair. "You'll be great, okay?" I said.

He nodded.

I knew it was time for me to go when Greg appeared in the doorway. He didn't say anything, just stood there while Kit and I finished our conversation.

"Hey, I gotta take off, okay?" I said, and Kit stared at me and nodded. "I'll stop by this weekend and drop off your birthday present, okay? I got you something special."

He smiled. "Okay," he said quickly.

I knew then that he'd been preparing for me to leave, that he'd been warned that I could only stay for a little while, and that he

226

knew he shouldn't make a big deal about it.

I gave him a hug and followed Greg out onto the front porch. From his body language, I could tell that he was going to say something.

"You talked to Lara about dropping off the gift?" he asked.

"No, but I didn't think she'd have a problem with me bringing —"

"You could've brought it today," he said.

"But I didn't."

He sighed. "You know this isn't going to last much longer, right?"

"What?"

"Look, man, I'm seriously not trying to be a jerk, okay. Really. But this can't continue."

"This isn't between you and me," I said. "It's between me and Lara."

He chuckled. "And that's where you mess up. Thinking that there's anything between you and Lara that's not between you and me," he said.

I wanted to kick him in his smug face, but the problem was that he wasn't just smug. He was also probably right.

"Look," he said. "I'm going to do what Lara wants me to do, because you're right. This is her choice. And she is worried about Kit, and it's obvious that you two had something. But you have to know that it's not going to last forever. If Lara doesn't start pulling back, Kit will. He's seven. He's got to move on with his life. He needs someone who's there for him, and that's me now. I'm sorry it was you before and that things didn't work out, but that's life. You gotta grow up, man."

I balled my fists at my sides and stopped myself from responding.

There was nothing I could say that would help things.

He turned to go back into his home, and I walked down the stairs, feeling exhausted, sad, and angry all at the same time.

Because, of course, he was right.

I just didn't think that made me wrong.

And he certainly didn't have to be a *dick* about it.

*I'll show you how grown-up I can be.*

On the way down the stairs, I let my fingers close around one of his perfect roses.

Ripping the flower from the stalk, I crumpled it in my fingers and scattered it on the pavement as I walked back to my car.

# CHAPTER EIGHTEEN

"You all right?" Gayla asked me, the following day.

I looked over at her, and she nodded toward the steering wheel. I followed her gaze and saw that I was tapping my fingers quickly against it without noticing it. I stopped, gripping the wheel tighter, and I tried to slow my racing thoughts.

We were heading back out to Piper Woods. I didn't know what the hell we were going to find out there, but we had to keep looking for some sort of clue as to why Emily had been out there.

Another team had been dispatched to the site, and Gayla and I were heading out to help with the search. And I could barely sit still. What if I saw the man in tan again?

And worse, what if I saw him and nobody else did?

It was hard enough facing my visions and nightmares on my own, but it was exhausting trying to make sure that nobody else knew what was going on.

As I pressed down on the gas pedal and sped toward the lake, I peeked over at Gayla again. She was staring at me with that sort of peaceful, inquisitive expression that said "I'm not judging you, but of course, I am."

Mary gave me that look a lot, sometimes when she didn't want me to know what she was thinking. I hate that look. It's equal parts sympathy, pity, and yes, judgment. I had to deal with it from Mary — that was her job — but I didn't need it from Gayla, too.

"Steven?"

I looked over at her, and she was watching me with a frown on her face. I realized she'd been talking for a while, but I hadn't heard a single word she said.

"Hey," she said. "What's wrong?"

"Nothing," I said with a shrug, hoping my expression was neutral enough. "Sorry, just lost in thought, but I'm okay."

"What were you lost in thought about?" she asked.

"Just trying to process this whole case. I'm not sure if there's anything left to find out here. It seems like it's been gone over with a fine-tooth comb."

"Yeah, maybe not," she said. "But I guess

230

it's worth taking at least one more look. Not like we have many other leads. What we need is to find her car."

We pulled up to the site about twenty-five minutes later and got out of the car. The air was humid and sticky today, and the sun was blazing down. I flashed back to two days ago and the man I'd seen in the woods. The itchy sensation started again in my arms, and I tried to fight it. I looked over at Gayla, but her gaze was glued to her surroundings, and she didn't seem to notice how uncomfortable I was. I swallowed. I'd been hiding the images from people for so long. I'd always told myself that I would try to get to the root cause — to *get rid* of the nightmares and the images instead of just dealing with them. But then a year went by, and another. I found a new way to tackle it, and when that got old, I found something else. I knew that I should do something about it, but just getting through each day was hard enough.

We stepped through the trees and branches, and I was overcome with a sense of déjà vu from my experience the previous day.

"Steven?"

I looked up at Gayla. "Let's head back to the search team," I said. "There's nothing out here."

We began to walk away from the lake and back toward the main road. As we walked along, we came across a few members of the search team, and I could hear the sound of a dog barking in the distance. We didn't know what we were looking for. The car. Some signs of why she'd been out there.

And of course, any further signs of Ryan Griggs.

I saw a woman walking up to me, and I sighed when I saw that it was Eleanor Griggs. She was dressed in a bright-pink terry cloth jumpsuit, and she wore a pair of expensive-looking sunglasses. She was clutching her purse to her side, a huge, black leather bag with short handles, no strap.

"Nice purse to bring out on a search party for your missing husband," Gayla whispered.

Eleanor was standing with a man who it took me a second to recognize. Philip Jameson, the Kelium executive. He was dressed more reasonably, in jeans and a polo shirt, but somehow, he still seemed out of place.

"Why are they always together?" Gayla whispered. "Think something's going on there?"

"I don't know," I said as we came within earshot.

"Thanks for coming," Gayla said, changing her tone, her gaze darting to me before she turned back to the pair. "But it might be a good idea if you are home in case your husband returns. We have some great teams out here searching the area, and they're very capable."

The woman nodded. "I don't doubt it. That's not why I'm here. I couldn't just do nothing. I can't stand to just sit at home," she said. "I was going insane. The least I can do is come out here to help."

"Do you have your cell phone with you?" Gayla asked. "In case your husband calls?"

"Of course I do," she said.

I looked over at Jameson. He was standing next to Eleanor, his hands in his pockets, his face ghostly white, his entire body shaking.

"Are you all right?" I asked.

He looked at me and blinked a few times, and I could tell that he was far from all right. But after a moment, he looked over at Eleanor and nodded.

I took a glance at Gayla, who was watching them both with a frown on her face. It was clear that there was more between the two of them than they were admitting to, but the question was, how much more?

And did that have anything to do with Griggses' disappearance?

Jameson cleared his throat. "Are you sure the blood couldn't have come from something else?" he asked, his voice breathy, and I could tell that being out here in the woods looking for his partner was the last place he wanted to be. "Maybe it was animal blood or something. Not that it wouldn't be cause for question, but maybe it wasn't a person."

"No, it was from a human," I said slowly, trying to read him. We locked eyes, and he looked away. He was definitely shaken up, and I couldn't tell if it was just the circumstances around why we were all out there or something more.

We were turning to walk away when, suddenly, the barking got louder.

The sound of the dogs had been there before, a background noise that reminded us about the morbid truth of our search. But the dogs' sudden increase in volume stopped us all in our tracks.

It was a jarring, ominous sound out there in the woods, and everyone froze. My body jolted, and I could see an expression of dread descend on the faces of the people standing in front of me. My eyes darted from Jameson's face, to Eleanor Griggs's, and finally Gayla's.

Gayla didn't get easily rattled, but her eyes had widened, and her lips were parted slightly as we all listened to the dogs barking loudly, anxiously.

They'd found something.

We all took off at the same time, racing through the trees toward the noise. I was pulled back to the previous day when I'd followed the man in the tan suit, but this was different. The sound of the dogs barking was crystal clear, and more important, there were other people around to hear them.

No question about it — this was real.

I felt short of breath, but I kept going, just an inch or so off Gayla's heels. I could hear Eleanor and Philip scrambling behind me. We came into a small clearing where a crowd of people had formed. We were only about ten feet or so from where we'd parked our cars, close to the main road.

The small group stood in a circle, and they were all leaning forward to get a better look at what was going on. Their bodies blocked our view, and for a moment, we were able to guess, to make up theories about what we'd see once we had a clear line of sight. The images that flashed through my head were brutal, and I felt a lump growing in my throat.

As we approached, I turned back to Eleanor Griggs, who was scanning the scene in front of us with watery eyes, her chest heaving.

"You might want —" I started.

But she pushed past me and raced toward the crowd. I knew I should stop her, but she was too quick. She did pause, though, as she reached the edge of the crowd, and Gayla and I nearly collided with her back.

And peered over her head at a pile of leaves. Someone was moving them aside.

Then I saw what everyone was looking at.

Something small, tan — and almost certainly *human* — that dangled from the investigator's fingertips.

# CHAPTER NINETEEN

The news reporter's expression was grave as she stared into the camera.

"The body part was recovered in the woods near Piper Lake, and it has been identified as belonging to Ryan Griggs, CEO of Kelium Pharmaceuticals. Authorities have yet to release any further information, but Channel 4 can confirm that this Griggs was known to have had a tumultuous relationship with Emily Lindsey, owner of the *Carmen Street Confessions* blog, who was attacked in her home earlier this week." The anchor looked off camera for a moment and nodded almost imperceptibly before turning back to the camera. "Like I said, we will have more to share with you about this story as the details come in."

It was a piece of ear.

I'd encountered a lot of body parts during my time as a detective. People seemed to lose body parts in the most ridiculous places, and it's one of those things that you never get used to, even after you've seen it happen a few times. Fingers were a dime a dozen, but I'd also heard about an entire hand in a Dumpster, a human knee bone in a stovetop broiler, and a tongue in a toilet.

Still, I wasn't prepared for the ear.

As we'd stood outside in the woods, peering in at the officer, everything seemed to pause for a moment. Then the reality of what he was holding seemed to sink in for everyone at the same time, and there were collective screams of disgust and horror.

"Is that a toe?" someone asked.

"No, it's a finger."

"It's an ear!"

It didn't matter. Whatever each person believed it was, it was enough to confirm that we weren't out there for nothing, that there wasn't going to be a polite and decent ending to all of this. The gruesome truth changed absolutely everything about the case, adding as much confusion as it eliminated.

We were back in the station an hour later, and I rubbed my temples as the news reporter tossed the segment to commercial. The sixty minutes after the discovery of Ryan Griggs's ear had been a flurry of activity. His wife had crumpled to the ground in

238

the middle of the woods, and when I reached out to help her, I could feel her entire body shaking.

"It's his," she'd said, the tears running down her face. "That's Ryan's."

"You don't know that," I'd said, holding her up, but she shook her head.

The problem for Eleanor Griggs was in the shading of the ear — pale on one side and dark brown on the back of it. The second she'd gotten a closer look, she'd known. Unbeknownst to anyone else there that day, Ryan Griggs had a birthmark that extended all the way down the back of his ear. His long, messy ponytail usually hid it, but she'd seen it almost every day for the thirteen years they'd been married.

And she'd known.

The ear had been sent away for a full lab analysis, but there was little question about who it belonged to.

Ryan Griggs, or at least some part of him, had been out in the woods with Emily.

And something terrible had happened to him.

I still couldn't wrap my mind around *what*, though.

What motive did Emily have for killing or even hurting Ryan Griggs? Sure, they didn't like each other, and there had been a sea of threats on both of their sides, but could she really have it in her to do something like this? They could have gotten into some sort of fight, but there hadn't been a scratch on her when she was brought in.

It didn't make any sense.

Emily was a small woman, and it seemed impossible that she could have overtaken Griggs on her own. Had she had help? Her husband? The webmaster?

Philip Jameson?

The pieces of the puzzle were there, but they didn't come together to make any sort of logical picture. Which must mean that we didn't have all the pieces.

I could think of only one person who could help fill in those blanks — and she was sitting silently in a hospital bed, too scared to talk to anyone, including her own husband.

An officer had escorted a nearly hysterical Eleanor Griggs home, and Jameson had left, his face stony, his breathing labored. He'd been nervous enough when they'd first arrived, but he seemed to reach breaking point once they found the ear.

Gayla had headed home, and I'd gone back to the station alone. As I sat there watching the news on a small box television, I tried to figure out exactly what it was that

I was missing.

There had to be something.

I grabbed my things and left the station, heading toward McKinney Memorial. I didn't know if Emily and Dan had seen the news yet, but it was time for someone to start talking. If not Emily, then her husband. One of them had to know something, *anything,* whether Emily was responsible for what happened to Griggs or not. You didn't get that much blood on you without having some idea where it came from.

Twenty minutes later, I was walking down the sterile, white hallway that led to Emily's room. It was more time than I'd spent in a hospital in a long time, and I tried not to let my imagination wander. I nodded to the guard near the door, a young cop named Simpson, who I'd known for a few years.

"She awake?" I asked.

He nodded, stepping back to let me approach the door. It was open, just slightly, but I knocked on it anyway. It was completely silent inside, and I knocked again. A moment later, Dan Lindsey pulled the door fully open, a frown on his face. He sighed before stepping back and letting me inside.

He looked exhausted, as if he hadn't slept in weeks. His hair was crumpled on his forehead, and his wrinkled clothes were the same ones I'd seen him in for several days. His eyes were bloodshot and puffy.

"Thanks for letting me come in. I won't stay too long," I said. "How is she doing?"

He shook his head. "Not much better."

"How long has she been awake?"

"A couple of hours. She still won't eat anything."

"Has she said anything?"

"No, she won't talk to me," he said. "Which means she's not going to talk to you. They've had shrinks up here and everything. Do you know when I can take her home?"

"They said that anytime someone touches her, she screams," I said. "I don't know how you'd get her home."

"We could sedate her," he said, and he shrugged as my eyebrows lifted. "I know," he said. "It's not my first option, believe me. But I can't imagine that being here in this place is going to make her much better. Can't you help me? She wants to go home."

"No, you want to go home," I said. "The doctors are just trying to do what's best for her." I looked over at Emily, who sat perfectly still on the bed. "Until she says she wants to go home and they think it's okay, they're not going to let you drug her and take her out of here. You do understand that, right?"

His eyes narrowed. "Yeah," he said sullenly. "I understand."

"Can I talk to her?" I asked. "I have a few questions for her."

"She's not going to talk to you," he said, but he saw my expression and shrugged. "Be my guest."

I stepped closer to the bed and stared at Emily. She was looking straight ahead, and she didn't seem to notice that I'd moved closer to her. She was wearing a blue hospital gown, and I was happy to see that her hands were folded on top of the blankets.

"Emily," I started. "Can you hear me?"

It was a futile try but worth a shot. I knew better than to touch her, but I took another step, getting as close as possible. Part of me felt like she could hear me, and I just needed to work harder to get her to respond.

"Emily," I started again. "I hope you remember me. I'm Detective Steven Paul. My partner and I are trying to figure out what exactly happened to you on Sunday. I know you're not able to talk right now, but can you give me any indication that you can hear me?"

I waited, barely hopeful, and I took a deep breath when she didn't move. I didn't want to hurt her, but I knew I was going to have to keep going. To say something that would get to her. Shock her. I cleared my throat.

"Emily, we're looking for your locket," I said. "The heart-shaped one that you wore all the time." I looked up and locked eyes with Dan, whose eyes widened briefly. I couldn't tell if that was surprise about the locket being missing or that I knew about it.

"Emily," I said, looking back at her. "We're trying to figure out what happened to it, since you're not wearing it and it's not in your house. Did you lose it?"

Silence.

"Emily?"

Still nothing.

"What happened to the necklace with the photos of your parents in it?" I asked. "Your mother? Your father?"

Dan Lindsey was staring at the floor in confusion. "I thought it was at home somewhere," he said to no one in particular. He looked up at me. "How do you know it's missing?"

"It hasn't been found in the house," I said. "And her webmaster told me that she never took it off. It isn't odd to you that she's not wearing it?"

"No," he said. "And that's an exaggeration. She took it off at home sometimes. How the hell would he know that?"

"Still," I said. "It didn't concern you at all?"

"I didn't think about it," he said. "I guess I had a few other things on my mind."

I turned back to Emily, who hadn't moved. "Emily," I tried again. "That locket meant a lot to you, didn't it? What happened to the locket with the pictures of your parents?" I asked. "I know it meant a lot to you."

She didn't respond, but I saw the first sign that my questions were affecting her at all. Emily began to shake her foot beneath the sheet, and I didn't know if it was because of the locket or because I'd moved into her personal space.

"Did someone steal it?" I asked quietly. "Did it fall off your neck?"

"That's enough," Dan said, stepping closer to the bed.

"Come on, Emily," I said. "You have to help us. You have to tell us what you know. A man is missing. What happened to the necklace?"

"A man is missing?" Dan said, frowning. "Who is missing?"

I had to make a split-second decision

about whether it was time to play all of my cards.

"Ryan Griggs is missing," I said.

Dan Lindsey looked up in surprise. Emily reacted, too. She stopped shaking her leg beneath the covers, and her entire body froze. She hadn't been moving much before, but right after the words came out of my mouth, she seemed to stop breathing, too.

Which confirmed what I thought.

She could hear me.

"Mrs. Lindsey, we found remains of Ryan Griggs out in the woods where the cabdriver picked you up," I said firmly.

"That's enough," Dan said, but it was a whisper.

"We found them not too far from where the cabdriver said he found you on the side of the road. We'll soon be able to confirm that the blood found on you that day is a match for his blood."

"I said that's *enough*," Dan said, a little louder this time.

"So we know something tragic happened out there, and if you don't start speaking, people are going to start asking if it happened *to* you, or *because of* you."

"Detective!" Dan said. He moved quickly around the bed and stood next to me, breathing hard, his eyes on mine.

Emily was shaking in the bed, her eyes watery, her breath coming out in shallow gasps again. I was taken back to the first day I met her, and I knew I'd gone a little bit too far.

"I told you that's enough," Dan said. "Don't you see how this is affecting her? I get it, that's what you're going for, but you've got to know that this is not the time or place."

"I'm not just trying to help her," I said. "I'm trying to find out the truth."

Emily started moaning, and luckily, her hands were above the sheets still, so I could see them.

"I'm going to go get a nurse," Dan said, looking at me accusatorily before giving his wife a final look and turning to run out of the room.

A second later, Simpson stepped in. "What happened?" he asked, looking uncomfortable.

I walked closer to the bed, and I knew that I should maybe stop. That last time, the closer we'd gotten, the more she'd howled, and I couldn't take the chance that she was going to hurt herself again. But she had to know something about Griggs, about the blood that had covered her body, about the symbol we both saw at night. Without thinking, I stepped forward and put my hands on both sides of her face, holding her gently. She began to sway softly from side to side, and I could tell she was beginning to relax.

Her face settled into my hands, and I saw her swallow, her eyes coming to mine. Just like she had the first time I came, she looked directly at me, and the cloudiness went away.

"Emily, I know you can see me," I said. "You're okay. You're safe here in the hospital. Nobody can hurt you."

Dan Lindsey had returned, and I felt him step closer, but I didn't look up at him. The shaking had subsided almost completely, and Emily leaned back, staring up into my eyes.

I couldn't believe it. It was working.

Simpson echoed this. "What are you doing?" he asked. "Whatever it is, don't stop. She's calming down."

Sure enough, Emily rested her head in my hands, and her breathing began to slow down. Dan Lindsey looked like he wanted to protest, but he stopped when he saw how she was reacting.

Emily had stopped making noise altogether now, and she relaxed back against the bed, her face resting in my palms. I started to step back, but her expression changed, and she began to moan again in pain, so I stepped closer, cupping her face. It was an odd, intimate gesture, her skin soft against my fingertips, and I looked back over my shoulder at her husband, who seemed to be more shocked than angered.

I kept my hands on her face and sat down on the edge of the bed. We were just inches apart. Emily was almost silent now, staring into my eyes as her breath escaped her in pants.

I saw what was about to happen way too late. As I held my hands up to her face, my sleeves slipped down a few inches, the edges of my scars suddenly visible. Emily looked down and stared at them, curiously, blinking a few times before looking back up into my eyes.

I jumped up quickly, stumbling back, yanking my sleeves down. She started to moan again, but her eyes never left mine as both Simpson and her husband rushed toward the bed.

# CHAPTER TWENTY

*Then*

Gumball was trying to hide it, but she was upset.

She was really, *really* upset.

She stood in the back of the elevator, clasping her books to her chest, glad that nobody could see her face. If they could see her, she was sure they'd know immediately. They'd ask her what was wrong, why she didn't seem like herself, or what they could do to help.

And she wouldn't be able to lie, at least not well. Her expression would give it all away.

And then they'd know.

They'd know what she was doing, how she was planning on doing it, why she was doing it, and when.

Gumball watched as the numbers slowly increased as the elevator ascended to the fifth floor.

*Breathe.*

She didn't get upset easily — she knew by now that there wasn't much use getting upset and stewing over things for days and days. She tended to address problems with the other kids upfront, quickly, and with an eye toward resolution. She was different from her sister in that way. She liked things tidy, simple, clean. Her sister was a tornado of emotions and actions.

Still, today, Gumball was having trouble keeping her cool.

She liked Jack — she even liked him a lot. He was a smart boy, and he was passionate, traits she had a hard time ignoring. But the truth was, he'd tricked her into helping him. He knew it, and she knew it.

If it wasn't for Brat . . .

That wasn't to say that she wasn't curious about what went on up on the eighth floor on June 2. She always had been. The children spent plenty of time up there for weekly assemblies, but that one day was still a big mystery. Part of her felt like there must be a good reason why she and the other kids were kept from whatever it was that happened up there on that day.

All that aside, she was willing to go along with Jack's plan. Until he told her what she had to do.

She had to break into Mother Beth's office to find the gate key.

It had been an odd process of elimination, one that she hadn't seen coming and that had been over before she'd really realized that it had started. Perry had done the drawing, so he was out. Lill and Jack had some sort of plan to get the stairwell key, and Jack said he already had something planned for Brat.

So that left Gumball.

She'd wanted to protest, but she stayed silent when Jack said she should do it. She was a part of the team now, and she wanted to contribute.

She was just so *nervous.*

Gumball tried to calm down as she walked with the other children out of the elevator and down the hallway.

The plan was simple — Gumball was to head to class and then fake a stomachache. On the way down to the nurse's office, she'd go by Mother Beth's office. She had to time it just right — Mother Beth was out of her office at the same time every day, and she was out for no more than fourteen minutes and as few as eight minutes.

Gumball was going for six.

She looked down at the drawings in her hand. Perry had actually done a really good

job. Gumball had heard about what happened in class. If Mother Beth were to see
it now, she'd definitely know that it was a
picture of her office.

Gumball walked out of the elevator and
headed toward her classroom. As she walked
past Mother Beth's office, she took a quick
peek inside. Sure enough, Mother Beth was
hunched over her desk, looking at a stack of
papers. Gumball averted her gaze and kept
walking until she reached her classroom.
Walking inside, she took a seat near the
front of the room and pulled out her notebook.

And then she waited.

The waiting was the hardest part. Mother
Mary was leading the class, and she was
talking a mile a minute about ecosystems.
Gumball kept her gaze on the clock above
the woman's head. She had to time it perfectly.

The good news was that she didn't have
to work too hard to pretend that she wasn't
feeling well — her stomach was flipping over
with nerves, and when she put her hand on
it and leaned back in her seat, it wasn't
*entirely* for show.

Gumball saw Mother Mary's gaze dart
toward her, but the woman didn't say
anything. The second hand seemed to crawl

around the clock, and Gumball bit her lip as it approached nine forty-five.

*Go.*

"Mother Mary?"

The woman stopped talking and looked over at Gumball, concern on her face. "Yes?"

"I'm not feeling well. Is it okay if I go —"

"Yes, of course," Mother Mary said. "Go see the nurse. Do you need someone to go with you?"

"No, I'm fine," Gumball said, standing quickly and grabbing her notebook. She turned and raced out of the room, afraid that everyone could see the word *liar* printed on her forehead.

Mother Beth had the exact same routine every morning. Her first class was at 10:00 a.m., and by then, she'd already had at least two huge mugs of coffee. She left her office around nine forty-five to run to the bathroom and stop by the main office, where she'd head inside to turn in her paperwork from the day before. She also spent a few minutes chatting with the other mothers there for approximately eight to ten minutes.

Then she headed back to her office for a few moments to gather her things before heading to class.

As Gumball rushed toward her office at

nine forty-five, she hoped that they'd gotten it right. If she got there and Mother Beth was still at her desk, Gumball would keep walking and head to see the nurse.

The hallway was empty, and she moved quickly toward the door, which, from twenty or so feet away, she could see was still closed.

As she walked up to the door, she struggled to breathe normally. She slowed just a bit as she came to the glass, and she took a quick peek inside.

Empty.

Gumball stopped and looked behind her. The hallway was still empty. She put her hand on the door handle and fully expected it not to move as she pushed.

But of course, the handle spun easily, and the door pushed open.

It wasn't until that moment that Gumball realized she hadn't really been planning on following through. That she was hoping that the door would be locked. Or that something else would get in her way.

But as she stepped inside, she knew there was no turning back. She pushed the door closed behind her and took a deep breath.

*Go.*

Gumball flipped to the back of her notebook and pulled out the sheet of paper with

Perry's drawing on it. He'd had to start over when Mother Beth confiscated the first one, but after that, he'd finished quickly. Gumball examined the drawing in her hands, once again impressed by how good it was.

Jack had circled every place where the key could be and numbered them in order of likelihood.

Only seven places to check, and then she'd be out of there.

Gumball rushed over to the desk and opened the top drawer. It was filled with receipts, scraps of paper, and Post-it Notes with scribbles.

She shut it and walked quickly over to place number two — the brown-and-black vase on the filing cabinet behind the desk. She rifled through the contents. There were paperclips, trinkets, but no key.

She kept moving through the rest of the areas that Jack had circled on the page. Underneath a corner of the carpet. In the bottom drawer of the filing cabinet. She looked in the next place and the next until she'd looked in five out of the seven places.

But there was no key.

Gumball clenched her fists tightly and spun around the room.

It didn't make sense. They'd plotted it out so well. The key had to be there.

Gumball was scanning the drawing again, looking at the last two places she hadn't checked, when she heard a noise in the hallway.

It was rapid footsteps, getting louder by the second, and she knew she needed to hide. It couldn't be Mother Beth, could it? And even if it wasn't, Gumball knew she needed to get out of sight in case whoever it was looked in the office.

Gumball raced across the room to the other side where there was a small closet. Opening the door, she stepped inside, leaving it open just a crack. If Mother Beth did come in and if she had any reason to go in the closet, Gumball knew she was finished. It was barely large enough for her to fit standing completely upright — there'd be nowhere for her to hide.

With her hand on the doorknob, Gumball peered through the crack and out into the office. She had to stifle a gasp when she heard the door open and Mother Beth walked into the room.

It hadn't even been five minutes!

Gumball's breathing had turned into a near wheeze, and she placed a hand over her mouth.

She wasn't going to make it. There were still at least nine or ten minutes left before

Mother Beth had to be in class. It was way too long to stand quietly in a closet without the ability to take a full breath.

*Calm down.*

There were only two places on Perry's map left.

Would she even have a chance to check them?

She watched as Mother Beth sat down at her desk, picked up a file folder, and began flipping through a stack of papers. She uncapped the thick pen that she kept around her neck and leaned over the papers, marking them every now and then. Gumball wondered if it was the assignment from earlier that week.

It was so quiet in the room, Gumball worried that the sound of her breathing would carry out into the office. She removed her hand and opened her mouth wide, letting the air slide directly — and quietly — in and out of her lungs. She gripped the doorknob tightly. She was glad to be able to see Mother Beth, to know what was going on out there, but part of her wanted to pull the door closed and sink down on the floor.

Mother Beth leaned back in her chair and held a piece of paper up in front of her face. She had a half smile on her face, and she seemed to like whatever it was that she was reading. Gumball watched as Mother Beth stuck the other end of the pen in her mouth and chewed on it. Gumball grimaced. She always thought that was a disgusting habit.

The phone in Mother Beth's office rang, and she picked it up.

"Hello?" she said into the phone.

Gumball watched as the woman listened for a bit before responding.

"That won't be necessary. She's too new. I don't see any reason for her to participate this year, and I don't know who gave her the idea that it's her choice."

She waited again.

"I'm not changing my mind. Tell her that she'll have to wait until next year."

With that, she hung up the phone. Mother Beth continued to read the paper she'd been holding, but she seemed agitated now, upset. Gumball wondered just what it was that the person on the other end of the line had been asking for.

Gumball watched as Mother Beth continued to make marks on the paper, and she almost let out a sigh of relief when she finally put the pen down and pushed her chair back.

*Please don't come to the closet. Please don't come in here.*

But Mother Beth had just realized that

she was running late, and she rushed out of the room in a hurry.

Gumball waited a few moments before finally opening the door and stepping out, taking in a huge breath of air.

She couldn't believe how close that had been.

She looked down at the last two places on Jack's list. Jack had seemed so confident that the key had to be in one of the places he'd circled. Gumball would actually feel bad going back and telling him that he was wrong. There were two options: on the floor against the wall behind the filing cabinet in the corner of the room, or beneath the small rug at the foot of Mother Beth's desk.

She took a deep breath and rushed over to the filing cabinet.

She shimmied it forward just a little and then leaned forward and let her fingers trail along the dusty floor behind it. She grimaced, feeling the dirt bunnies as they danced between her fingers, and she was about to give up when she touched something cold, hard, and small.

And incredibly *key*-like.

With a gasp, she pulled the object out and let out a startled laugh.

Jack had been right.

His crazy plan just might work after all.

# Chapter Twenty-One

*Now*

As I drove toward Lara's house, my mind was still on Emily and her face as she sat in the bed. I'd had the same feeling I did when I first went to the hospital on Sunday night.

Like behind her blurry, unfocused eyes, she could see me.

Really see me.

And only me.

I was learning that there was a lot I didn't know about Emily Lindsey of *Carmen Street Confessions.* The angry letters had surprised me — they went far beyond typical hate mail or rogue internet comments. These people really hated Emily.

And in some cases, it seemed like they had a reason to.

I found a spot on the street two doors down from Lara's.

She'd called me the night before to see how my visit had gone before dropping the bomb that she was having a small get-together for Kit's birthday the next day and that "I could come if I wanted."

"On a Wednesday?" I asked. "I was planning to bring his gift by this weekend." She was silent for a moment, and I felt the need to continue. "I was going to call and make sure that was all right."

Lara sighed. "We have the play this weekend, and then we're going out of town," she said. "It's summer, so we figured we could get enough of his friends to come."

"What friends?" I asked.

"Look, we're having the party, and I just thought I should tell you."

I didn't bother to get upset about the last-minute invite or her obvious reluctance. There was no way I was going to miss his party.

As I got out of the car and shut the door behind me, I saw two girls race around the house, screaming with laughter as they tore through the front yard and looped their way back around to the back of the house. Who were these kids? I knew that Kit didn't have that many friends, and I wondered whose idea it was to invite so many people over.

I walked through the back of the house and immediately saw Lara laughing next to a tall woman. The woman saw me first, and her eyes narrowed, and she said something to Lara. From a distance, I could see her lips asking "Is that him?" and I knew that Lara had been talking about me.

And for a moment, I let myself imagine that the friend had recognized me because Lara had said something like "My ex-husband is a tall, built, hot detective. You'll know him when you see him."

"Hey," I said when I got to Lara. "Thanks for letting me come by."

"Yeah, of course," she said.

That was the thing about Lara. She could be so abrupt on the phone, and she'd avoid me for days or weeks, but when she saw me, I saw the softness in her eyes, could see that she had a hard time saying no to me. I shouldn't take advantage of her intense pity on me, but I didn't have enough pride left for that.

"What a turnout," I said.

She nodded. "There are so many people here who I don't know," she said. "Greg has a big family, and it seems like everyone brought somebody."

The conversation was dead before it started, and we rocked back and forth for a moment. Before I could say anything else, she spoke again.

"Kit is inside," she said. "Feel free to go

in, though I think he might be playing."

I nodded and hesitated for a moment. I hadn't seen her in months, and I wanted to ask her how she was doing, have her ask me, do the little small talk, because it seemed like the chances for it were so few and far between, but her crazy friend just stared at me, ready to fight by all appearances.

"Hello," I said, but she didn't say anything, just continued to stare at me with a challenge in her eyes. "Okay," I said and looked back at Lara. "Thanks," I said before turning to walk into the house.

As I did, I spotted Greg sitting on the patio next to another couple, beers in all of their hands. I tensed myself for a conflict, but all he did was lift his beer slightly and go back to his conversation.

What was his plan? Kill me with kindness? With classiness? Fuck that.

I stepped into the house.

"Kit?" I called out, holding the gift box in my hand.

There were a few kids playing in the living room. I walked past them and hesitated before going upstairs. I walked through the narrow hallway at the top where there were pictures on the wall of the three of them.

*What, did you run out to take new family*

*pictures as quickly as possible?*

Kit's door was partially opened, and I pushed it open, tapping on it. I was surprised to see him sitting on his bed, holding a tablet in his hands.

"Hey," I said.

His eyes lit up, and he jumped off the bed and barreled toward me. "Hi," he said. His eyes went to the gift.

"What's going on? Why are you up here alone?"

"I don't know, just didn't really feel like being down there."

"Are your friends down there?"

He shrugged.

I touched his hair. As he sat there in his room, I was pissed at them for making him have a party that he didn't want and ignoring the fact that he wasn't having a good time.

He ripped open the gift, a fifty-piece science kit. "Oh, awesome, Dad, thanks," he said.

I felt my chest tighten. "How's it going with the play?" I asked.

He shook his head. "Not good. I forgot all of my lines yesterday. In front of everybody."

"That's okay," I said. "It was just practice. You'll remember them for the real thing."

"Will you be there?" he asked. "It's next

week on Sunday."

I cleared my throat. "Of course," I said. "Front row. You won't be able to miss me."

He smiled a toothy grin, and I gave him a hug. As he put his headphones back on, I left the room to head back downstairs and broach the subject of the play with Lara.

As I reached the top of the landing, I saw a movement at the bottom of the stairs.

*No.*

I felt a shiver run through my body, and for a moment, I was paralyzed.

There were a lot of people down there — children running back and forth, a pair of women talking while their eyes remained trained on the little ones that weaved between them.

But there was someone else.

Standing behind them, there was a man in a tan suit.

Watching me.

I froze at the top of the stairs, and his beady eyes bore into mine, daring me to come down. I felt the chalkiness on my tongue, the sweat forming beneath my arms, and I let out a growl before racing down the stairs.

He was in Lara's house.

*Kit's* house.

The man turned and walked quickly away.

I reached the bottom of the stairs and spun around, but he'd disappeared.

"That man," I said to the two women who were talking at the bottom of the staircase. "Do you know who he was?"

"Which man?" one of them asked, frowning.

"The one in the tan suit."

She looked around and shrugged. "I don't know. I didn't see anyone."

I raced through the house and toward the front door where there were more children running and playing. The front door was wide open, and I stepped out onto the porch, searching in every direction. I jogged down the steps and back around the house where Lara and Greg were still in the yard, laughing and drinking beers.

"Did you see him?" I asked, racing up to Lara.

She turned to me, a frown on her face. "See who?"

"The man . . ." I said, out of breath. "The man in the tan suit."

She looked at her friend and then back at me.

"I don't know who —"

"There was a man in your house, Lara," I said, and I saw her expression change. Greg had stood up and was working his way over to us.

"What's going on?"

"I saw someone . . ." I took a moment and cleared my throat. "I saw someone in the house who wasn't supposed to be there."

"Who?"

I couldn't figure out how to answer the question.

"Someone from one of my cases," I said. "Someone dangerous. He was inside."

"Oh my God," Lara said, and she turned to race into the house. Greg was not far behind her.

I ran back to the porch, my gaze searching in every direction for the man. After a few moments, Greg and Lara both came out onto the front porch, followed by a few of their friends.

"There's no one here," Greg said.

"I think he left," I told him. "I'm going to call it in."

I was reaching for my phone when I saw Greg and Lara look at each other.

"We spoke with Meg and Julia," he said. "Nobody saw anyone in a tan suit. They just saw you bolt out of there."

I blinked. The way he said it — softly, slowly — it was as if he didn't believe me.

"Who did you ask?" I asked, feeling defensive. "A bunch of seven-year-olds? Because there sure are a lot of them in the house right now, Kit included, with just Meg and Julia watching them. No wonder they didn't see him."

Lara put a hand on Greg's arm. "Just let him call it in," she said softly.

I frowned. She said it as though they were doing me a favor.

*Just let him do this.*

*Don't question it.*

It was almost as if . . . he knew.

As soon as I thought it, Greg confirmed it, on a porch surrounded by all of their friends.

"Go ahead and call it in or whatever," he said. "I'm trying to be cool here, but we don't have time for your visions or hallucinations or whatever it is. You're upsetting everyone."

I saw Lara's eyes widen, and I felt as if I'd been punched in the gut.

"I told him I wouldn't tell anyone, ever," she hissed at her husband.

I staggered back and walked quickly to my car, my cell phone still in my hand.

As I did, I heard him tell her loudly — for my benefit mostly, I had to assume — that he wasn't just *anyone.*

# CHAPTER TWENTY-TWO

I had a hard time concentrating as I drove toward Enid Greene's house. When I called in what happened at Lara's house, I'd asked Dori for the address of the Kelium patient who lived in the area. I needed something else to take me away from what I'd just found out, something to keep me focused on the case.

But Lara had told that plant-loving asshole about the visions.

It felt like she'd betrayed my biggest secret, the one she'd promised she would never tell anyone. She could've told him anything else about our relationship, that I was selfish or bad in bed.

But not the visions.

I tried to put it out of my mind and continued driving toward Greene's house.

She'd been one of the last people to see Ryan Griggs before he went missing. At worst, she could tell me what he'd wanted, what his disposition had been, if he'd seemed nervous or upset.

At best, she could tell me if he'd had all of his body parts when she saw him.

If Philip Jameson and Eleanor Griggs were to be believed — which I still wasn't entirely sure about — Griggs had driven to Greene's home first before getting on the road. And then, instead of going to Philadelphia to see the next patient as intended, he'd changed his mind and met up with Emily Lindsey.

Greene had to know something.

She lived in a sleepy town about twenty miles from the highway. I pulled up in front of her house and turned off my car. I sat there for a few moments, not moving, wondering exactly what I would say to this woman who'd had her life turned upside down in the last few months.

I got out of the car and walked up to the front door. I knocked and immediately heard a cough, and then there was noise on the other side. It opened, and there was a woman standing there, staring at me through the iron door. She was a small woman, five foot one at most, and she peered up at me through the bars. She held up a key, but she didn't say anything.

"Detective?" she asked, and I showed her my badge. She took it through a gap in the bars and examined it, then looked at my face. She nodded before handing it back to me. She finished unlocking the door from the inside and finally pulled it open, stepping back to let me inside.

I was greeted by a wall of hot, stale, musky air that crept up into my nose and seemed to settle into my pores. She coughed and walked back into the living room, motioning for me to sit down on a brown paisley couch covered in thick plastic.

"You called me," she said suddenly, as if my presence had just registered. "You're the detective."

"Yes," I said. "Do you live here alone?"

"I sure do," she said. "I've lived alone for the past thirteen years, since Adam . . ." She shook her head. "My daughter, Julia, comes by to check on me once a day, but she misses sometimes. That's okay. I know she's busy with her husband, and she has two little ones. She can't be worrying about me too much, now can she?"

I smiled softly. "I'm sure she worries about you very much. So I guess you've had a lot of visitors in the last few weeks, huh?"

She nodded. "Yes. You and the man from the drug company. Julia was so mad at me when I told her he came by, because she didn't want me to meet with him alone. And because I'm not always well. I get forgetful sometimes, you know. But I'm not totally gone yet, you hear me?" There was a sparkle in her eye, and in that moment, I believed her.

I nodded. "Why was your daughter so upset that you were meeting with Mr. Griggs?"

"Well, she's the one who agreed to talk to that reporter or blogger or whatever it is you call them these days," she said. "I didn't know anything, you know. I just tried to remember to take my medications when they told me to. But she talked to my doctors, and they looked at my numbers and knew something was wrong."

"What kinds of symptoms did you experience?"

"Well, I'm already not doing great," she said. "But they said it made me worse. I can't say for sure, but I trust my doctors. Even better, I trust my daughter. They said that the drugs were making me sick, and I believe them."

"Why did you let him come by?"

"I guess I wanted to hear what he had to say," she said. "I wasn't going to deny myself that opportunity. So when he showed up at my door, I let him in. I recognized him from the TV. He sat right there," she said, pointing to where I was sitting.

"And when was this?" I asked. "You said he came on Wednesday afternoon?"

"Yes, Wednesday," she said, staring at my seat, almost right through me, and I wondered if she was seeing Griggs. "I shouldn't say this. I know I shouldn't because he's a bad man, but he sure is a *handsome* man. With the suit, and so tall. He was charming, too. Told me he liked the dress I had on that day, and that dress wasn't anything to write home about, just a plain old white cotton dress. But he did. I'll have to give that to him, if nothing else. He's a charming man."

I cleared my throat. "So what is it that he wanted to talk to you about?"

"Well," she said slowly. "It seemed like he just wanted to come and check on me. To see how I was feeling and to tell me that he was concerned about my well-being."

"How long did he stay?"

"About twenty minutes or so. He got up several times to get me water, in my own house. I have these coughing fits," she said, placing her hand on her chest. "Anyway, we talked for a while, about my background, my health, my life out here. He told me about this healing retreat in India that he thought would be good for me. Nothing that could cure me, of course, but which could improve my symptoms."

"A healing retreat?" I said. "In India?"

"Yes," she said. "He told me that a friend of a friend who has cancer like mine went there." Her eyes lit up. "He also said they have amazing food, and being the foodie that I am, I think I talked his ear off about my recipes and all the things I could try there. He listened patiently and then got me more water."

"So he suggested that you actually go to India?"

"Yes," she said. "It really does sound wonderful."

"How would you —"

"Pay for it?" she asked. "Well, he said that there may be some opportunities with Kelium and some of their community service."

"He said that?" I asked.

"Yes," she said. "And honestly, if I thought it would actually help my health, I'd consider it, of course. I could get that amount of money, or more, through a legal battle, or I could get less or nothing at all. And who knows how long and painful that would be?"

I swallowed, watching my words. "Ms. Greene, you're a material witness in an open investigation about Griggs and his company," I said. "I don't know how to put this, but what he was doing was against the law. He was offering you . . . offering money, it seems, to keep you from testifying against him."

She didn't say anything for a moment, and then she smiled. "I told you, I'm forgetful sometimes," she said. "I get it. Sometimes I ramble on, or I talk about things that make people think I'm completely silly. I don't do it on purpose, but sometimes it happens, and I can sense them trying to stop me, or *put me in line.* I can't think of any other way to describe it. And I hate it."

"Ms. Greene?" I started, but she held up her hand.

"I might be old, and I might be sick, but I'm no fool."

"You mean . . . you knew that's what he was doing?"

"Like I told you when you first arrived, Detective, it *seemed* that he came by just to check on me. But I could smell the truth the minute he walked in. And trust me, I would have considered his offer if I thought I would get better. Because better people than me have compromised their morals for much less. But my doctors have already told me that my health has nowhere to go but down from here."

"I thought —"

"I know what you thought, Detective. You thought I'd let his charm interfere with my simple logic. That I'd forgotten how to read people."

"I'm sorry I —"

"That's what he said, too," she said. "That he was sorry for underestimating me."

"Wait," I said. "You told him that you knew what he was doing?"

"I sure did," she said proudly. "And he apologized for that, too. Said he shouldn't have tried to bribe me." She stood up and walked over to a small filing cabinet and pulled it open. Reaching in, she pulled something out and turned around. "He was really upset when he saw this."

She held up a small black box, and it took a moment for me to realize that it was a tape recorder.

"You recorded him?"

"I sure did," she said. "He was so upset. He stormed out and went and sat in his car. Think he was making a phone call. Sat out there for ten minutes or so, then left."

"You don't know who he called?"

"Nope," she said. "But I bet he was calling his lawyers to tell them what happened."

"What did he say before he left?" I asked. "Anything? Anything at all?"

277

She shook her head. "No, nothing. What could he have said?" she asked, a sparkle in her eye. "I'd just handed him his fanny. Wasn't much left to say after that, now was there?"

# CHAPTER TWENTY-THREE

*Then*

"Twen-tee sec-unds?" Brat had exclaimed earlier that day, her eyebrows raised, her hands on her hips, her mouth scrunched up in disbelief. "You mean like two zero? Twenty. Ten measly seconds and then just another ten. That's not possible!"

Brat's expressive face was one of the things that easily distinguished her from her sister. Even though they were nearly identical, it seemed that Brat had three times as many emotions — and corresponding expressions — as Gumball. When she was happy, Brat's face lit up, and her eyes beamed. When she was sad, she pouted, and you could see the anguish in every single line on her face. Gumball, on the other hand, rarely seemed affected by much, her gaze constantly cool and neutral as her jaw worked away at the ever-present gum.

Now, Brat was standing near the wall at

the north end of the large gymnasium. Her sister was a few feet from her, hanging on to the monkey bars, not really moving.

The gym was located on the third floor of the building. It was a large, rectangular room with designated areas for exercising, basketball, and handball. Brat stood at one end of the structure, her back to it, her eyes narrowed as she watched Jack on the other side of the room.

"Stop looking at him," Gumball said in a conversational voice, a fake smile on her face in case anyone was watching her. "Just get ready to go again."

The other kids were spread out around the gym. They didn't want to say it, not yet, but they agreed with Brat. The activity course was designed for the older kids, and at twenty feet long, it took up a sizable amount of the room.

And Jack wanted Brat to get through it in twenty seconds.

First, she'd have to scale a seven-foot ladder stretching up to the wobbly bridge. She'd then have to crawl on all fours through a tight tunnel. Once she got out of that, she'd have to race up a small staircase and go down a long slide.

To avoid suspicion, Jack had said that only the twins should stand near the jungle gym while Brat practiced. He and Perry would sit on the ground a few feet away from them, their backs against the wall, as they fiddled with their warrior projects. Jack's eyes were trained on the large clock directly across from him and Brat's stumbling progress through the gym.

Lill was playing basketball at the southern end of the long room, but she hadn't made a single basket, so focused was she on what was going on across the room.

When Jack had first told the others about his plan, they'd been at lunch, and Brat had been chewing, which had been a bad idea.

"You want me to do what?" she'd asked, bits of corn and potato going everywhere.

"There's an air duct that goes from the girl's bathroom to the supply room behind the auditorium. You're going to have to climb through it in twenty-five seconds."

Brat had looked around the table, waiting for someone else to weigh in, but everyone else was staring at Jack as if he were crazy.

"Before I get to how," she said, "*why* in the world would I need to do that?"

"It's a long story, but for now, you just have to trust me. I need you to practice."

"How?"

"On the jungle gym. That's a lot easier, wider, and much better lit than what you'll

281

be doing in the air duct. So you should be able to get across the jungle gym in twenty seconds."

"It'll take me that long just to get up the steps and across the bridge," she said. "No way. Why do I have to do this anyway? Why can't somebody else? Why do I get the hard stuff?"

"What, like sneaking into Mother Beth's office?" Gumball asked.

"Yeah, or almost getting caught *drawing* her office?" Perry asked, and everyone looked over at him in surprise. "What? It's true," he said sheepishly.

Jack smiled. "You're right, Perry. Everyone is contributing a lot. But yes, Brat, this is one of the most important jobs. I'm giving it to you because I know you can handle it."

Brat tilted her head to the side and seemed to consider it, at least for the moment. But the flattery wasn't enough to quell her concerns. "But what if I can't do it? Or what if I can do the jungle gym but can't do the air duct? Who knows what's up there?"

She was pouting, and when Brat pouted, her voice got loud. The rest of the group shushed her, looking around nervously to make sure that none of the mothers were in earshot.

"We'll figure that out," Jack said. "But first things first. The jungle gym. Tomorrow, when we go down for gym, will you at least try it? I know you can do it. It's just going to take some practice."

Now, as they all sat around the gymnasium, their coordinated movements were barely noticeable.

Gumball was on the jungle gym, not just because it made sense that the twins would be there together but because she was tasked with watching for Jack's signal.

Jack still held his warrior in his hands, but he was gazing up at the second hand on the big clock. Gumball pretended to swing casually from the monkey bars, but she watched him closely. His right hand was wrapped around the top of the warrior, and she paid special attention to his fingers. As the second hand wound around, Jack extended all three fingers.

"Three," Gumball said to her sister.

Brat turned back to the jungle gym and took a deep breath.

With the second hand, Jack tucked in one finger, leaving just two.

"Two," Gumball said.

Brat balled her fingers at her side.

Jack pulled another finger so there was only one left.

"One," Gumball said, a little louder than she should, but there was no one around to hear her. "Go!" she said.

With that, Brat took off.

To anyone else watching, she was just a kid having fun, playing on the new jungle gym. But to the four kids watching her intently from different parts of the loud gymnasium, it was maybe one of the most important parts of their plan. Lill stopped in the middle of the basketball court, oblivious to the game going around her. Jack and Perry had both paused, their art projects in their hands. Gumball had dropped down from the monkey bars, and she watched as her sister tore through the jungle gym.

Brat reached the other side and stopped, turning to face them, her mouth open as she gasped for air. She spread her arms. All of the kids looked up at the clock, and then they turned to look at Jack, who'd been drawing his eyes back and forth between Brat and the clock.

His expression didn't change, but he shook his head. Then he looked directly at Gumball and mouthed a number.

Thirty-seven.

Brat saw it, too, and she kicked her foot against the jungle gym, causing one of the mothers to look over.

"Are you okay?" Mother Bella asked.

Brat nodded. "Yeah, sorry," she said, walking back over to her sister.

Thirty-seven seconds was way too much. She held a glance with Jack for a moment and then turned to Gumball.

"I told you guys, I can't do this," she said. "Maybe you should try it."

"There's a reason Jack wants you to do it," Gumball said. "I think you just have to keep trying." She looked up, because Jack was walking over to them.

Brat shrugged her shoulders as he approached. "See, I told you," she said.

"You can do this." Jack motioned toward the start of the gym with his head. "Ready? Hope you're not tired yet. We have a long way to go to get down to twenty."

Brat rolled her eyes. But without a word of complaint, she took her position at the bottom of the ladder as Jack walked away and joined Perry again. He looked up at the clock.

Brat turned to her sister and waited for her countdown.

It was going to be a long afternoon.

The twins sat across from Jack two periods later in art class. They were all working on their warrior projects.

Brat held her doll in her hands. "Are you going to tell me what the whole plan with the jungle gym is? The air duct in the girl's bathroom that you talked about? Are you gonna explain?" she whispered as she glued a piece of metal on her warrior's jacket.

"Not right away," Jack said. "I promise, I will tell you when the time is right. For now, I just need you to focus on decreasing your time."

"But I want to know," Brat said, frowning, her forehead scrunching, her fists balling up. "You should just tell me now. Maybe it will help me," she said.

"No, it has to work this way," Jack said, gluing a piece of stiff straw to his warrior's head. He glued it slowly and made sure that the hair stood straight up.

"That looks terrible," Brat said as she began braiding a long piece of her doll's hair. "Look, Jack, I know you think that there's some better time to tell me, but I think it could help. I'm going to keep trying, but I'm not sure we're going to get down to twenty seconds. When are you going to tell me what I'm doing this for?"

"Soon," Jack said, gluing another piece of straw down. His warrior was taller than the girls'. It stood at about three feet tall, and it was incredibly thin. Nothing about the creation signaled a warrior, but the mothers tried hard to foster a spirit of encouragement.

"That's great," one of the mothers said as she walked by.

Brat rolled her eyes. "No offense, Jack, but that is not great." She held up her own doll. "Now this, this has warrior written all over it. She's fearless."

Jack smiled but didn't say anything — he just continued to glue on pieces of hair.

"Okay, everyone, time to pack up," Mother Bella said, and the students all stood, grabbing their dolls.

"I hope you're right," Brat said. "We're all trying to stick to your plan, but I don't see how it's all coming together."

"You will," he said with a soft smile. As he stood, he grabbed his warrior. He hadn't planned on showing her yet, but it seemed that they needed some kind of reassurance.

He held the warrior in both hands as the other children watched him.

Then he flipped it over.

The stiff hair stood straight up, and he held the warrior by the feet. If he bent over, just slightly, the hair would touch the floor.

Lill was the first to figure it out, and she gasped.

Jack smiled. "I want you all to know that

we can do this," he said.

At the same time, Lill breathed out, "The broom."

# CHAPTER TWENTY-FOUR

*Now*

Gayla's phone call woke me up at two in the morning.

I was in the middle of the nightmare, my finger trailing along the symbol in my dark cell, the smell of rot stinging my nostrils. As I stared past the bars, a woman's face appeared, and it took me a moment to recognize that it was Emily, her eyes hollow and her skin covered with thick, caking blood.

I gasped as my cell phone vibrated near my head, pulling me out of the dream. I picked it up and saw that it was Gayla. Like most times when the phone rings at 2:00 a.m., I knew immediately that something was wrong.

"Hello?"

"Someone found the car."

I sat up in bed, blinking in the dark room, my heart rate speeding up, one hand clenching the sheets. I winced at the pain in my freshly bandaged arms. My brain struggled to put together the words that she was saying, to understand what it meant.

"Emily's car?" I asked. "Where was it?"

"About eight miles away from where she was picked up," Gayla said. "I just got the call."

"Eight miles?" I said. "You don't think she walked that far, do you?"

"We don't know, but there's no blood in the car, so wherever she got it had to be somewhere in between there and where Cruise found her. That narrows it down. At least we have someplace to search."

"Did they find anything in the car?"

"Her laptop," she said. "There were some weird stains all over the driver's seat, but we're not sure what they are yet."

"Stains?" I asked. "You sure it's not blood?"

"Don't think so. The team said they're too dark. Could be old, but we'll find out what they are."

"Okay," I said. "Anything else?"

"They're going to continue the search in the morning when it's a bit brighter outside. Just wanted you to know. The car seemed clean enough, but it did have some sort of weird smell."

"What kind of smell?"

"According to the officer who first got to the car, it smelled like garbage. Like something rotting."

I swallowed, a weird sensation rushing over my body, and I thought back to the nightmares.

"Is that how he described it?" I asked, trying to keep my tone neutral. "Like garbage?"

"Yeah, he said it smelled like garbage or rotting eggs or something."

I froze, sitting there on the bed, the phone still pressed against my ear, and I tried to figure out what it was that was bothering me about what she'd just said.

It wasn't just that it made me think about the nightmares.

It reminded me of the smell upstairs in the Lindseys' home.

"You going out there?" I asked Gayla.

"No, I'll wait until morning. Derrick is on his way, and he said he'd call to let us know if they find anything else. He asked me to give Dan Lindsey a call, so I'll do that. Right now, it's just a missing car, but I think he'd appreciate knowing that."

"Okay," I said. "Let me know if you hear anything else."

We hung up, and I sat there a little while longer. But I knew I wasn't going to be able to go back to sleep. Something wasn't right, and I needed to go back to the Lindseys' house to figure out what it was that was bothering me so much.

I got dressed quickly and left my apartment. I stopped by the station and grabbed a pair of keys to the Lindsey house before heading there. As I drove, I tried to picture Emily in her hospital bed. How would she react when her husband told her that they'd found her car? Could she even hear him, and would his words register?

When I pulled up in front of Dan and Emily's home, I stopped my car on the street and sat there for a few moments. My throat felt dry, and I realized I hadn't been back to the house since my first visit, when I ran out because of a couch.

I got out of the car, walked quickly to the front door, and rang the doorbell. I knew Dan was likely still at the hospital with his wife, and after a few moments of silence, I unlocked the door with the key I'd taken from the station.

The place looked almost exactly the same. The teams had taken a few items for evidence, but the blood-covered couch was still there. I averted my eyes as I walked farther into the living room, moved to the staircase, and began to ascend.

The top of the stairs faced a small, second-floor window with sheer curtains in front of it. As I reached the top, I could see directly out of the Lindseys' home and into a similar window in the home of their neighbors, the Paxtons. I frowned when I noticed that a light was on.

And there was a figure standing in the small window.

I crept closer to the window in the Lindseys' home and finally put my face to the glass.

It was a woman's figure, and when I squinted, I could make out her features — it was Jane Paxton, the woman Gayla and I had spoken to our first night.

*I had an audience.*

She was standing in the window, and suddenly, she caught sight of me. I expected her to pull back since I'd caught her spying on me, but instead, she lifted one hand and waved before quickly turning and walking away.

*What the hell?*

I turned and walked down the stairs and out the front door. I walked over to the Paxtons' house and knocked on the door.

It took a few minutes, but it opened, and I stood face-to-face with Jane Paxton.

"Mrs. Paxton, I'm sorry to bother you so late, but I saw that you were up."

She didn't say anything for a moment, and I thought she was going to protest, but then her entire body swayed to one side, and a slow smile spread across her face.

"No problem, Detective," she said, and she was just too chipper, too focused and blurry at the same time.

She was wasted.

"Sorry to bother you and your husband —"

"Oh, he's not home," she said quickly. "Believe me, if he was, do you thin —" She wavered and then smiled. "I saw you when you got here. Why are you here so late?"

"I came back to check out a couple of things at the Lindsey home," I said.

"In the middle of the night?"

"Sometimes, inspiration hits you," I said, and she smiled broadly. "What are you doing up so late, if you don't mind me asking?"

She shrugged.

"Just wanted to check, since I saw that you were up. Is there anything else you remember about the night that you found Emily in her house? Anything that sticks out?"

She blinked a few times. The alcohol seemed to be pouring off her skin. "Not really, Detective," she said, slurring her words together. "I told you, I went over there to get the vegetable peeler that Emily borrowed, and the whole night spiraled after that. To tell you the truth, I wished I'd just left it, because then I wouldn't be a part of this, you know? I mean, maybe I would have had to give an interview later or something, but all that blood — I wouldn't have it burned in my mind."

Something about what she said bothered me, and I frowned.

"Detective?" she said when I hadn't said anything for a moment.

"What did you say it was that Emily borrowed from you?"

She bit her bottom lip, and even though her eyes were unfocused, I could see a flicker of worry in them.

"Um, a vegetable peeler?"

"Last time, you said it was a can opener."

She frowned and looked down at the floor. "Did I? I must have slipped and said the wrong thing," she said. "It was a stressful night. Sorry, I meant vegetable peeler. That's what she borrowed."

"Why did she borrow it?" I asked. "Does she not have one?"

"Uh, I guess not," Jane said. "Otherwise, why would she borrow it from me?"

She looked so nervous, she was practically

shivering where she stood. I knew that this was my best chance to get the truth from her.

"You know, Jane, in an investigation like this, where it's clear that someone has been hurt, you could get in a lot of trouble for making things up and not being completely honest with us. Are you sure that's what she borrowed from you?"

She sighed and shook her head.

"I wish you'd just . . ." She took a deep breath. "I wish you'd just talked to me in private, rather than in front of my husband."

"Why do you say that?" I asked.

"Because I couldn't tell you the truth, not with him standing there."

"What's the truth?"

"That I went over there to borrow something, not the other way around. Ever since I started my twelve-step program, we got rid of all alcohol and alcohol-related utensils in the house. But he doesn't know that I picked up drinking again, just a little. Not a lot, just a couple of glasses here and there. I keep the bottles hidden in my closet. So I bought a couple of screw-offs and had one of those that night, but then I had another bottle that I got from a work party that we didn't use. It wasn't a screw-off. So I went next door to ask Emily to borrow her cork-screw."

"How much did you have to drink that night?" I asked.

"Just the one bottle."

I coughed. "An entire bottle?" I said. "And nobody noticed?"

"It's the cigarettes," she said with a sly smile. "Works every time." She took a deep breath. "This alcohol, it's my demon, Detective," she slurred. "I know you don't believe me, but I really do know it, deep down. If I hadn't gone over there, I wouldn't have seen her like that, with all that blood on her face. To tell you the truth, I couldn't really focus that well. I was so horrified about what was happening. And the woman who stood in that living room — I don't know, she just wasn't the Emily I know. Her face, covered in all that blood, she didn't even look like herself. I'm never going to be able to get that picture out of my head."

I paused as her words sunk in.

I felt nauseous all of a sudden as a thought crossed my mind, one so ridiculous and absurd that there was no way it could be true.

I backed away slowly from the door and then turned to run back to the Lindseys' house.

"Detective?" I heard Jane Paxton say, but I was rushing back to the house now, my legs wobbly, a sinking feeling in my gut.

*She didn't even look like herself.*

I raced upstairs and turned into the extra bathroom where I'd found what I thought to be Emily's toothbrush. I turned on the light and stood in the room, my hands shaking as I braced them on the bathroom counter.

It couldn't be.

The smell was gone, but I could remember it clearly.

It *wasn't* the rotting smell from my nightmares.

The smell in the bathroom had been different.

Not mildew, but garbage.

Rotting eggs.

*Sulfur.*

As I stared at the black marks on the vanity, my heart skipped a beat, and I thought I might pass out.

The dark streaks on the counter.

The ones in Emily's car.

I knew what they were. I'd seen and smelled them before.

Nell had started covering her gray hair in her late thirties, and I didn't know what was worse — the chemical, sulfur-like smell that filled the house when she used them or the evidence left behind in the bathroom. Black streaks of dye embedded into the porcelain, on our towels, on the back of the door.

The smell in the bathroom and in her car confirmed it — Emily Lindsey had dyed her hair.

Recently.

And judging by the color of the marks on the counter, she'd dyed it *black.*

Black dye on her sink and on the driver's seat in her car.

I fished my cell phone from my pocket and tried to call Gayla, but it went to voice-mail. I called Derrick King, but he didn't pick up either.

I raced back down the stairs and out the front door of the Lindsey home. I jumped into my car and peeled away, heading for Piper Woods.

I made it two blocks before my phone buzzed, and I saw that it was Gayla.

"Hey," I said, out of breath. "I just left —"

"Wait," she said, cutting me off, her voice hoarse. "I was just on the phone with Derrick, and you're not . . . you're not going to believe this."

"No, I know —" I started.

"They found a body. In between where

they found the Jeep and the site Cruise told us about."

And then, from the pure shock in her voice, I knew she was about to confirm the suspicions I'd had in the bathroom just moments before.

"I can't believe it," she whispered. "Derrick said it's a woman he's never seen before. Black hair, blue eyes, twenty-two stab wounds, most of them in the chest. And he thinks it's —"

"I know," I said, cutting her off. "He thinks it's the real Emily Lindsey."

# CHAPTER TWENTY-FIVE

When I could find words, they tumbled from my lips.

"Did you call them?"

"What?" she asked.

"Did you call Dan Lindsey? Did you tell him you found the car?"

"Yes, I called him earlier tonight —" She stopped. "Oh my God."

"I'll head there now," I said, hanging up the phone.

Moments later, I was flying through the streets, my siren blazing, my breath escaping my body in shallow bursts. I held my phone up and dialed Simpson, but it went to his voicemail. Cursing, I hung up and dialed the main number to McKinney. The phone tree came on, and I spent a few moments listening to the different options before hanging up. I cursed again and jammed down on the gas.

I couldn't believe it.

The blood had been Emily's.

We'd just missed that the woman covered in it hadn't been *Emily.*

A few blocks away from the hospital, I lifted the phone to try to call Simpson again. No luck.

When I burst through the doors of the hospital a few minutes later, I immediately saw why Simpson hadn't been answering my phone calls. He was standing near the check-in desk talking — no, *arguing* — with the man sitting behind it. Simpson was waving his arms, his face filled with anger.

He looked up as I approached, and I saw his eyes get wide.

"Where are they?" I asked.

"It was just a second!" he said, shaking, his voice pleading. "I went for a piss —"

"Yeah right. You've spent the last hour outside smoking, even though smoking isn't allowed within twenty-five feet of hospital entrances," the attendant said.

Simpson looked down angrily at the man.

"Where are they?" I asked again, my chest heaving, knowing what his answer would be but needing to hear him say it.

Simpson looked back up at me, and I knew that he'd be heading right back outside for another smoke the moment we were done. "They're gone," he said.

"What happened?" I asked.

"I told you, I just stepped away to go to the bathroom. When I came back, the room was clear. You gotta believe me. I take my job seriously, and that was the only time I left them alone. Really."

The attendant snorted, and Simpson looked back at him with a scowl. "Hey, you're the one who let a man drag his unconscious wife out of here," he said.

"Wait, how do you know she was unconscious?" I asked.

"Well, you saw her," Simpson said. "You've seen the way she acts. She doesn't let anyone get near her, especially not the husband. And when I got to the room, there was a needle on the bed. He must've given her a shot before picking her up and carrying her by here."

"I told you before, nobody carried anybody out this way. They must have gone out another exit. If anyone had come this way, we would've stopped him," the attendant said. He looked up at Simpson. "If that man goes home and murders his wife, it's on you."

"You little —" Simpson said, launching toward the man, but I stretched out my arm, holding him back.

"Show me the room," I said.

He took a deep breath and nodded.

We took one of the elevators up toward Emily's floor. As we walked down the hall, I replayed the events of the last hour in my head.

*How did we get this so wrong?*

As we walked inside the room, my gaze scanned the bundled sheets, the dining tray lying on the ground, and the syringe that Simpson had mentioned, sitting in the middle of the bed.

I held up a hand as we walked inside. "This is now a crime scene," I said. "Call it in."

I looked up as Dr. Suda walked up to the door. "Your team was supposed to protect her," she said, and I could see the anger in her eyes. "Our job was to give her medical treatment, but your job was to make sure that she was safe. Emily was in a very delicate state. I can tell you for certain that she did not go anywhere with her husband by choice."

It wasn't the time nor the place to tell her the truth. She may have been right about the fact that the woman in the bed didn't want to go anywhere with the man.

But that woman was *not* Emily Lindsey.

And it seemed pretty likely that the man was not Dan Lindsey either.

"Is the person who checked Dan and Emily in Sunday night here?"

Dr. Suda frowned. "I'm not sure," she said. "We can check in the ER. I was here when Emily was brought in, though. Her husband checked her in."

"So he had her identification?"

Dr. Suda frowned. "I don't know," she said, shrugging. "Maybe? I mean, probably. Actually, I think he was carrying her purse, so yes, probably. What's that got to do with anything?"

"Nothing," I said. "Is there another way to get off this wing? Something else besides the front door? The attendant swears that nobody went out that way, so there has to be another option."

Dr. Suda seemed to think about it for a moment. "Yes," she said suddenly. "I guess they could have used the staff exit, at the end of the hall."

"How would they have known about it?"

"Oh," Simpson chimed in. "He probably saw it. Dan Lindsey has walked all of these halls like a madman. Whenever Emily slept, he walked."

"He was scoping the place, looking for a way out," I said. "He was waiting for you to give him that opportunity."

"I thought I was supposed to focus on not

letting people get *in,*" Simpson said.

For a moment, I actually felt bad for the guy.

As we walked out of the room, I looked up at the dark plates embedded in the ceiling. "Pull whatever video footage you can find for this hallway," I said, staring at the security cameras.

We walked down a long corridor toward a big door. I tried to imagine Dan Lindsey carrying an unconscious woman.

At this time of night, it would be impossible for him to do that without being seen and stopped. No, he had to have some other way.

As we reached the end of the hallway, I figured out exactly how he did it.

Pushed against one of the walls, blending in with the background of chaotic hospital life, was a wheelchair.

"Should that be there?" I asked.

Dr. Suda frowned. "Anyone could have left it here, I guess," she said. "But are you suggesting that he could have wheeled her in it?"

Dr. Suda lifted a badge from her chest pocket and held it against a reader near the door. It beeped, and the light turned green. She pushed on the door so we could all walk through.

"Wait, so he would have needed one of those to get through here?" I asked.

Dr. Suda nodded. "Yes, it locks back within five seconds. He definitely couldn't have wheeled Emily through without someone noticing. He must have had a badge."

"Okay, we'll need to check the floor and see if anyone is missing a badge."

"No, we won't," Simpson said, walking forward and bending down to pick something up. He straightened, holding a badge on a light-green lanyard. "Seems like we've figured out pretty quickly that" — he paused, looking at the badge in his hands — "Edward Covel will be missing his."

"Okay, so he steals a badge, finds the employee exit, grabs a wheelchair, injects the woman, and wheels her out here," I said. I looked around the small break room. "Where does this go?"

We all walked to the far wall and then around a corner and down a narrow hall toward the door. Dr. Suda pushed it open, and we were standing in a narrow alley, the smell of garbage wafting up into my nose. Across from us was the employee parking garage.

The alley was empty except for a couple of men working on repairing a sign in front of the hospital's child care center, which was a few feet down.

"Excuse me," I said. "Did you see anyone leave here in the last hour?"

The man frowned, wiping his hands on his pants. "Yeah. Lots of people. Nurses and doctors and stuff."

"How about a man, not in uniform? He was with a woman. He might have been carrying her, and she may have seemed drowsy or been asleep."

"Ooh. Freaky. Naw, I didn't see nothing like that."

"I saw something," the other man said. "I saw them. I thought it was weird, but you know, I didn't want to get involved."

"Where did they go?"

"They got into a car," he said.

"Did you happen to see what the car looked like? Or get the license plate?"

He chuckled. "Yeah, and I wrote it down." He shook his head. "No, I didn't see nothing like that. It was black, but that's about all I saw."

I called Gayla to tell her that I was on my way, and moments later, I pulled off of hospital property. The events of the past few hours were making my head pound, and the only good news was that I was not making them up. I wasn't the only one who knew what kind of shit storm we were in.

I'd heard it in Gayla's voice as we hung up. She sounded scared, even defeated.

I had a feeling we were both asking ourselves the same question: *How could we have missed this?*

How had we looked both of those people in the eye and not questioned if they were who they said they were? We'd questioned everything else — why they were there, what had happened to them, and how it happened.

But never *who* they were.

I got off the highway and followed Gayla's directions to the scene. We were about seven miles away from where the blond woman had been picked up by the cabdriver. Not an impossible walk, but in her state, hard to imagine.

There was a clustering of police cars, fire trucks, and emergency vehicles gathered. I parked on the outskirts of the crowd and made my way to the center, my gaze darting about for Gayla.

I spotted her, talking to Derrick King. She saw me and waved, eyebrows raised.

I shook my head. "No sign of them," I said softly as I walked up.

"You're kidding me!" she said with a hiss. "They got away? Who . . . How —"

"It looks like he drugged her, and they

left out an employee exit."

"He being Dan Lindsey?"

I didn't say anything, and she closed her eyes. "That wasn't Dan Lindsey, was it? Of course it wasn't. What the hell is going on?"

I looked over at the figure lying at the base of a tree. I took a few steps closer. The body seemed small from this angle, almost doll-like. The real Emily Lindsey was lying on her back in a pile of leaves, her torso bloodied, her insides showing through the stabs and slits in her shirt. Her eyes were closed, and blood coated her cheeks almost like blush. Her hair had been dyed jet-black, made obvious by the smudges along her hairline and the dark strands clumped around her face.

As I stared at the body, I felt my vision get blurry, my arms itchy. I swallowed and turned away.

"You all right?" Gayla asked.

I nodded. "Yeah."

"What the hell happened to her?" she asked, staring down at Emily Lindsey's body. "How the hell did we let this happen?"

# Chapter Twenty-Six

*The Last Day of Emily Lindsey*
*Saturday night — twenty-four hours left*
The black actually looked really good.

That wasn't the point, of course. She could have dyed her hair anytime she wanted to, but she never had, not once in her thirty-nine years. She'd never really thought about it, to be honest. She'd gotten in the habit of plucking the errant grays that danced along her temples. If it was true that it made them grow back twice as fast, then she'd just have to pluck more quickly.

As Emily stood in her spare bathroom and stared at her new black strands in the mirror, she couldn't help but feel that beyond the fact that she was about to break the biggest story of her career, she looked *hot.*

She leaned forward and peered more closely at herself, brushing a few strands out of her face. She was distracted by a glob of black on the mirror. She'd managed to get dye everywhere, which was ridiculous, because she'd used gloves and tried to be careful as she applied the jet-black hair color kit that she'd gotten from the drugstore. Still, there were smudges on the sink and on her skin.

She wet her palm and wiped at a few, but the dye seemed only to seep further into the porcelain. Shit. Dan was going to be pissed off about it, but she didn't have time to go find any bleach to clean it up.

She had work to do.

Emily walked back into her bedroom and picked up the clothes she'd laid out on the bed. After pulling on the oversize shirt and a pair of jeans, she grabbed her purse and raced down the stairs.

She'd never felt as passionate about a story as she did about this one. She'd never been much of a writer, but she had a lot of writer friends. They could take words and make them flowery, even if they didn't have much to say. They weren't willing to *dig.* They weren't willing to expose, to tell the truth. They didn't want to do the dirty work.

Emily could do it.

She could do it, because the internet let her. She could say anything she wanted to say. Sometimes, she stretched the truth if it meant that she was getting her point across.

And they came back with anger and yelled at her, but the truth was already out there.

The power of words.

She'd never felt powerful until she'd started *Carmen Street,* and then she'd suddenly had people who counted on her, who trusted her. The number of emails she'd saved from people begging her not to paint them in this light or that was astounding.

But this one was going to be the story that made her career.

All she needed was for *two* women to talk.

She was going to see the first one tonight. Her name was Amanda, and she ran a grief support group every Saturday night at a church about an hour away from Emily's home. Emily looked at her watch. She needed to leave in the next fifteen minutes if she was going to make it.

She walked into her office and picked up her laptop, stuffing it into its case. Armed with it and her purse, she headed out the door.

She didn't know what to expect from Amanda. They'd talked on the phone several times, and then the woman had stopped returning her calls.

But Emily did know what to expect from the *other* woman.

She was going to try to meet with Matilda

tomorrow, and it was imperative that nobody recognized her when she arrived. She'd been thrown out twice already, and they'd throw her out again without a second thought. The black hair, the glasses with clear lenses. She wanted to do a hat, but that seemed too suspicious. Like she was trying too hard.

Emily slipped into her car. She wasn't really nervous. When she sat behind her computer and cranked out stories, she knew that what she was doing was important. When she was on the road like this, she felt *invincible*.

She settled into a groove, hair flowing over the seat, streaks of not-dried hair dye leaving little black smudges on the headrest that were dark in the middle and lighter as they branched out.

# CHAPTER TWENTY-SEVEN

*Now*

"Brick wants us to come in," Gayla said into the phone as I pushed it against my ear the next morning. I'd been sprawled on my back, staring at the ceiling since I'd arrived home about an hour after we found Emily Lindsey's body in the woods.

"Okay, I'll meet you there."

I walked into the station about twenty minutes later, and I saw a few people look up at me before quickly looking away.

Word had gotten around.

I saw someone standing near my desk, and I frowned when I saw that it was Mary. She nodded hi to both of us and then turned to Gayla, who was already sitting at her own desk. Gayla and I locked eyes, and I could tell she hadn't gotten any rest either.

"Can I speak with you?" Mary asked Gayla, who nodded and stood. They turned and walked away, heading into one of the offices that lined the walls.

"Detective Paul, in here," I heard a voice say, and I looked up to see Brick standing in his office. I walked over to him.

"Where did Gayla go?" I asked. "You're splitting us up now?"

He narrowed his eyes as we sat down. "You guys aren't ten years old, and I think this conversation would be better suited as a one-on-one."

"What *conversation*?" I asked. "You need us to tell you the details about what happened, right? Why do I get the feeling that this is a test to see if we're going to give you the same story?"

He didn't say anything for a few moments. I felt angry, caged, and attacked. I knew what Mary was talking to Gayla about. It wasn't about the case.

It was about me.

Brick shifted in his chair. "Look, I'm just going to put this plainly," he said. "The woman you have been investigating for the past three days has just been found, sliced open from head to toe, and she's been out there for as long as you have been working this case. This isn't just a small mistake."

"I didn't say it was —" I started.

"The only thing you need to be saying is what the hell is going on, and start figuring out how the hell that woman could be in two places at one time," he said angrily. "*Especially* if, in one of those places, she's dead."

Mary was waiting for me when I walked back out to my desk.

Brick had grilled me for about an hour, asking for every detail of the case and my mental state. "I need you to be honest here about these blackouts," he had said. "No more beating around the bush."

"I haven't had any," I had said. "Nothing like that."

Mary was standing with her arms crossed against her chest, her back pressed against one of the large columns in the middle of the station. I couldn't read her expression, but I was sure she could read mine.

I wasn't angry at her, not really. But a part of me wanted her to think that I was. Childishly, I held up a hand as if to say hello and continued to walk past her without stopping.

"Seriously?" she asked, spinning toward me as I moved by her.

"Oh, hey. What's up?" I said, and she rolled her eyes. "Sorry, I figured you got everything you needed from Gayla." I walked over to my desk and sat down.

Gayla was at her own desk, not even pretending to work. She stared at us openly, not saying a word.

"Steve, you know why Brick wanted to talk to you alone," Mary said.

"Yeah," I said. "I know exactly why he did. Doesn't help."

Mary walked closer to my desk and bent down in front of me. "Can we go talk?"

I nodded and stood, following her into one of the interrogation rooms. Gayla stared at us the whole time until I closed the door behind us.

Mary sat down, but I stayed standing in a corner of the room.

"Let me guess," I said. "You're like Brick, and you think that crazy-ass Steve is responsible for all this."

"No, I don't think that," she said. "That would be ridiculous, given that Gayla was with you the whole time, and she was fooled, too."

"Okay, then what are we doing here?" I asked, frustrated. "Why aren't Gayla and I out there, searching for the two people who are pretending to be other people and who are most likely responsible for Emily Lindsey's death?"

"You really don't know?" she said.

"No, I don't," I said. "What's the problem?"

"I wasn't sure if he was going to tell you, but I guess he didn't. Steve, we know that what happened with Emily Lindsey wasn't your fault. That's not why you're here."

I frowned. "Okay, then, why am I here?"

"What did Brick say?"

"He just kept asking me if there was anything else I wanted to tell him, any problems I'd been having recently. I guess he wanted to know if I had any more blackouts, and I told him, like I've told everybody, that I haven't."

"He wanted you to tell him about this," Mary said abruptly, reaching into her pocket and pulling something out. She placed it on the table in front of me and moved her hand back. When she did, I felt my stomach flip over and then sink, deep into the pit of my abdomen.

It was a tin of Altoids.

*My* tin, to be more exact.

I blinked a few times.

"Okay," I said. "Um, mints? He wanted me to tell him about what? Some mints?"

"We ran them," she said, staring at me. "Not a mint in sight. Seventeen pills, all lorazepam, often used for treatment of anxiety disorders. Quick-acting pills that slow the central nervous system."

I swallowed again. "Okay —"

"Before you think that we were snooping around, you dropped them in Gayla's car the other day. She found them and went to steal a mint when she noticed that they weren't mints at all."

My throat was dry. "I have a prescription for them," I said. "Nothing wrong with that."

"No, there wouldn't be," she said. "But the drug is known to have a high level of dependency. I have at least half a dozen witnesses who claim that they saw you with the tin almost every day for the past year. And that you definitely had it with you on the day of the bank shooting."

"What are you saying?" I asked.

*Don't let her see you flinch.*

Mary cleared her throat and straightened. "I'm saying that the Glenwood Bank shooting is being reopened because of concerns that you were under the influence of very strong benzodiazepines on the day that Patricia Michaels was shot and paralyzed," she said. "I'm saying that you need to talk to me, Steve, because you could be in real trouble."

"I pushed the gun out of the way," I said. "He was going to kill her."

"I know but —"

"I can't believe this," I said, standing up and yanking the door open before walking out of the room.

I bolted past Gayla, who stood up, knocking her chair back as I moved toward the door.

"Steve," she started, but I drowned her out as I stepped out and let the door slam behind me.

I drove back to the Paxtons' home, on the way missing four calls, two from Mary and two from Gayla. When I arrived, I walked up and knocked on the couple's front door. It took a few moments, and then the door opened, and the couple stood there, expressions of concern on their faces.

"Is something wrong?" Jane asked. She looked at me meaningfully and lifted her cigarette up to her mouth. "How's Emily?"

"Do you know what time it is?" her husband asked, turning to look at a clock in the hallway. "It's not even seven thirty yet."

"I'm sorry," I said, "but this is important. Can I come in?"

They both stepped back and waited for me to say something.

"Well," Ed said, "what's wrong?"

"I have some bad news," I said. "I'm sorry

to say that Emily was found very early this morning in the woods by Piper Lake. She's been murdered."

They both looked as if they'd been hit by a train. "What?" Ed croaked out. "But —"

"How —" Jane started, and she closed her eyes and shook her head hard. "But she was at the hospital, and you said she was okay!" she said.

"I don't understand —" her husband started.

I knew this next part was going to be tough. "There are a lot of unanswered questions, I know," I said. "But I need to ask you a few very important questions. I need to know more about the man and woman you saw next door on Sunday night."

Jane wiped at her face and frowned, looking at her husband. "What do you mean the man and woman? You mean Emily and Dan?"

I cleared my throat. "Unfortunately, it's come to our attention that the two people you saw were almost certainly not Emily and Dan Lindsey."

"What are you talking about?" Ed asked. "Is this some kind of joke?" He stepped forward and put his arm around his wife. "If it is, it's not a funny one, Detective."

"No," I said. "I wish it were." I pulled the

photos that we'd gotten from the hospital security camera out of my back pocket, along with Emily's driver's license. I showed them the license first. "This woman, this is Emily Lindsey, yes?"

Jane looked at it and nodded. "Yes, of course," she said. "That's her driver's license. It says it right there."

I put it back in my pocket. "I need you to think really hard about that night. Is there any chance that the people you saw were not Emily and Dan?"

"Of course not," she said. "I know what I saw."

I unfolded the paper with the picture of the man and woman who checked into the hospital and held it up in front of her. "Is there any chance that they were the man and woman you see in the picture?"

She squinted. "Yes, that's him. That's Dan . . ."

"No," I said. "That's the man you saw, but it's not Dan Lindsey. You said you never met him before, right?"

"Well, no," she said.

I raised the paper again. "And could this have been the woman?"

She swallowed and took a deep breath. For the first time since I arrived, I could see that she was giving it some actual thought.

She took the picture from me and looked at it closely. "I don't . . . I don't think so," she said softly, staring at it. "I mean, I'm pretty sure it wasn't. I guess . . . I guess there's a chance it could have been. She was so far away. And there was so much blood on her face, I didn't . . . Oh, I can't believe it."

"I need you to come with me, back to the house, so that we can recreate exactly what happened. It would be helpful if we go back to that night with new eyes and think about the possibility that the man and woman you saw were not Dan and Emily Lindsey. Can we do that now?"

The couple looked at each other, and they both nodded.

"Let me get our keys," Jane said.

I walked with the couple into the Lindseys' home. We moved straight through into the living room, and I walked back to open the patio door.

"Please, step outside," I said. "I want you to walk up to the house the same way you did on Sunday."

Jane nodded and stepped out, looking hesitantly at her husband. I knew she was worried that I would tell her husband about our conversation the previous night.

I walked over to the couch and stood near

it. As she approached, I called out. "Is this where he was standing?"

"Over," she said, gesturing with her hand.

"And where was Emily?"

She pointed to the couch. "Right there. He was leaning over her at first and jumped up when I walked up."

"Where did he go?" I asked.

She frowned, staring at the room.

"This is very important," I said. "I need you to really think about it. The moment you walked up to the glass, what did you say, and what did he do right after that?"

She stood at the glass. "I don't know," she said, frowning. "I think I said his name. I said 'Dan?' and he turned and looked at me."

"You asked if it was him?"

"I mean, sort of," she said. "I told him who I was and asked what was wrong with Emily."

"So you said his name, and then what? Then he moved?"

"Yeah, I guess," she said. "He was right next to her there, and then when we started talking, he moved here."

She pointed to a spot right in front of her, on the other side of the patio.

I nodded. "So he started there, and then he realized you didn't know him, and he walked over to you."

"Yeah," she said. "What does that mean?"

"I think he was blocking her," I said. "How well could you see her after that?"

"Not that well, I guess," she said. "I don't know. It's all kind of fuzzy. I was so freaked out. I can't believe I missed it."

"You're not the only one," I said.

I thanked them for their time and headed back to my car. As I sat down, I pulled out my phone and called Gayla.

"Steve," she said shakily, and I knew something had happened.

"What is it?" I asked.

"Brick wants to know where you went. I'm still at the station. He said that given the recent events, the tests, Mary's report . . ."

"What?" I said.

"He's taking you off the Lindsey case. I'm really sorry, Steve. I think he's blowing this out of proportion, and I tried to explain that to him. But he's made up his mind."

My fingers were starting to hurt from gripping the wheel so hard. I let go and, in a fit of rage, banged both hands against the steering wheel.

"So he thinks what?" I asked, feeling the anger rise up and trying to push it down. In the back of my mind, I knew she was on my side, and yet I still felt attacked. "He thinks I was so high and out of my mind on drugs that I was responsible for Pat getting shot? Deep down, he thinks I'm the one who's responsible for the Emily Lindsey mix-up, right?"

"Maybe it's not such a bad thing," she said quietly. "This needs to blow over, and I know it sucks, but maybe you should just take a little time."

I opened my mouth to fire something back, but I stopped myself. The decision had been made, and she was just trying to help me catch up to it.

"I told him it wasn't your fault," she said. "And that if he's going after you, he has to go after me, too."

"Look, Gayla, I need you to help me," I said. "This case is really important to me. I can't tell you why. But I can't give up on it, not now."

"Steve . . ."

"Please," I said. "I need your help. And if I have another episode — if anything like that happens at all — I'll tell you immediately and stop. Right away. I promise."

She didn't respond, and I knew she was thinking about it.

"Please," I said again. "I just need to know

what was on Emily's computer. Can you do it?"

I heard her sigh, long and deep, and then she whispered into the phone, "Fine. What do you need?"

# CHAPTER TWENTY-EIGHT

Gayla met me at my apartment a few hours later. When I opened the door, she was staring at me with an expression that seemed both worried and annoyed, but she was holding a file folder in her hands.

"I owe you one," I said, taking it from her.

It had taken her three hours to access the files on Emily's computer. "Look, I'm going to continue the search for Dan Lindsey, because that's Brick's primary concern," she said. "Let me know if you find anything, and, Steve?"

"Yeah?" I asked, looking up from the folder.

"If you have another blackout or episode or whatever it is you want to call it, and you don't tell me about it, that's it. I mean it." She said this firmly, but I could see the softness in her eyes.

I nodded. "Okay," I said. "I'll tell you, I promise."

She nodded and left.

I sat down and splayed the papers out on my coffee table. Emily's desktop had been filled with articles and pictures for *Carmen Street Confessions.* Gayla had printed out the contents of a folder called Notes. I flipped through the Word documents; one was a transcript with an unidentified client of the Kempton Food Pantry. Near the end, the interviewee began to describe, in vivid detail, some of the things he or she'd seen in the basement of the food pantry. I cringed and kept moving.

I flipped through another document, and then another, and I cursed as each one seemed to be about a story that had already appeared on her blog. Some were controversial — like the Kempton Food Pantry — and others were not, but there was nothing that shed any light on where Emily had been that weekend or what may have happened to her.

The fourth item I got to, however, made me pause.

It wasn't a transcript but instead a scanned image of a dark-blue flyer. There wasn't that much text on it, but it was designed well — it had obviously been created by a professional. The flyer was for an organization called Friends of Frank, and at the bottom, there was a phone number listed in tiny print. I tried to remember if I'd seen anything on Emily's blog about the organization, but it didn't ring any bells.

Reaching over to grab my cell phone, I dialed the number on the flyer.

I frowned when it didn't ring, but a second later, a woman's robotic voice filled the line.

"The number you have reached is out of service. Please hang up and try again."

I sighed and hung up the phone, scrolling back through my recent calls to make sure I'd dialed it correctly.

I flipped the flyer over and continued rifling through the folder. A few more Word documents turned up nothing of interest. I slowed down to read a few articles. Some were newspaper clippings about missing people in the area. I made a note of their names and continued reading.

One thing was for sure — Emily had obviously had a lot of projects brewing. That made it all the more difficult to figure out which one she'd been pursuing that weekend and which one could have gotten out of control.

I flipped yet another page and saw that it was filled with a list of names and phone numbers, though there weren't any indications about which stories they were connected to. I scanned down to the bottom of the list. If she was using this document as her Rolodex, chances were the ones at the bottom had been updated most recently.

I picked up my phone and dialed the first number. It went to the voicemail of a woman named Kimberley Bell, and I remembered that she was one of the patients who Emily had talked to for her Kelium story. I hung up and called again, but still no answer.

The next number had even less information than Kimberley's — there was no last name. I dialed the number for someone named Amanda and waited. I fully expected it to go to voicemail, like the number before it, but after five rings, a woman picked up.

"Kendall Community Church. This is Amanda."

"Hello," I said, caught off guard and suddenly realizing that I hadn't thought through the purpose of my call or what I was going to say. "My name is Detective Steven Paul, and I'm with the Douglas County Police Department."

"Okay," the woman said slowly, and I could hear a definite shift in her tone. "How can I help you?"

"I'm sorry to get right to the point," I said,

"but I am hoping you can provide me with some information for a murder investigation."

She didn't respond the way I expected her to. No surprise or confusion. Instead, she sighed.

"I don't have anything to tell you," she said.

"But you don't even know —"

"I don't know anything."

"I'm sorry, Ms . . ."

The woman didn't say anything for a moment. "Pearson," she finally muttered. "Amanda Pearson. Look, I'm sorry. Like I told the blogger, I don't know anything about a murder."

"The blogger?" I asked, startled. "Do you mean Emily Lindsey from *Carmen Street Confessions*? Did she call you?"

"Yes, she called me asking about some murder, and I told her I didn't know anything. Please stop calling me —"

"Wait," I said. "I don't know what murder Emily was asking you about, but I'm not calling about the same one."

"You're not?"

"No."

"Whose murder are you calling about then?"

"Emily's."

I heard her inhale sharply, and there was silence on the line for a few moments. "What are you talking about?" she asked hoarsely. "She was just here."

"Wait, she came to see you?" I asked. "I thought she just called. Where are you located?"

"The church is in Ashland," she said. "I'm sorry, Detective, but I have to go."

I could hear the panic in her voice, and I could tell that I was about to lose her.

"Wait," I said. "Please. I'm trying to figure out what happened to her. When was Emily there?"

"A couple of days ago," she said. "Really, I don't know anything. I'm sorry to hear that happened, but I don't have anything else to tell you. Please, don't call this number anymore. I've told you everything I can."

"Wait —"

I slumped back in my seat as she hung up. I dialed again and was unsurprised when it rang several times with no answer. I hung up my phone and spun it around in my hands a few times.

I looked up the address to Kendall Community Church and added it to my notes. Amanda Pearson wouldn't be happy to see me, but I needed some answers.

My cell phone vibrated, and I glanced down at it. It was a number I didn't recognize.

"Hello?" I said, answering.

There was a brief pause, and then a man's voice filled the line.

"Detective. It's Philip Jameson."

"Mr. Jameson," I said. "What can I do for you?"

"I need to talk to you," he said. "I —"

"Is everything okay?"

"They said they found the Emily woman. Dead."

"Yes," I said. "She was found about twenty minutes away from Piper Lake."

He was silent again for a moment. "Something is really wrong here," he said. "I don't know what's going on, but something is not right."

"What are you talking about?" I said. "Tell me what's going on."

"The day at the lake," he said, and then he stopped.

I thought back to when he'd joined the search party at the lake and the team had found Griggs's ear. I'd never seen someone look so terrified. "What is it?" I asked. "What happened that day at the lake?"

"I saw her," he said. "She reached into her p-purse . . ." He stopped, and I could hear him swallow.

"Who reached into her purse?" I said. "Mr. Jameson, I need you to calm down and tell me what's going on."

"Eleanor Griggs. I was with her. And she thought I wasn't looking. She turned and threw something in the woods. I saw it. It was small and soft, and she threw it right where you found it. When she first asked me to lie — to say that Ryan had called me — I thought that it just had something to do with Emily and the blog, and I wanted to do what I could to help —"

"Wait, you saw her throw what?" I asked, grabbing the phone tightly and leaning forward, sure that I couldn't have heard him correctly. "What did you see her throw in the woods?"

"The ear," he said. "I watched her reach into her purse and throw her husband's *ear* into that pile of leaves. She zipped her purse up quickly, but not before I saw the blood on the inside. Who does that?" he asked. "Who the hell does that?"

# Chapter Twenty-Nine

I banged on the Griggses' front door with the palm of my hand and waited.

One the one hand, what Jameson had told me was simply too ridiculous, too far out in left field, to be true.

On the other hand, he didn't have any reason to make it up.

Still, I had a hard time wrapping my mind around what he was saying.

I banged on the door again and pressed the doorbell a few times. I'd tried calling, but no one had picked up. I started to head around back when I heard footsteps, and finally, the door opened slowly.

I stood face-to-face with the Griggses' assistant.

He frowned. "Sorry, but it's not a good time, Detective."

"This is important," I said. "I need to speak with Eleanor. Now."

"I can't —"

"It's all right," I heard a woman's voice say.

Eleanor Griggs appeared, her eyes red and puffy. She was holding her phone in her hands. "You can come in, Detective."

"What's wrong?" I asked. "Was that him?"

She frowned and tilted her head to one side.

"Was that who?"

"Your husband," I said, suddenly out of breath, the anger making it difficult for me to speak normally. "Was that him on the phone?"

"What?" she asked, the frown deepening. "Of course not. What's going on? Why are you asking ridiculous things like that?"

"Was that your husband?" I asked again. "Is that who you were just talking to."

*"No,"* she said firmly, anger creeping into her voice. "I just told you. Besides, I would have called you if I'd heard from him." She turned and walked into the living room, sitting down on the couch. She looked down at the phone in her hands and took a deep breath. "That was my mother. She called to ask me if I'd heard anything from Ryan. What are you doing here, Detective? What's going on?"

"What's going on is that I need the truth, Mrs. Griggs," I said. "Did you put that piece of your husband's ear in the woods?"

Her eyes widened, and the phone tumbled out of her hands. She sat there for a few moments, her mouth open, and she stared at me as if I had snakes growing out of my head. I knew that I should be more delicate, that I shouldn't have tossed the question out there so quickly, but I couldn't push down the feeling of anger about being lied to.

"What are you talking about?" she whispered, her eyes wide. "What do you mean did I . . . put his ear there?"

"I received a report that someone saw you reach into your purse, pull it out, and throw it in the woods," I spat out, barely able to wrap my mind around it. "As ridiculous as it sounds, I think it's true."

She coughed, putting her hand to her stomach.

"I think I'm going to be sick," she said. "I can't believe you're asking me that. Are you serious?"

"I'm completely serious," I said.

"Then are you crazy?"

I didn't say anything.

She shifted in her seat. "*No,* Detective," she said. "I have no idea what you're talking about. Why would I —"

"What if I told you that I talked to Philip

Jameson just half an hour ago, and he told me that you came to him and asked him to lie about your husband contacting him?"

It was as if I'd reached over and slapped her. She reeled backward, jolting against the back of the couch, and inhaled sharply.

"Well, I'd say he's lying," she said hesitantly, and I could see her choosing the words as they fell from her lips. "I'd say that he's making things up, and I truly don't know why."

"So that never happened?" I asked. "Could he be misconstruing it? Maybe you asked him to exaggerate? Really, you'd do best to give me a straightforward answer about this."

"I don't think so," she said quietly, but her hands were shaking. "I mean, I don't know what I could have said to make him think that he should make that up."

"What if I told you that he would swear to it? That he said that he even had a voice-mail of when you first called him to tell him about it. What would you say then?"

I watched as she swallowed. She reached over and picked her phone up off the floor, rolling it over in her hands. And just like that, I knew she was lying. I could see it in her eyes, in the way she moved her jaw, in the way she twirled the phone slowly through her fingers.

"Mrs. Griggs, please," I said. "This is important. I need you to tell me what happened between you and Jameson."

Her eyes filled with tears again, but this time, they spilled over onto her cheeks.

"I'm sorry I lied," she said, and a deep, guttural sob escaped her. "I didn't really . . . I guess I wasn't thinking. I asked Philip to help me. You're right. I asked him to lie and say that Ryan had called him and that he was going to follow Emily."

"Why did you do that?" I asked.

"I guess I thought it might help us," she said. "I wasn't thinking straight. When you told me that they found her with a knife, covered in blood . . . I guess I thought I could gain some sympathy votes for my husband, for Kelium, if people thought that maybe . . ." She shook her head. "I honestly don't know what I was thinking."

"Did your husband have anything to do with this?" I asked.

"No," she said. "Nothing at all. I figured I'd hear from him, that he'd come home soon and then everyone would know that he was okay. But before then, we would have maybe helped to hurt her image a little, you know? It was a stupid idea. That was before we found his . . ." She shuddered. "Before we found his ear."

"So you deny that you had anything to do with that?"

"Of course," she said. She stood up and began to pace back and forth in front of the couch. "I can't believe he said that. He must have seen something else, though I don't even remember reaching into my purse that day. You have to believe me," she said, wiping her face with the back of her hand. "I have no idea why Philip would say such a thing." She was breathing hard and staring at me with desperation — she was practically pleading with me to believe her.

I had to admit, it sounded ridiculous. But the certainty in Jameson's voice earlier that day was hard to deny.

"What reason could he have for saying something like that?" I asked. It wasn't really a question meant for her, but I said it out loud.

She stopped pacing. She stood in front of me, shaking her head slowly back and forth. "I have no idea," she said. "Philip has always been a devoted board member and friend to us. I . . . He doesn't have any reason to lie." She walked over to the table near the front hall and reached for a tissue. Wiping her face, she walked back over to me. "It doesn't make any sense."

Her whole body was shaking, and I felt bad for starting so strongly.

"Look," I said. "Maybe we can clear this up pretty easily. Jameson said that he saw you take something that looked like the, uh, remains out of your purse. There's no way that could happen without a considerable mess. Perhaps if you showed me the inside of your purse, we could clear this all up."

"You still don't believe me," she whispered. "I don't know how I can prove to you that I'm telling the truth."

"You could just show me the purse," I said again.

She shrugged and let out an exasperated sigh. "Of course," she said. "Fine. If that's what it's going to take, I'll show you the purse."

She walked out of the living room without saying a word, and I wasn't sure if I should follow her. I walked back into the foyer, but she'd begun to walk up the stairs. She turned around and looked at me.

"I'll be right back," she said.

I waited at the bottom of the steps. So she'd asked Jameson to lie for her — for her and her husband — and hadn't felt the need to come clean when her husband's ear was found in the woods. I wanted to believe her; what Jameson was proposing was pretty hard to stomach. I looked up as Eleanor appeared again and began to walk down the steps, a large brown bag in her hands.

She walked over to me, her hands still shaking, and she held the bag out.

"See," she said. "There's nothing in there."

I took the bag from her but didn't bother to look at it. It was a bold move but not too surprising; she didn't have any reason to think that I'd paid too much attention to the purse she'd been wearing the day before. But Gayla's comment about Eleanor's purse that day — her large, black purse with no strap — hit me, and in that instant, everything became clear.

Jameson was right.

Eleanor Griggs had something to hide.

"I think you're going to want to try again," I said.

"What?"

"The purse. This isn't the one you had the other day. I know that, and you know that. So do you want to go upstairs and get the right one?"

"This is the one I had," she said, looking at it with a frown. "At least I think it was . . ."

"No, you know it wasn't," I said. "The purse you had yesterday was black. I remember because my partner thought it was an odd choice to bring to a search party. I think you know which one I'm talking about, though. Now, do you want to go get that one, or do I need to get a search warrant for your house?"

Her eyes narrowed, and there were no traces of the tears left. "I told you, Detective, this is the purse I had with me. There's no other purse for me to give you."

I handed the purse back to her and nodded. "Okay," I said. "I guess I'll have to come back. Trust me, we will find it. I don't care how deeply you've hidden it."

"There's no other purse," she said again firmly. "Look, I have a lot of black purses, and if you think I'm going to go upstairs and search through them for your little witch hunt, you're mistaken. And I'm really offended that you would come here and talk to me like this when my husband is missing and that smug bitch is sitting in a hospital, not saying anything."

Eleanor's entire demeanor had changed. Gone was the sniffling woman from moments before; now, her eyes told me that she knew more than me, that the purse was someplace where she was sure I'd never find it.

Which meant I was going to have to

convince her to give it to me.

"That's all well and good," I said. "But you should know that the smug bitch you just mentioned? She's not sitting in any hospital bed. She never was. She was found earlier today on the side of the road, not too far from where your husband's ear was found. And she'd been stabbed — twenty-two times — in the chest. Oh yeah, and as you can imagine, that makes your husband one of our primary suspects."

Eleanor's faux surprise before had nothing on the real thing.

All of the color drained from her face, and she gasped. She blinked several times, and I could practically see her brain processing the information. Finally, she straightened her shoulders and pulled her cell phone out of her pocket. She pressed a few keys and then held it up to her ear, her eyes trained on mine.

"Hey," she said into the phone, her voice strong and in control. The sniffles from a moment earlier had disappeared. "No, wait. Stop. Never mind that. You need to come home. No, *now.*"

# CHAPTER THIRTY

*Then*
*6:54 p.m.*

Brat pushed her dinner around on her plate. The peas had grown cold, and the mashed potatoes had hardened, since she'd been pushing them around over the past hour. She looked at her sister's plate across the table. Gumball's didn't look much better, since it was still more than halfway filled, too.

Neither of them had much of an appetite. Brat continued to swirl the peas as she looked across the room at Jack. Unlike the twins, he was chomping away quietly, and he didn't look the least bit nervous. Brat wished she could handle things the way he did.

She didn't need to worry, though.

If the children were acting weird, none of the mothers would recognize it. Everyone was quiet tonight — that's what happened on June 2. The air felt different, the mood tense, the mothers' faces void of any hint of a smile.

Brat stared down at her plate. They'd been working toward this day for so long, and now that it was finally here, she felt both relieved and terrified. She couldn't wait to get started — she was only an hour or so away from learning just what it was that took place upstairs every year.

And yet, part of her wanted to call it off, to go back to her room like everyone else and just wait until morning.

"Finish up dinner, and then head to your rooms. Remember, no library visits tonight. You're all expected to be in your rooms by seven thirty," Mother Ann said, walking through the aisles of the cafeteria.

Brat looked down and continued making patterns in her food. She was drawing an *S* when she felt a hand on her own. She looked up and saw her sister peering at her.

"You all right?" Gumball asked. "You know, we don't have to do this," she said. "We can just tell Jack we changed our minds. He'll be disappointed —"

"No," Brat said, squaring her shoulders. She wasn't doing a great job at hiding her nerves, but she wasn't ready to back out. Not yet. They'd all started this together, and they were all going to finish it together. "I'm okay," she said to her sister as she put her fork down and pushed her chair back. "It's time to go."

*7:21 p.m.*
Mother Ann opened the door to the stairwell and pulled it open so that the children could walk through. She followed them and then moved ahead to open the second gate. The children remained in line as they moved through that one and then dispersed to head to their rooms. It was completely silent on the children's wing, and the kids all moved with purpose — stepping into their small rooms and closing the doors.

As he closed his door, Jack looked across the hall at Perry's room. Perry nodded just slightly and closed his own door. Jack was proud of Perry. He'd really come through for the team. He felt bad that he hadn't been completely honest with Perry or any of the others.

He hadn't told them that he was pretty sure they'd get caught.

He would do everything he could to keep that from happening, for their sakes. But what they were doing was risky, and the truth was that even if they were able to get upstairs unnoticed, it was going to be very hard to make it back down.

Jack was okay with that. He hoped the rest of them were, too.

He closed his door and then stood at the window and watched as Mother Ann walked by quickly to the end of the hallway. He waited a few seconds, and then he heard the swishing sound of her broom hitting the floor. Seconds later, she walked by, her head down as she swept long lines into the sand. Jack couldn't see from where he stood, but the long sweeping noises sounded like she was making her signature feathers.

He could do feathers.

He walked over to his bed and sat down on the edge of it to wait.

*8:02 p.m.*

Jack stood up from his bunk bed. He tiptoed over to the door and reached down to pick up his warrior. He cracked the door open slightly. There was no movement at all in the dim hallway. He took a deep breath.

Exactly one minute later, Perry's door across the hall opened. A few doors down, Gumball and Brat's door opened, and they appeared. They were dressed exactly alike, and their hair was braided the same way. Gumball wasn't chewing her gum, and in the dimly lit hallway, it was impossible to

350

tell them apart.

The children all stepped out of their rooms at the same time and closed the doors behind them.

Jack looked at the kids' faces in the dim light of the hallway. He was proud of them. Brat looked nervous but determined. Perry shifted back and forth in his spot, but he held Jack's eye contact and actually looked excited. Gumball was standing just behind her sister, her hands at her sides, and she chewed her gum slowly.

Everything was in place.

They would meet Lill upstairs — she was upstairs helping out in the nursery tonight. She'd convinced Mother Deena to let her stay up there and sing to the children.

They were ready.

Jack moved first. He walked quickly down the hall, past the twins, and then turned back. He looked at Brat and nodded.

Brat and her sister darted away from their room, Gumball walking a foot behind her sister and taking care to step in her footprints when possible. When they got to Perry's room, he stepped out, too.

Jack trailed all of them. Flipping his warrior over, he leaned over and began to flick the sand lightly, covering up his own footprints and that of the other kids. He could only sweep the top layer of sand — anything else would be too loud. But the top layer was enough.

In less than ten seconds, all four of them had reached the first gate, and the floor of the dusty hallway was perfectly swept, as if it had not been stepped on since Mother Ann left.

Still holding the warrior broom, Jack nodded at Brat. She had the key that Gumball had found in Mother Beth's office in her clenched fist, and her hands were shaking — they could all see it in the dim hallway light. Brat inserted the key into the gate and turned it. There was a resounding click — and they all held their breath, waiting for any movement from the wing they'd just left behind or Mother Ann's room in front of them. But nothing happened. They pushed the gate open and stepped through, and Jack turned around and swept the sand again. He closed the gate, and they began to walk slowly and carefully toward the second gate.

Jack nodded at Brat, and she stuck the key into the lock and turned it. This time, they all pulled up as hard as they could on the gate while swinging it open. They walked through, and they all turned back to pull it closed. Right before it clicked into place, the gate let out a loud, high-pitched squeal.

They turned to each other, their faces covered in shock.

"Hurry!" Jack whispered, and they pulled the gate closed before scurrying to either side of Mother Ann's door. The four children stood with their backs against the wall, two on either side of the door, and they held their breath as Mother Ann stepped to the glass and peered out into the shadowy hallway.

# Chapter Thirty-One

Jack didn't know how long to wait. He'd seen movement in Mother Ann's room just as he'd launched himself against the wall. If she came out, they'd be toast.

But her door didn't open.

As they stood there against the wall, looking at each other across the doorframe, Jack wondered if Mother Ann was still standing there. He couldn't very well lean forward and see. He looked over at Brat, who had her eyes closed, her head back against the wall. Gumball was standing next to her sister, and she spread her hands and mouthed something.

"Okay?"

Jack shook his head. But he knew they couldn't stay there all night. He closed his own eyes and counted to twenty before opening them again. Slowly, he leaned away from the wall until he could see into the room.

There was no one standing there. He stepped fully away and motioned for the others to follow him. They all crept into the small elevator bank and let out a sigh of relief.

Brat lay on the floor, flat on her back, and covered her face with her hands.

Her sister leaned over her and mouthed the words, "Get up!"

Jack walked over to join them and reached out a hand toward Brat. "Come on," he whispered.

Brat finally stood back up. She still seemed seconds away from bolting back through the gates and into her room. She fidgeted, wringing her hands together in front of her.

Gumball saw it, too, because she reached out and put one arm around her sister. "You okay?" she asked.

Brat nodded.

Jack was still shaken, too — they'd been so close to getting caught. It wasn't the fact that they'd get in trouble; he wasn't worried about that. It was the fact that if they got caught, he'd lose all chance of getting upstairs and finding out what was going on.

But he couldn't show them how he felt. They were depending on him to be the leader.

"Let's keep moving," he said. "Lill is waiting."

He nodded toward the stairwell, and they all walked over to the door. Jack pushed it open and stepped inside. The others followed him, just a few steps behind each other.

Jack had known the stairwell would be dark — they all had. Still, they weren't prepared for just how dark it would be. It was pitch-black, and somehow, that made the air feel heavier and thicker and the trek they were about to attempt even more impossible. They couldn't possibly make it all the way up eight floors in complete darkness, could they? Jack felt his stomach flip over as the door to the children's wing closed behind them with a resounding click. He knew he needed to keep going, to charge ahead before one of the others decided to back out.

Jack reached behind him and grabbed Brat's hand. It was cold and clammy, and she gripped his fingers so tightly, he began to lose feeling.

"Everybody locked?" he asked in a loud whisper.

He heard a resounding yes from the group, and he couldn't help but smile. If they were thinking about backing out, they sure weren't showing it. Jack took a deep breath and tried to calm his nerves. Then he began walking up the stairs, concentrating on not falling over.

Left foot, right foot.

He was walking so softly that his shoes barely made a sound on the tiled steps. The others did the same. They moved in perfect synchrony, slowly and deliberately.

The first section of the stairwell wasn't so bad. They all continued to hold hands — Jack and Perry were at the front and back of the group, and they each used their free hands to hold on to the bannister.

They kept going for what felt like forever. Jack counted the steps in his head and softly said every fiftieth step so that the others could know what was going on. He hoped no one was getting too nervous and thinking about jumping ship, but it wouldn't surprise him if they were. Even he was wondering if there was any way they would actually get away with this.

When he reached what he knew was the third floor, he stepped up to the glass and peered out onto the floor. It was dark, like most of the others, but at the very end of the hall, he could see the light of the nursery.

Exactly ten seconds later, he saw the light

in the front of the nursery go out. And then turn back on. It happened twice. He took a deep breath. Lill.

"Let's go," he whispered softly, and he kept walking.

They all reached the top, and he only then heard the soft wheezing from Perry. "Hey, are you okay?" Jack said. "Perry?"

"Yes," he heard the boy say between breaths. "I'm fine. Let's keep going."

"We made it."

"Oh . . . good."

Jack turned to the stairwell door. There was a little green light next to the keypad. Reaching into his pocket, he pulled out the key that Mother Deena had given Lill. He used it to unlock the door before pulling it open, and they all walked through.

As they stepped into the soft glow of the eighth floor, the four children squinted at each other, their eyes still sensitive. They couldn't believe they'd made it this far. Even if they didn't get any further than this, they didn't miss the significance of the fact that they were on the eighth floor on the night of the ceremony. It should have been impossible. In that moment, aside from their fear, they were proud — of themselves, and of each other.

"Okay," Jack said. He turned to Brat. "Are

you ready to go?"

She nodded. "Absolutely," she said in what was mostly a croak. She looked over at her sister. "You ready?"

"Yeah," Gumball said, and they hugged.

Jack and Perry walked back toward the locked supply room at the back of the auditorium as the twins headed toward the guard station.

"We'll be waiting for you," Jack said.

Brat braced her shoulders and walked over to the guard station. She'd been so nervous when they were getting through the gates and up the stairwell. But now she felt different. They'd gotten this far, and she felt ready.

She had a job to do, and she couldn't let her nerves get in the way.

She peered around the corner at the guard station. Her sister was right on her heels, and Brat reached back and squeezed her hand. She could see Mother Beth there alone. Brat wished that there was anyone else there today — Mother Beth was going to be a hard sell. But there was no going back now. Brat knew she was going to have to put on the acting performance of a lifetime.

Giving her sister's hand a final squeeze,

Brat took a deep breath and moved quickly toward the station.

Mother Beth saw her almost immediately and jumped up out of her chair.

"Brat!" she hissed, her nostrils flaring, eyes open wide. "What in the world are you doing up here?"

"I'm sleeping in the nursery tonight, and I was having a bad dream," she said, like they'd practiced. "I was looking for Mother Grace. And I didn't want to wake any of the babies up."

"That's still no excuse," Mother Beth said. "Mother Grace is busy. I hope you know you're in a lot of trouble."

"Okay, sorry," Brat said. "I'll go back downstairs."

"I'll come with you," she said.

Brat had expected it, but she pretended to be surprised. "Oh, you don't have to," she said. "I'm just going back down to the nursery. I was helping out there overnight. I'm really, really sorry," she said, her eyes welling up. "Please, I'll go right back down."

Mother Beth broke, just a little. "Brat, you know better," she said. "I'm so disappointed in you."

"I just wasn't thinking. I'm really going to get it, aren't I?"

Mother Beth sighed. "Look, let's just get

you back downstairs, okay? Come on."

Brat trailed in front of her slowly, her head down, hoping she could pull this next part off. As they moved past the eighth floor bathroom, she slowed down.

"Could I go to the bathroom really quick?" she asked. She saw Mother Beth's eyes widen.

"No!" she said. "You need to get back downstairs, right now."

"But the thing is, they don't like us going to the bathroom down there once the babies are asleep because it can wake them up. I mean, we can, but . . . It'll be real quick, Mother Beth, I promise. Please?" She hopped back and forth a little. "I really have to go."

"Oh, Brat," Mother Beth said. "Okay, two minutes, and I'm serious."

Brat nodded, turned, and raced into the bathroom. When the door closed behind her, she leaned against it and let out a deep breath.

Two minutes.

Her sister had two minutes.

Brat walked down to the last stall and stepped inside, closing and locking the door behind her. Then she looked up at the wall above the toilet.

Just as Jack had said there'd be, there was

a metal grate covering an air vent.

Now she just needed her older sister to come through.

Gumball had trailed her sister and Mother Beth, ducking behind corners as she watched her sister's performance. She smoothed her hair down. It was braided exactly like Brat's, but she still didn't know if she was going to be able to pull this off.

She watched as Mother Beth stood outside of the bathroom door, tapping her foot as she waited for Brat to emerge.

Gumball inched closer until she was just a few feet away from her. She knew she had to time it perfectly.

She waited for an opening, for Mother Beth to turn her head just slightly, and Gumball rushed toward her back. Mother Beth spun around and looked down at her, then back at the bathroom door.

"You're done?" she asked.

Gumball nodded. "Yep," she said, raising her voice high to match Brat's. "Thanks."

Mother Beth stared at her for a moment and then nodded. "Let's go." They walked toward the elevators and got in. Mother Beth pressed a button for the third floor.

When they got out, they walked down the hallway toward the nursery. As they opened the door, Lill came out from the back. She was holding Hiccup in her arms, and the small boy swayed back and forth, watching her intently.

"What's wrong?" she asked.

"Nothing," Mother Beth said, frowning at the boy. "Why is he awake?"

"You know hiccups," she said, and she turned and nuzzled his cheek.

"Huccuppp," the boy said, the giggle escaping his small body.

Lill hummed softly, but as she did, she locked eyes with Gumball.

Mother Beth cleared her throat, and Lill stopped. "Lill, I'm counting on you to make sure that any other children in the nursery with you stay here for the entire night. And make sure he gets to sleep."

Lill nodded, frowning at her friend. "Yes, of course," she said.

Mother Beth returned to the elevator, and the girls went into the nursery.

"Everything go okay?" Lill asked as she placed Hiccup back in his bed. He stirred and stared up at her, and Lill hoped he wouldn't start crying when they left.

"Yeah, everyone is in place."

They walked back out in the hallway and then to the stairwell and crept up to the eighth floor. When they got there, they peeked through the glass. Perry was standing there, and he opened the door to let them in. All three of the children crept back down the hall toward the locked storeroom where Jack was still waiting. He let out a sigh of relief when he watched them walk up.

"Any sign of her?" Gumball asked.

"Not ye—" He stopped as they all heard a noise on the other side of the storeroom door.

Suddenly, it flew open, and Brat stood there, her clothes wrinkled and dirty, her hair tumbling out of her braid, but her face covered in a proud smile.

"Come on in," she said.

They walked through the storeroom toward a door that led into the back of the small auditorium.

"You ready?" Lill asked the group, but she was mostly talking to Jack.

"Yeah," he said, and for the first time, he wasn't the cool, confident Jack they all knew. His hand was shaking as he reached up to open the door. "I'm ready."

# CHAPTER THIRTY-TWO

*The Last Day of Emily Lindsey*
*Sunday — twelve hours left*

She woke up feeling tired, her eyes heavy and head thick, as if she'd had too much to drink the night before. Her newly dyed hair was matted around her face, sticking out in every direction, and she finger combed it down as she sat up in her hotel bed.

The White Swan Inn was an inappropriately named motel about ten minutes from the church she'd visited last night.

She glanced at the clock.

*Time to get up.*

She'd shown up at the church the previous evening after the meeting had already started, and Amanda had been at the front of the room. When she'd spotted Emily hovering in the back, she'd smiled and reached out a hand, beckoning her.

"Come join us," she'd said softly. "Everyone is welcome."

Emily had walked forward and sat down. There was no need to tell her who she was just yet. She'd get Amanda to talk to her after everyone had left.

As the meeting ended, Emily lingered near the back of the room.

"Amanda Pearson," the woman said, reaching her hand out to shake Emily's. There was only a handful of people left in the room.

"I'm Emily of *Carmen Street Confessions,*" she said softly, not letting go of the woman's hand. "I'm sorry for surprising you like this."

"You've got to be kidding me," Amanda said, her face falling. "What are you doing here?"

"You stopped returning my calls. I really need your help. I'm trying to learn more about Friends of Frank."

"I told you, I don't have anything else to tell you."

"You're the one who contacted me," Emily said, finally stepping back. "Don't you forget that."

"I didn't forget it," Amanda said. "But when I read the draft of the article you sent me, it's not what I wanted at all . . ." She shook her head. "If I'd known what you were going to do, I never would have reached out to you. I never would have told you about Friends of Frank in the first place!"

"Look," Emily said. "I just came by to let you know that I'm moving forward with my story no matter what. And I'd really like you to be a part of it."

"You must be nuts," Amanda said, looking around her. She raised a hand as the final couple left the room and headed back upstairs. Amanda shook her head and pushed past Emily, walking toward the door. "Leave me alone, okay? I wanted your help, but I should've known your own self-interest was more important."

"Fine," Emily said. "It took a lot of searching and a lot of questions, but I finally got the names of two other people who can help me, two other people who can shed some light on what Friends of Frank really is." She reached into her pocket and let her fingers graze the Post-it Note where she'd scribbled down two names.

"Well then, I guess you'd better go get them to help you," Amanda said firmly. "Now please, just let me be."

# CHAPTER THIRTY-THREE

*Now*

It took some convincing, but Gayla was able to convince Brick to let me sit in on the interview with Ryan and Eleanor Griggs.

"He's the one who found out they were lying," I heard her say as I stood outside Brick's office while she plead my case.

"He shouldn't have been talking to them in the first place," Brick said loudly, turning to look at me through the open door. "But it's fine. I'll allow it, just this once."

The five-hour interview with the Griggs was tedious, exhausting, and embarrassing for everyone involved.

It also confirmed a few things.

One, they were liars, and not in the harmless, little-white-lie sort of way. They were willing to go to any and all lengths to protect themselves and their business, even if that meant making up the most outlandish story I'd ever heard.

Two, they were certifiable. Nuts. Both of them. As they held hands and explained what happened with tears in their eyes, I had to wonder if everything was all there upstairs.

Three, and most important of all —

They were probably not murderers.

Ryan Griggs had joined us at the station just two hours after his wife called him from her foyer. He'd walked in, his long, shaggy hair hanging down around his shoulders, a thick beard covering half his face, his eyes alert. As he turned to one side, his hair moved to reveal a large bandage on the side of his head.

"You have got to be kidding me," Gayla said.

Ryan and his wife embraced, and then the protests were falling out of his mouth before either Gayla or I had a chance to say anything.

"Look, I know what we did was a bit unorthodox, but we didn't have anything to do with that woman's death," he said. "Nothing. I had no idea until my wife called me. I swear."

He looked about fifteen pounds lighter than the picture I'd seen of him, and he was jittery, tapping his fingers quickly against the table in front of him while he held on to his wife's hand with the other. He seemed scared, nervous, and not 100 percent sober.

But he was very much alive.

"All right, well, why don't you take a stab at telling us what's going on?" I said. "You know, give the truth a chance?"

He nodded and looked over at his wife, who sat there with a steely expression on her face. She seemed angry, but Ryan Griggs looked relieved to be telling us the truth.

"I drove out to see one of the patients who Emily interviewed for her blog," he said. "Enid Greene."

"Yes, I met Enid," I said.

"You did?" he asked. "What did she tell you?"

"Why don't you tell us what happened?" I said. "And again, you might want to err on the side of telling the truth here."

"Okay," he said. "It was horrible. A big mistake, really. I went out there just to talk to her . . ." He slowed his speech when he saw my face. "And yeah, maybe I wanted to see if there was anything I could do to change her mind about the lawsuit," he said.

"You tried to bribe her."

"No," he said. "I tried to . . . give her something that she wouldn't be able to have otherwise?" He shrugged his shoulders. "I just feel like *bribe* is a strong word. It was probably not the best idea, but it's not like it worked anyway."

"Yeah, given that she recorded you."

"What?" Eleanor asked.

"Yeah, that's when I realized it was getting out of control. I didn't feel like coming home right away. I don't know. I knew that Eleanor . . ." He looked at his wife. "I knew how much you wanted me to talk to them, to stop all of this, and I knew how disappointed you'd be," he said. "I just wasn't ready to come home yet, but I didn't feel like going to any of the other meetings. So I missed my flight."

"Wait, so you were never in Philadelphia?" I asked.

"No, I grabbed a hotel out near Enid's, this absolute hole in the wall, but it was nice to be alone, nice to not have to deal with any of it or to explain why I didn't want to try anymore."

"But if you just talk to them —" Eleanor started.

"What? They'll record me trying to bribe them and make it all look even worse?" he asked. "It's not worth it."

"So what was your plan?" Gayla asked. "Just hole up in your hotel room and hope it all went away?"

"You know, that was pretty much as far as I got," he said. "I was just lying there in my hotel room, wondering if I should go get a bottle of whiskey. It seemed like too much effort. That was the only thing that stopped me. The worst part is that I really wanted to snatch that tape recorder when I saw it. I thought about it, for just a moment, and then ran out of there." He shook his head and looked at his wife. "I'm a lot of things, but I'm not a violent person," he said firmly.

I nodded for him to go on.

"So I'm lying there, having missed my flight. I'm thinking about getting drunk, and I can't even think about calling Eleanor."

"Ryan . . ." his wife said.

"I just stayed there for a few days, not doing anything. I knew that she thought I was traveling and that she'd be pissed at me for not calling, but she always got over things like that. But then I got her message."

"Which one?" Gayla asked.

"She said that Emily from *Carmen Street* had been found in her home, covered in blood and holding a knife. And that there was no body, and nobody knew who she'd hurt. And that's when I saw my opportunity."

"How's that for an opportunity?" Gayla muttered to me, her eyebrows raised.

"So you decided, what, to stay hidden?" I asked.

"Yeah," he said. "I know how crazy it sounds, but you have to understand the state I was in. I just couldn't deal with all of the scrutiny and the questions. That woman was relentless. I figured, if people thought she was a crazy psychopath, I could stay hidden for a few years, and the company would rebound."

"A few years?" I asked. "How would you do that?"

"It's not that hard actually. My wife and I have three homes and a couple of properties across the globe. I knew people would figure it out soon enough, but maybe by then, they'd start to see that there was something wrong with Emily, you know, something not quite right."

"There was no way your plan would have worked," Gayla said.

"But it did," Ryan said. "For a little while, right? I know it was ridiculous, but you have to understand — it came from a place of passion. That business was my life. Do you know how many people we help at Kelium? How many people's lives we've saved or prolonged with our medications?"

He looked down at his hands and swung back and forth in the chair, his face twitching, the tears just starting to roll down his cheeks. His wife sat stonily beside him. "She wanted to ruin that because of one bad batch."

"But you didn't stop there," I said, pointing at his ear. "What were you thinking?"

He looked at his wife and shrugged. "We weren't," he said. "We got desperate. When we heard about the search teams in Piper Woods, we figured . . . it was the most definitive way to prove that I'd been out there with her." He shook his head. "Like I said, we weren't thinking."

"How did you do it?" I asked, and he looked at his wife again.

"I did it," she said softly. "With a brand-new pair of garden shears." She laughed humorlessly. "You know, infections and stuff."

"My brother-in-law is a doctor," Ryan said. "He gave me the numbing injection. He didn't know why, though. I don't want him getting mixed up in any of this."

We wrapped up the interview with the couple a few hours later. Gayla and I walked back to our desks and dropped into our chairs.

"I've seen some crazy stuff," she said, "but this takes the cake. Where the hell do we go from here?"

I closed my eyes and rubbed my temples. When I opened them, I straightened in my chair.

"We go to a church out in Ashland," I said.

Gayla frowned. "What?" she asked.

"Come on," I said, standing. "I'll explain on the way there."

# CHAPTER THIRTY-FOUR

We drove forty-five minutes up to Kendall Community Church. Gayla was quieter than usual, and I didn't know if it was because of the whole Griggs fiasco or because of what happened with Mary earlier.

Or both.

"You all right?" I asked, my gaze on the road. Gayla and silence simply didn't go well together.

"Yeah," she said quickly. "I'm okay. Are you?"

"Yeah," I said. Then nothing again for another few minutes. "Look, about Brick and Mary —"

"It's okay," she said. "We have a deal. As long as you're okay, I won't say anything to them."

I glanced over at her and nodded. "Thanks," I said. "Any luck with Dan Lindsey?"

She shook her head. "Nothing. Nobody's seen or heard from him. It's not looking good."

We pulled up outside the church a few minutes later. It didn't look much like a church at all. Kendall Community Church was a small, one-story building with a fading facade and boarded-up windows. If it wasn't for the sole light on in the building, I would have assumed that it was the wrong place.

Gayla must have shared my sentiments. "You think that's it?" she asked.

"It's gotta be," I said. "Worth a look around at least?"

Gayla nodded, a frown on her face as she opened the door and stepped out. I did the same, and we walked together up to the door. It was only seven, but the street was eerily dark. There was just one other building on the block, and a huge vacant lot separated it from the church.

I pulled the door open, and we stepped inside. The small, warm foyer we stood in certainly smelled like a church. I hadn't been to church in a very long time, but they always smelled the same. We stepped forward.

"Hello?" Gayla called, but there was no answer.

We reached the end of the hall and looked into a small room with hard-backed chairs facing a stage. The room was empty, and we both turned around and headed back toward the front of the building. A staircase led down into the basement, where there were more lights on.

Gayla turned and began to make her way down. "Hello?" she said again as we walked down the stairs.

We stepped into the basement, and the heat improved, if only slightly. The floor was filled on both sides with boxes, trinkets, tables, and chairs, pushed out of the way and forgotten. We walked to the end of the hall where a door was pushed partially closed, and as we got closer, I could hear light chatter on the other side.

I stepped up to the door and peered through the glass. Inside, I could see about half a dozen people milling about the room. A man and a woman were standing just a few feet away from us, talking. The other people in the room were arranging chairs and settling in.

Gayla opened the door, and we both walked in. Everyone looked up, and the couple that was talking stopped, leaving the room in complete silence.

"Hi," I said. "We're looking for someone

named Amanda."

A woman near the front of the room stepped forward. "I'm Amanda," she said. "Are you here for the seminar?"

Immediately, I recognized her voice from our phone call. "No," I said. "I'm Detective Steven Paul, and this is Detective Gayla Ocasio. I talked to you earlier today on the phone. I was wondering if you had a few moments."

The already quiet room got impossibly quieter as everyone stopped moving and stared.

Amanda looked like she'd been hit by a truck. She frowned and bit her lip and then quickly crossed the room until we were standing face-to-face, her back to the rest of the room.

"I thought I asked you not to call me," she said in a low hiss. "You can't possibly think that showing up here is any better."

"I just want to ask you a few questions," I said. "Please, it's extremely important."

"You can't just barge in here," she said. "I'm about to host a meeting."

"Are we going to do this or what?" one of the women asked from behind her. "It's seven o'clock, and I have places to be."

"I'm sorry. I can't do this right now," Amanda said to me, turning briefly to the crowd behind her and raising up a finger. "We have to get started. I wish you hadn't come."

"Is this seminar open to the public?" I asked. "If so, you won't mind if we join?"

She balled her fists at her side but didn't respond. Finally, she turned and headed back to the front of the room.

She sat down in her chair and watched Gayla and I warily as we made our way farther into the room and sat down in two empty chairs. Some of the other participants watched us for a moment, but they turned back to the front of the room, seemingly ready to begin their session more than they were worried about us.

"Thank you all for coming," Amanda said, still watching me, and I could see that our presence had rattled her. I didn't feel good about making her uncomfortable, but that fact alone let me know that she knew something. She had to. She was the best lead we had on what exactly Emily had been looking for right before her death.

"I want to talk to you about grief and overcoming that emotion," she said. "Grief is an important part of our lives, something we all experience at some point, in varying degrees of severity. It's how we deal with it that really matters. Because like I said, it's going to come. It's how we find inner peace, where we turn for sanctuary, that can help us through it."

Amanda wasn't looking at me anymore, and she was engaging with her audience. She was a natural, and I could tell that she'd done this before. She opened the floor up, and then the room began to share stories about things that happened to them. The stories were all incredibly painful — a mother who'd just lost her daughter to stomach cancer, a man who'd lost his wife in a car accident. I realized very quickly that you didn't show up for grief counseling on a Saturday night if you didn't have a good reason for it.

"Now, under your seats," Amanda said, pointing, "I've placed a pad of paper and a pencil. I want you to sketch something. Absolutely anything that makes you upset. And I'm not grading based on artistic talent here."

A chuckle went around the room as everyone reached under their chairs and picked up the pad of paper.

Amanda leaned to one side and looked at Gayla and me. "You too, Detectives. If you're going to sit in, you have to participate. This is a safe space. Nobody gets to sit and watch."

Gayla and I both leaned down slowly and picked up our notepads.

"So I want you to draw something on one side that makes you upset, something that troubles you. Maybe it's something in your past that still brings you grief. Maybe it's something you're afraid of. I want you to draw that on one side of the paper. I'll give you a few minutes to do that. Don't take a lot of time. Just draw the first thing that comes to mind."

She sat back in her chair while the participants all bent over their papers. I wanted to get up and use this time to ask Amanda more questions, but I knew it wouldn't be appropriate. Besides, she'd made it perfectly clear that she didn't want to talk to me anyway.

I looked at my blank paper. Gayla was busy drawing, and I smiled at how easily she let herself get involved in things like this. I didn't know what to draw. Truth was, there were so many options. I was trying to think of something to put down, something to be able to say I'd done the exercise, when the image of the steel bars came to my mind.

Amanda had said, "Draw the first thing that comes to mind."

Before I knew what I was doing, I'd drawn the bars, long and narrow, almost covering the page.

Gayla looked over. "What's that?" she asked. "Prison bars? You're scared of prison?"

I shrugged. "Something like that." I don't know what compelled me, but I leaned forward and drew a tiny picture of the symbol on the bottom of one of the bars. When I was done, I quickly flipped my paper over and cleared my throat. I looked over at Gayla, who was hunched over her own paper. "What's that?" I asked.

She sat back and lifted her paper so I could see it.

She'd drawn two people far apart on the paper. "Loss," she said. "I'm constantly afraid of losing someone I love. I think about it all the time."

We stared at each other for a moment. Gayla was probably the strongest person I knew, and this revelation surprised me. I was about to say something when Amanda spoke again.

"Now, if you're done with that, I ask you to flip it over, and on this side, draw something, just one thing, that makes you smile," said Amanda. "Anything. Take some time with this one. Whereas on the other side, I asked you to draw the first thing that came to mind, on this side, I want you to think of the last thing that made you smile, really smile this week, and draw that."

I stared at the paper. The last thing that made me smile this week. I knew that it was at the end of my meeting with Pat, when I'd told her I'd see her next week. I drew her standing at the door, and then suddenly, I wanted to hide it. I tore off a clean sheet of paper and covered it up, because I didn't want the prison bars facing up either.

Amanda stood up and began to walk around the room. "Here's what's interesting to me," she said. "Some of you have flipped the paper over so that the bad image is facing up. And some of you have chosen the good image. What does it say if you're more willing to let people see what you're afraid of than what makes you smile, or vice versa?" She stopped next to my seat and looked at the paper I'd used to cover up my drawings, but she didn't say anything.

The class wrapped up a few minutes later, and I stood, crumpling the paper up and putting it in my jacket pocket. There were a lot of people waiting to speak with Amanda, and Gayla and I hung around to talk to her. She looked up at us, and I could see the exasperation in her eyes.

"Come on," Gayla said. We headed upstairs and waited by the front door. We watched as the attendees walked up one at a time, giving us a brief nod as they walked out the door. Finally, we heard footsteps, and Amanda was there, carrying a milk crate full of supplies and her bag on her shoulder.

When she saw us, she sighed. "You're still here?" she asked.

"We need to know whatever you can tell us about Emily Lindsey," I said. "All we want to know is why she came to see you."

She shook her head. "I really don't want to talk about this," she said. "I don't understand why you can't respect that."

"Because a woman is dead," I said. "And the people who did it got away. That's why we can't respect your wish not to talk to us. I'm sorry."

We all heard a buzzing sound, and Gayla dug her phone out of her pocket. She looked down at it. "Sorry," she said, nodding at Amanda before opening the door and stepping out.

Amanda walked past me and out the door. She held it open. "Are you coming? Or are you going to stay in there all night?" she asked.

I followed her out into the night and stood behind her as she locked the front door to the church.

"I'm sorry," she said. "I don't know anything, and I can't help you."

As we stood there in the night, her with a milk crate perched on her hip, me with my hands in my pockets, I felt desperate. She was the only lead I had, and I needed to understand just what had happened to Emily — and who that woman was at the hospital.

And why she'd drawn the symbol.

My fingers connected with the paper I'd balled up and stuffed in my pocket only minutes ago.

I took it out and unrolled it before handing it to her.

"What's this?" she asked, shifting the milk crate before continuing to unroll the paper. Her face scrunched in confusion as she looked down at the picture I'd drawn of Patricia.

"Turn it over," I said.

She flipped it over and stared at the picture of the prison bars that I'd drawn. I watched as her gaze dropped down to the small symbol I'd added in the corner. Her eyes widened, and she looked back at me.

"That symbol," I said. "I think the woman who drew it is the woman who killed Emily. Have you seen it before?"

She blinked a few times, and I knew immediately that she was hiding something.

"No," she said. "I've never seen it before. Now, Detective, please — *please* — I'm begging you. Let this go."

When I got home that night, I dialed Lara. She picked up on the last ring.

"Hi," she said. "Look, Steve, I'm sorry about what happened at the birthday par—"

"Is it okay if I come to the play?"

"What?"

"Kit's play. He wants me there. But I wanted to make sure it's okay with you."

"I don't know . . ."

"I mean, it is a public event," I said, and I winced as the words came out of my mouth.

She cursed under her breath. "Then why even call me? Huh, Steve? I hate when you do things like that."

"I'm just telling you that it's a public event —"

"No, it's not. It's for parents of students at the school —"

"And community members and friends, but if you don't want me to come —"

"I don't want you to come."

She said it softly but firmly, and I choked on nothing but air.

For months, I'd been pushing her, daring her, knowing she wouldn't be able to actually say the words. Relying on the fact that she'd loved me once.

But she'd finally called my bluff.

"Well, I guess that's that, isn't it?" I said.

I hung up and headed straight for my bedroom. The guilt was rushing over me in waves, and I knew I should stop, but my feet kept going, leading me toward the side of my bed. I opened the drawer to my nightstand and leaned over it, breathing heavily.

I didn't bother to get out the towels or tissues. Instead, I lifted my sleeve and placed the razor against my arm, my fingers shaking as I pulled it slowly against my skin.

The pain was gratifying, and it replaced the guilt. I sat there, watching the blood as it slowly rose to the surface of my skin. At the same time, the tears welled in my eyes, and I waited as the droplets balanced in both places — one on my arm, and one at the top of my cheek.

I felt the tear rolling down my face, and I tilted my head down to wipe it on my shoulder. As I did this, the droplet of blood suddenly rolled, as if it were trying to get away — and landed on my sheet.

I felt an overwhelming sense of panic as I stared at the tiny, dark-red spot on my sheet.

"Fuck," I said out loud, dropping the razor back into my nightstand and standing up. I raced into the bathroom and wet a washcloth before running back to the bed to scrub it away. It was evidence of everything dark and terrible in my life, and I wanted it *gone.*

But it was too late.

I wiped at the stain, but it just smeared slightly and stayed there, taunting me. All of the guilt rushed back to the surface, and I screamed, tearing the sheet off the bed. I carried it and the razor blade into the kitchen and pushed both of them down into the trash can.

Then I grabbed my cell phone and dialed a phone number.

"Mom," I whispered when she answered. I hadn't called her like this in a long time, but immediately, she knew.

"I'm on my way," she said.

# CHAPTER THIRTY-FIVE

*The Last Day of Emily Lindsey*
*Sunday — two hours left*

Not for the first time during this trip, Emily glanced into the rearview mirror and stared at herself for a few moments before letting her eyes drift back to the road. She liked looking at herself with her new hair and flushed cheeks and barrels of new-found, reporter-extraordinaire confidence.

She felt *alive.*

She pushed down on the accelerator and let the needle go five, then ten, then fifteen miles over the speed limit. She slowly eased her foot off until she was back in a safe zone and then did it again.

The meeting was being held at a small coffee shop in a town not far from the hotel where she was staying. Friends of Frank held meetings three Sundays out of every month with interested women. They never held them at their home — that place was reserved for women who made it past the several-month-long recruiting process.

And those women were few and far between, Matilda had told her several times.

"Only certain women are destined to be a part of our group, and I feel like you're the one," she'd said to Emily on just their third meeting.

They'd met more than a dozen times over two months, and within just a few weeks, Matilda had been eating out of her hands. Emily saw in her a woman who was yearning to be free from her past, searching for acceptance and childlike in her friendship.

And apparently, Matilda saw in her some desperate woman who was yearning to be in a mind-controlled world. Emily smiled at the thought as she pulled into a space a few blocks away from the café. Maybe, if this whole blogging thing didn't work out, she could go into acting.

As she parked, her jet-black hair hanging around her cheeks, she felt more confident and more nervous than she had that first day. She was more confident, because she had a plan and she knew what she was doing, but she was more nervous for the same reason.

That first day, Matilda had walked timidly into the restaurant to meet her, and Emily had been surprised at how normal she looked. It was a cult after all, and she'd expected the woman to have ankle-length hair and beady eyes or to have some sort of religious symbol painted on her forehead. Instead, she actually didn't look too different from Emily herself, with long, blondish-brown hair and an athletic build. They were even about the same height. Besides her overtly pale skin, Matilda could have been any of the girls in the neighborhood who Emily worked so hard to avoid.

"Emily?" the woman had asked her. "Welcome."

As she sat outside the recruitment event three months later, Emily knew she had to find a way to get close to her without the men seeing her. The men were always watching; that's one thing it took her a while to learn. During her regular meetings with Matilda, she'd seen them lurking, usually the tall one who sort of looked like a vampire John Travolta.

And then there was the man in the ill-fitting tan suit, Bill Boyd, the one who'd been watching her for a while.

She'd noticed him after her second meeting with Matilda, trailing her home. A few harmless questions, and Matilda had admitted that Bill was the organization's personal private eye — he followed prospective women around to make sure that they were who they said they were. Emily had spotted him early and had managed to keep him at bay, for a while. He was the one who'd broken her cover to Matilda.

Still, Emily knew she had to find a way to get the woman alone.

If they saw her again — she'd already tried to get close to Matilda twice since they'd banned her — they'd get Emily out of there right away, and she knew she'd never see Matilda again.

She got out of the car and walked quickly into the drugstore next to the café. In case anyone was watching her, she wanted to appear like a normal woman running some errands who stopped for a coffee. She walked around for about ten minutes before leaving and heading to the café. She was early. She opened the door and walked inside. She crept to the side of the room.

She just needed a chance, an opening.

She took a seat at a table near the back.

A teenaged waitress appeared, a smile on her face. "What can I get you?" she asked.

"Um, just some hot tea, with lemon."

The girl nodded and walked away. Emily brushed her hair in front of her face and slumped in her booth, her eyes on the door.

About fifteen minutes later, she watched as the door opened and a young woman walked in. Emily knew immediately that this was the woman who was meeting Friends of Frank. She was young — she had to be under twenty — with waist-length brown hair and big, brown eyes.

And she looked scared out of her mind.

She walked over to a table near the back of the café and sat down. Emily turned her head and pretended to read the café menu that was scribbled on the wall behind the counter, but she watched as the woman reached into her purse and set something out on the table in front of her.

A small, red dictionary.

That must have been the item they told her to bring to identify herself. For Emily's first meeting, it had been a blue notebook. Emily turned back and watched the door.

"Here's your tea," a voice said from behind her.

Emily jumped. "Oh, thanks," she said, leaning back so the girl could place it in front of her. As she added sugar, Emily saw that her hands were shaking. She was reaching for another sugar packet when the door opened again, and two women walked in.

Emily recognized Matilda right away, and she quickly averted her eyes to the table. If

Matilda recognized her before Emily had a chance to get her alone, she'd be gone. Emily stared down into her tea as the women walked to the back of the café and joined the woman with the dictionary.

The meetings usually lasted a while, and Emily settled in to wait. All she needed was for Matilda to go to the bathroom, to get separated from the other two women for just a moment, and she'd seize her opportunity.

"Ma'am?" Emily looked up. The waitress was standing there, frowning.

"Oh, sorry?"

"I said do you want more hot water?" The girl peered over into the cup. "Oh, never mind. Looks like you're still full there," she said loudly before walking away.

Emily turned to look at the table and felt her heart skip a beat. Matilda wasn't talking to the other two women.

She was staring directly at Emily.

There was a frown on her face, and that frown turned into something else — fear, anger, or something close to it. She stood abruptly, leaned down, and spoke quietly to the woman she'd come with. They both stood, said something to the woman with the dictionary, and then turned to walk toward the door.

"Wait . . ." Emily croaked out, scrambling from her seat. She reached into her purse and grabbed a few bills for the tea, dropping them on the table. Then she rushed toward the door where Matilda was leaving.

"Wait, Matilda," she said. "Mattie."

The two women at the door shared a glance.

"I told you to leave me alone," Matilda said. "What did you do to your hair?"

"They're here, aren't they? Somewhere out there waiting?"

"You need to leave me alone, Emily," Matilda said quietly but urgently. "Please. Leave us alone."

"Who is this woman?" the lady standing next to her asked.

"Nobody."

They turned, stepped through the door, and began walking quickly down the street. Emily stumbled along behind them.

"Wait!" she said. "Mattie."

The women kept walking. They were heading toward a black car at the end of the block. Emily watched as the door opened and a man got out, peering in their direction. He scowled when he saw Emily, and he began heading toward them.

"Mattie, wait!" Emily said again, and then, because she had no more tricks up her sleeve, she used her last one. "Mattie, remember what you told me! You told me. I'm not going to stop."

Matilda stopped in her tracks and looked at the woman beside her and then at the man who was walking toward her. He reached her and put his arm on her shoulder, looking over her head at Emily.

Emily stood there, her shoulders square. They were in the middle of the street in broad daylight. She had the information she needed. They couldn't do anything to her.

She watched as Matilda leaned forward and whispered something to the man. Then Matilda turned and, with both hands in her pockets, walked quickly back to Emily.

Her eyes were unfocused, her breathing shallow, but Emily knew she'd gotten through to her.

"Did you drive here?" she asked quietly.

"Yes."

"Let's go for a drive."

# CHAPTER THIRTY-SIX

*Now*

The next morning, I woke up in my bed on fresh sheets. I walked out into the living room and found both Nell and Mike in the kitchen making breakfast.

"Pretty slim pickings here," she said, turning to me with a smile. I watched as she sliced a green pepper and put the pieces in the skillet. Then she rinsed the knife and wiped it with a paper towel. She watched me carefully as she walked over to her purse and dropped it inside. "That's the last of them," she said.

I swallowed and nodded, taking a seat on one of my barstools. I glanced around the kitchen and saw that she'd taken the rest of the knives out of my knife block. I didn't have to look in my desk drawer to know that my scissors were gone, too.

"Thanks," I said as she put a plate of eggs in front of me.

She nodded.

Mike sat across from me and dragged his fork against his empty plate. He stopped and leaned back as Nell served him some eggs. I saw them share a glance, and I waited for whatever it was that he was about to say.

"Son . . ."

"I know," I said.

"No, I don't think you do."

I put my fork down and looked at him. "It really doesn't happen a lot," I said.

"Enough," he said. "Every time we end up here, you tell us it's nothing, that you're getting help. We've let it go on for so long." His voice caught, and his eyes got watery.

I felt a chill rush through my entire body.

Mike's voice didn't catch.

Mike's eyes didn't get watery.

"You need to do something about this. We thought that you were getting better, or that's what we wanted to believe —"

"I promise you, I just had a bad night —"

"Look at yourself!" he yelled, leaning over to grab my arm. In doing so, he knocked his plate off the table, and eggs went flying. He held my forearm roughly in one of his hands and lifted it toward my face. "Look at yourself," he said again. "Please." A sob escaped him, and then I was crying, too, because Mike definitely didn't *sob.*

And then suddenly, he was yelling again, and Nell joined him, and I sunk back in my seat as my parents screamed at me for the first time in thirty years. As a kid, I'd waited for this, waited for them to yell at me, to get angry, to send me away. But they never did. They were patient, loving, and kind. Now, at thirty-seven, I was childlike, cowering in my chair, the disappointment and pain in their eyes more hurtful than anything I'd ever experienced before.

When they didn't have any energy left, they both slumped back, Mike in his chair, Nell against the kitchen counter.

And as I sat there, all I could think about was how much my arms were on fire, how much I needed to release this pain, and how much I needed help.

Nell and Mike stayed for a while before saying goodbye in a fit of more tears, apologies, and prayers. They both squeezed me so close, I thought I would suffocate. I was ashamed and exhausted.

I sprawled out on my bed, my cell phone beside me, and I knew it was time to call Mary. To tell her what they all wanted to hear.

The truth.

I rolled over and was reaching for my phone when it rang. I frowned when I saw that it was a number I didn't recognize.

"Hello?" I said.

"Hi, Detective Paul?"

"Yes."

"This is Amanda, from Kendall Community Church. You came by last night?"

I sat up fully, gripping the phone tighter. "Yes, of course," I said. "How can I help you?"

There was silence on the other end of the line for a few moments.

"Hello?" I said. "Amanda? Are you still there?"

"Yes," she said quietly. "I'm here. And I'm ready to talk now."

# CHAPTER THIRTY-SEVEN

I knew that Gayla was on my side, but I didn't want to ask her to lie for me.

Not anymore.

It wasn't fair to her, and there was no way in hell I was just going to wait for someone else to figure out what was going on.

I'd go out to the church and listen to Amanda, and then I'd fill Gayla in. And, if Brick found out, I'd ask for forgiveness later. Within ten minutes of the phone call, I was in my car and heading toward the highway.

There was barely any traffic, and I made it back to the church in about half an hour. It looked exactly the same as it had when we'd left the previous night, except that it seemed even quieter now than before. I pulled up in front of the door and parked the car. I walked up to the door and knocked before trying the handle. Unlike the night before, it was locked, and I waited. Before I could knock again, I heard rustling and then a click on the other side of the door, and it opened.

Amanda stood in front of me, her expression cautious but also frightened. She stepped back to let me enter the church. I was struck by a sense of déjà vu as I walked into the corridor. Before she closed the door, she stepped forward and peered out, her gaze scanning the street. She pushed the door closed and turned two large dead bolts before turning back around to face me.

"Are you all right?" I asked. "What were you looking for?"

"I'm not really sure," she said. "Here, let's go into the office." She walked past me and led me back into a small office that Gayla and I had passed. Amanda took a seat and motioned for me to sit across from her in another metal folding chair. "Thank you for coming back," she said, staring directly into my eyes. "I'm sorry I made you make the trip twice. When you came here before . . . I was just so surprised. And I was scared."

"Why are we meeting here?" I asked. "I could have met you at your home."

She stared at me for a moment and didn't say anything, and it occurred to me that she was less concerned about convenience than she was about revealing where she lived.

"What are you scared of?" I asked, changing the subject. "You have to tell me what's bothering you so I can help you."

She continued to stare at her hands. "Maybe first, you could tell me something. Where did you get that symbol from?"

"Symbol?"

"Yes," she said. "The one you drew during my exercise last night."

"The one you said you'd never seen before?"

She didn't respond, just watched me carefully, and I sat up straighter in my chair before answering.

"I saw that symbol because the woman I met at the hospital who was pretending to be Emily Lindsey drew it all over her body," I said. It was the truth, if not the whole truth. "And now that I know that she may have stabbed a woman to death, I can't help but think it means something."

"So you have no idea why she drew that image?" she asked.

"None whatsoever," I said. "But something tells me you do."

She looked away again and didn't say anything.

"Look, if you know something, you have to tell me," I said. "Please."

404

She nodded. "Emily was looking into an organization called Friends of Frank."

I sucked in a breath. "I've heard of them," I said, frowning as I leaned forward in my chair. "I found an old flyer of theirs in her notes."

Her eyes clouded over. "So you do know about Friends of Frank?"

"Not really," I said.

She nodded. "Friends of Frank has been around for almost forty years. Of course, it doesn't have the numbers or presence it once did, but it's as influential as it's ever been, maybe even more so. It was started by a man named Frank Davies. Frank died in 1991. Today, it's run by his son, Ellis Davies. I'm not sure exactly where it is today — they moved about twenty-five years ago — but I know they're still in the area."

"Okay," I said. "And what does this organization do, and how come I couldn't find any information about it?"

"Because you're not supposed to be able to. Now, as to what they do . . . do you mean on paper, or what they actually do?"

"Both," I said.

She nodded. "Well, on paper, they're a shelter for women who are pregnant and in situations where they don't have anyone else to turn to and need support. Heavily underground, for women who have spouses or boyfriends who will stop at nothing to find them. It's an incredibly tight network of people, and very few people outside the organization even know it exists."

"And what does the organization provide these women?" I asked. "I'm guessing shelter? Food, supplies, safety?"

"All of the above," she said. And then she added, "On the books."

"Okay," I said. "So what about off the books, Amanda? What is Friends of Frank? Really."

"Off the books," she said slowly, gripping the sides of her seat tightly, "Friends of Frank is the most horrifying, vile community I've ever encountered. It's what nightmares are made of. It's why I haven't had a real night of sleep since I was a little girl. It's why I'm a grown woman who is scared to turn off her light at night."

"What are you talking about?" I asked. "I don't understand. You have to start from the beginning."

"Okay," she said, taking a breath. "Friends of Frank is a group that subscribes to the belief of communal parenting."

"Communal parenting?" I asked. "What exactly do you mean?"

"All of the adults are responsible for tak-

406

ing care of all of the children. No preferential treatment allowed. Of course, everyone knows whose child is whose, but there are strict punishments for showing it."

"How do you know all of this?" I asked. "Were you . . . were you one of the mothers?"

"No," she said quietly. "I was one of the children. A long time ago, a group of us escaped. There were five of us." She said this sadly.

"What happened to the other four?" I asked.

"I don't know," she said. "We left and split up, and I never heard from them again. Except my sister, of course."

"What happened to her?"

"She died three years ago," she said. "I couldn't help her."

"I'm sorry," I said. "What do you mean that you couldn't help her?"

"Gumball was —" She smiled sadly. "Sorry, Gloria. We used to call her Gumball. Gloria never fully came to terms with our childhood and what we saw the day we left the compound. It tore her apart. She couldn't sleep either, and it drove her crazy."

"She took her own life."

She looked down and then back at me and nodded.

"What did you see that day?" I asked. "The day you left."

She stared through me now, her gaze focused on something in the past, something I couldn't see with her, and I struggled to get inside her head.

"Amanda," I said. "What is it?"

"We saw them kill a child," she said, and her shoulders slumped right after she said it. "I've never told anyone that. Can you believe that? I saw it happen, and I've never told anyone."

"What are you talking about?" I said. "Who's 'them'? What child?"

"A little boy," she said. "I can still see his face. We snuck into this ceremony that they had every summer. I don't know if they do it anymore. But when I was there, they made sure that we were not allowed up on the floor where they had the ceremony. That year, five of us snuck up, and we saw it. We saw what they did. Frank used his hands — his bare hands — and suffocated a boy in front of some of the others. The rest of the adults just stood there and watched. It's an image I can't ever get out of my head. The boy was sleeping at first. He woke up and . . ." She took a deep breath, the tears falling down her cheeks. "I just remember them wrapping his body up and giving it to one of the mothers. That's the day we left."

"Where did you go?" I asked.

"We walked and walked until we found a truck stop, and they called the police. They took us in, and that's when Gumball and I got separated from the others." She blinked back tears. "I never saw or heard from them again."

"Did you tell the police what you saw?"

Amanda swallowed and shook her head. "We couldn't."

"Why not?"

She sniffed. "Because right before we left, we made a promise to someone that we wouldn't."

"Who?"

She bit her bottom lip and shook her head. "I can't . . . I'm sorry, I can't tell you that."

"But —"

"I can't," she said firmly.

I sighed. "Okay, then maybe you can tell me more about what Emily Lindsey wanted from you."

"It started with what I wanted from her," she said.

"So you're the one who contacted Emily?"

"Yes. The woman that we made the promise to . . . I just wanted Emily to check on her. I didn't even know if she was still alive, but since my sister died, I haven't been able to get what happened out of my head. I've read Emily's blog, and she's good. She can find out anything. So I reached out and asked her to check out Friends of Frank. But I told her she had to be careful, to be delicate. She promised she would look into it."

"And she did?"

"Yes," Amanda said. "She didn't tell me much, just that she'd found something. Found the woman I told her about. But instead of telling me how she was, if she was okay, she just kept asking me questions. Like she wanted to know more or wanted to interview me. Then one day, she sent me a draft of a story she wanted to write, and I almost lost it."

"What was the story about?"

"It was anything but delicate. It was mean, cruel, and one-sided. I don't have any love lost for Friends of Frank, but I do for some of the people we left behind. I asked Emily to help me, but she had her own intentions. She kept trying to call me for an interview. And I realized that she was only interested in her story. That's when I started ignoring her calls."

"So why are you telling me all of this?"

"Because I could tell that the Emily Lindsey case is very important to you. And I need your help. The woman who I asked Emily to look for — if you promise to help her, I'll tell you how to get in touch."

"I promise to try my best," I said. "But do you have another way to get in touch with them? Another number? Because I tried the one that Emily had, and an automated voice came on saying the number was disconnected."

"Oh," she said simply. "No, you made a mistake."

"You think I dialed wrong?"

"No," she said with a small, sad smile. "The number is not disconnected. You made a mistake in believing that 'automated voice' that said it was."

# CHAPTER THIRTY-EIGHT

Gayla tapped a pen against the coffee table as we sat across from each other in my living room.

Detective Franny Bates, a friend of Gayla's, sat next to me, her hands folded in her lap.

"Thanks for helping us out on this one," Gayla said. "I can't go in, because there's a chance the woman who pretended to be Emily will recognize me."

Franny nodded. "It's no problem," she said. "I just hope I can pull this off. Seems like they run a pretty tight ship."

We'd printed up a full page of notes, and it was sitting in the middle of the table, but nobody touched it. We all knew what needed to happen. We had one goal — get Friends of Frank to trust that Franny needed their help and to give us a location.

An address.

A landmark.

Anything.

Something to help us find the woman and man from the hospital.

Amanda had given us precise instructions for what we needed to do in order to set up a meeting with the women from this Friends of Frank organization — but it wasn't going to be easy.

"Whatever you do, you need to convince whoever picks up that phone that you found one of their flyers and you need their help," she had said. "It depends on who picks up the phone. Some of the women will probably give you a harder time than others. They never gave out that many of the flyers in the first place, and of course, that's what Emily said when she called."

"Won't they be suspicious?" I had asked.

"If you get the same person that Emily got, yes," she had said. "But I have a feeling from what Emily told me that they haven't shared that too widely. They don't want people knowing about the flyers."

Franny reached over and dialed the number. She put it on speakerphone, and we all listened silently as the phone rang four times, just as it had when I called the first time.

The same voice I'd heard the first time I'd called filled the line.

"The number you have reached is out of service. Please hang up and try again."

We all looked at each other, and then Franny cleared her throat and spoke. "No," she said. "I believe this is the right number."

There was still silence on the other line, and I stared at her. She bit her bottom lip and then spoke again.

"Hello?"

"Please hold."

I sucked in a breath. It was the same woman, but her voice was only slight less robotic than it had been a moment ago.

Nothing happened for a full minute.

"Hang up?" I mouthed to Gayla, and she was the one to shake her head this time.

A few moments later, a woman's voice came on the line.

"Hi, are you in danger?"

Franny looked at me as she spoke. "I think so," she said.

"Okay," the woman said. "Don't worry. We'll take care of you."

And just like that, we were on.

Franny and the woman arranged to meet later that day. The woman had insisted that Franny wait until the following week, but she'd done a great job in pushing back. I'd worked with her a few times and knew that she was pretty fearless, but she'd held her own on the phone with the woman.

"Please," she had said. "The flyer said you could help. I need to get out of here now. Please."

"Okay," the woman had finally said. "We have another meeting planned for today, so you can join us for that."

She provided an address and a time.

They were meeting at Jerry's Café. It was in the middle of the city square. To get to it, we'd had to descend a long flight of stairs and walk through a crowded patio filled with families, couples, and friends out enjoying the warm afternoon.

Gayla and I arrived half an hour early and were seated near the back of the café. I was facing away from the door; she sat across from me, carefully watching the door, ready to duck out of sight if necessary. She also had a line of sight to Franny, who was sitting by herself in a booth near the door. Franny was miked, and I had an earpiece in. Gayla wasn't wearing one, since she would be visible to anyone walking in.

I took a deep breath.

"Someone's coming," Gayla muttered. "A woman, white, late twenties, blond hair."

"Yes, I'm Franny," I heard the detective say in my earpiece.

And then silence.

"What are they saying?" Gayla asked.

"Shit, I can only hear Franny. The mike's not picking up the other woman. From body language, do you think it's the Friends of Frank woman?"

"No, probably the other recruit. She looks scared. Someone else is joining them," Gayla said. "Thin, redhead. Looks like she's never seen the sun a day in her life. She just sat down at the booth."

"Yes, I'm Franny," I heard over the mike.

"Well, my husband put me out yesterday," Franny said, answering a question I hadn't heard. "I was staying with my sister, and he came by and demanded that she let him in. She wouldn't, and he forced himself in anyway, looking for me. I hid in a closet. I was so scared of what he was going to do if he found me."

It was scripted, but Franny delivered it so perfectly that I almost believed her.

"Shit," I heard Gayla say.

"What?"

"The redhead keeps looking back here."

"At us?"

"Yeah. She looks real nervous. I think she's gonna —"

As she said this, I heard Franny speak again into the microphone. "Already? That's

416

all for today?"

"Shit," Gayla said, standing up. "She made us."

I stood, too, whipping around. But the redhead was already walking toward the door.

# Chapter Thirty-Nine

I jumped out of my seat and spun toward the front of the café. Franny and the other recruit were still seated in the booth, and they'd turned to talk to each other. There was a woman in a white blouse and jeans, her hair gathered back in a long braid, walking quickly out the front door. As she did, she turned back toward us, and we made eye contact.

Gayla and I moved quickly to the front of the room. "I'll stay here and talk to the woman who showed up, see how she got here, if she knows anything," Gayla said, stopping at the booth.

"Okay."

I rushed out the door after the woman from Friends of Frank. As I stepped onto the warm patio, the sun beating down on me, I blinked a few times. There she was, rushing through the middle of the square. I took off after her. There were people buzzing all around us. Families out playing, couples strolling slowly. I wondered if they'd picked the square because it would be so crowded. Had we underestimated them? This group was determined to stay hidden, and maybe we should have been better prepared.

I kept my eyes on the long braid bouncing against the white shirt. She wasn't running, but she was moving quickly and with purpose.

And then, suddenly, I felt the chalky taste in my mouth. I stopped abruptly, and a man walking behind me bumped into me.

"Hey," he said before stepping around me and continuing.

The heat, the people, the adrenaline. I knew that a vision was coming, and I longed for my mints, wished I could have that soothing sensation right then and there. I blinked a few times as suddenly, my vision doubled.

The family that had been playing just to my right multiplied, and there were two of each of them, standing side by side. The man who'd stepped around me a few minutes ago had a twin, and they hurried off in perfect synchrony. I blinked a few times.

What the hell?

I stared straight ahead, and the woman in

white was gone.

I felt my chest clench. I couldn't have lost her. Gayla had stayed behind to talk to the women. My job was to not let the woman out of my sight, and yet I had. I swallowed, trying to calm myself down, but it wasn't working.

A movement across the square caught my eye. I let out a sigh of relief when I saw that the woman was still there. She was standing near the bottom of the stairs that led out of the square. Her shoulders were hunched over, and I could see that she was talking on a cell phone. I inched closer, the doubles still moving all around me, and I tried to block them out. I was within ten feet of her, standing behind her, when suddenly, she took the phone away and turned to dart up the stairs.

Shit.

The chalkiness still in my mouth, the people still buzzing around me, I ran to the stairs to follow her. She was small and quick, and she ascended them easily. I was a few paces behind her, breathing heavily as I ran up the stairs after her.

She reached the top and then was just out of sight. I kept pushing until I made it to the top and then let my gaze scan the streets.

And then I saw her.

Not just the woman from the café but the woman she was talking to.

Standing ten feet away, next to a black sedan, was the woman from the hospital.

I froze, the visions still swimming around me, my head spinning, and watched as the woman from the café spoke quickly and excitedly to the other woman. She was dressed similarly, in simple, solid colors, with her hair pulled straight back from her face. She was listening to the woman, and then she let her gaze sweep the area by the stairs, immediately landing on me.

We stared at each other, and I couldn't tell if she recognized me or if it was simply the fact that I was standing there, out of breath, watching them. But she didn't move, didn't turn away, didn't try to get in the car. I leaned forward and tried to catch a glimpse of the license plate. I could just make out the numbers . . .

I heard a noise to my left, and I turned. Standing just a couple of feet away from me, just out of my line of sight, was a figure.

I gasped when I saw who it was.

The tan suit, the beady eyes.

It was the man from the woods and Lara's house.

I blinked a few times, the chalkiness oppressive now, and I was afraid that I would lose it completely.

He didn't say anything, just stared at me, and I began to run through the questions in my mind.

*One: Can anyone else see him?*

*Two: Can you touch him?*

*Three: Can you interact with him?*

Before I could stop myself, the words fell out of my mouth. "Are — are you real?" I whispered.

I saw something change on his face, and I realized what was happening too late.

His expression changed from anger to stunned surprise.

"No, I'm not, Detective," he said, his voice low, his hot breath on my face and undeniably real.

The minute I felt it, I knew that I'd made a mistake.

He leaned even closer to me.

"Boo."

With that, he lifted both of his hands and pushed, hard, and I only had a moment to hate myself before there was nothing below my feet, and I went tumbling back down the stairs into the square.

# CHAPTER FORTY

*Then*

There were five of them.

They stood shoulder to shoulder in the auditorium, their backs pressed against the wall. In the last few months, they'd plotted and planned and strategized. To anyone watching them closely during that time, they would have seemed much older than they really were. But now that they'd made it — now that they knew the truth — they'd reverted back to children, and they stood there shaking, none of them able to come up with a single idea for what they should do next.

Brat was the first to make a noise, a large gasp escaping her lips as she stared at the body of the small boy being carried away. Her hands flew up to her mouth. She was sobbing now, quietly, and it was only a matter of seconds before the cries exploded from her body.

Gumball looked up and saw what was about to happen. Darting to her sister's side, she put her arms around her and pulled her close. The girls cried together, their small frames shaking as they let out their fears and sorrow through the streaks of water that dripped down their cheeks.

Shy Perry was the first one to make a move toward the door. He was devastated like the rest of the children, but he knew they needed to get back downstairs before the auditorium emptied. He stepped forward. "Let's go," he whispered. "We have to get out of here."

Lill nodded. She wasn't crying but was staring off into space as if the events that had just taken place hadn't fully registered. She stepped away from the wall to follow Perry, and the twins followed her. As they moved in a line toward the exit, they noticed that Jack hadn't moved at all.

"Jack," Lill whispered. "Come on, let's go."

But Jack still didn't respond.

As he stood there, staring at the stage, Jack was completely still besides the tears that danced at the edges of his eyes. He finally knew the truth — Mother Breanna wasn't coming back.

In a way, he'd known it. He'd known that

he'd never see her again. But seeing what happened to the boy, he knew that she had seen it, too, and that she hadn't been able to handle it.

She really had left. And now he knew why.

"Jack," Lill said again, and she walked back over to the boy, who was a different child than he had been the past few months. That boy had been confident when the rest of the team was not, excited when they felt nervous, and calming when they got over-whelmed. The boy standing in front of her looked terrified and lost, and Lill reached out and put a hand on his shoulder. "It's horrible, I know. But we have to get out of here. Come on."

Jack looked up at Lill, and he could see the sadness in her eyes, but there was strength, too. He nodded. "Thanks," he said, and he followed the rest of the children through the door.

The children stepped into the storeroom behind the auditorium. It was strange — they'd been there an hour ago, and while they'd been nervous, they'd also been excited about what they were about to find out. Now, they moved through the store-room in a panic.

"Why did they do that?" Brat exploded. "What is wrong with them? I can't believe they all just sat there and watched it happen."

"Let's get back downstairs," Gumball said. "We can talk about it later."

Jack walked to the door and opened it slightly. Through the slit, he could see a group of the mothers standing next to the security table. "We'll have to go one by one and quietly," he said.

The others nodded. Shy Perry went first, inching along the wall and quietly opening the stairwell door before slipping inside. He left it ajar, just slightly, as Brat made her way, and then Gumball. Lill was next. She took a look at Jack over her shoulder before she stepped out of the storeroom and walked slowly toward the stairs. When she was safely inside, Jack took a deep breath and stepped out into the hallway.

When he stepped into the stairwell, they all breathed a sigh of relief as he shut the door behind him. The only bit of light in the stairwell was the soft glow that came from the small window in the door to the eighth floor.

"Let's go," Lill said.

"Wait," Jack said. He walked over to where he'd left his warrior behind the stairwell door. He picked it up and held it out to Brat.

"Take this with you. Get down there as quickly as possible, get inside, and make sure you sweep your footprints, okay?" he asked. "And be careful with the squeaky gate."

"Wait, where are you going?" Lill asked.

Jack shook his head, the tears filling his eyes again. "I don't know, but I can't stay here. Not now that I know what happened to Mother Breanna."

"You what?" she hissed.

"You guys go ahead," Jack said. "Don't worry about me."

"I don't want to go either," Brat said softly, and the others turned to look at her. Brat stared at her sister. "I don't want to go back down there."

"Okay, we won't," Gumball said. She looked at Jack. "We're coming with you."

"What are you talking about?" Lill asked. "Where are you going to go?"

"I don't know," Brat said. "There has to be somewhere else we can go."

Lill looked at Perry, and he was wringing his hands together in front of him quickly.

"Perry?" she asked. "What about you?"

"I don't want to stay either."

"Come on, Lill," Jack said. "I know it's scary, but we have to go. After that, how can we stay?"

Lill seemed at a loss, and finally, her shoulders slumped. "How in the world would we get out of here?" she asked.

"Up there," Jack said, pointing to a small ladder on the wall above their heads.

"The roof?" Perry asked.

"It's not the roof," he said. "It's the top floor."

"I thought we were on the top floor," Brat said.

"I heard some of the mothers talking about a ninth floor," Jack said. "They use it for storage. There's also an exit up there. But we have to be quick."

"You had this all planned," Lill said. "You never were planning to go back."

"I wanted the option," Jack said. "I needed it, just in case. You all ready?"

He looked around the small circle in the dim light. Brat and Gumball nodded emphatically. Perry crossed his arms over his chest and gave a quick nod. Lill and Jack stared at each other for a moment, and finally, she took a deep breath and nodded, too.

"Yeah," she said. "Let's get out of here."

# CHAPTER FORTY-ONE

*The Last Day of Emily Lindsey*
*The end*

Emily drove away from the meeting point with both hands on the wheel. She was having a hard time concentrating on the road. She looked back and forth between the open road in front of her and the woman sitting in the seat beside her.

Matilda had changed so much. Where she'd been encouraging, open, a friend before, now she sat sullenly in the passenger seat, her chest heaving up and down, her eyes unfocused. Emily felt bad; she really did. But the woman was nuts. Absolutely psycho.

"I'm only trying to help you, Matilda," Emily said.

Matilda was wearing a jacket, and both hands were shoved into her pockets, and she stared out the window, not speaking.

"We're friends, right?" Emily said.

This got a reaction, Matilda's head whipping to the side to stare at her.

"That's what I thought," Matilda whispered. "I wanted that more than anything."

"We are friends," Emily said, slowing down. She frowned when she saw a car a few feet behind them. It was completely empty on the road, and she slowed down a little more. When the car didn't go by, she had a sinking feeling it was someone from Friends of Frank.

"They really won't let you go anywhere alone, will they?"

Matilda didn't say anything, just continued to stare out the window. "You could've just left me alone," she said softly. "I thought you needed help, that we could help you and make you better. I thought you were my friend."

"Matilda, I am your friend," Emily said. "I've enjoyed getting to know you over the last few months. But that place is dangerous, you have to know that. You can't do what you did. The children, the boys."

"That's in the past," she said. "Don't you think it was hard for me to stay? I stayed because I know that we help people. We help women who need it. That's what Friends of Frank is, and I thought we could help you, too. Why can't you just let it go? If you don't want to be a part of the group, that's fine. But you could just let it go."

"Let what go?" Emily asked, glancing into the rearview mirror again. The car was still there, trailing them. "The fact that you killed nine babies? Maybe more?"

"Shut up!" Matilda said.

"That's not something you let go," Emily said. "I'm telling you, you're a victim here. I know you are, so you can tell them you didn't know anything about it. Tell them that when you joined the group, you were brainwashed, whatever. I really do care about you. I wouldn't be here if I didn't."

With that, she pushed her foot on the accelerator and rocketed her car forward again. In the seat beside her, Matilda gasped, but Emily ignored it. She made a hard right and sped through the dirt roads before turning again through the woods. She turned again and wedged her car into a small cove off the side of the road. Then she turned off the car and her lights and waited.

"What are you doing?" Matilda asked.

"Someone was following us. It was probably one of the men," Emily said. "Don't you understand that it's not okay that they won't let you out of their sight? It's controlling and disgusting, and it's a power thing that's not okay."

Matilda's eyes were wild now, and she looked around them, out the back of the car. "Let me out," she said.

"The door's ope—"

"Let me out!" With that, Matilda pulled out a knife from her pocket.

Emily jerked back. "What are you doing?"

"They told me you were dangerous," Matilda said, her eyes wild. "Let me out of here."

"Like I just told you, the door is open."

Matilda fumbled with the door and opened it. Emily sighed, reaching over to grab her purse and the car key before stepping out to follow her. Matilda had walked around the back of the car and was heading to the main road. Emily hoped that whoever was following them was long gone by now.

"Matilda!" she called out, running after the woman, but she wouldn't stop. "I'm just trying to help you. How come you can't see that?"

The woman kept walking, her small frame stumbling along, and Emily had to stop herself from grabbing her and dragging her back to the car.

"Look, just give yourself up. Come with me now. We'll go to the police. I know where the house is. You'll never get everyone out in time, and you're going down with them.

You can say that you didn't know anything. You can say that you just moved there. Nobody will know! There are no records."

She was just a few feet behind her now, and Matilda had slowed down, but she still wasn't stopping. Emily clenched her fists and stepped closer. "You've been lying this long. What's the harm in telling one more lie?"

Now Matilda stopped, and Emily felt a strong flood of satisfaction wash over her.

"I get it — you needed me to join. You wanted me to join because you thought it would make you normal. Me joining would validate that for you. That's why you started wearing your hair like me, acting like me. You're obsessed with me! You wanted me to join so badly that you made up this whole lie about you having just been pulled in. But that's not true, is it?"

Matilda still didn't move. She stared forward, her shoulders hunched over.

"You've been here much longer than that. You didn't think I'd find out, or at least not this soon, right? You've been here your entire life. You were one of the five who were supposed to escape. What did they call you back then, Lill?"

Still no response.

"What happened to you after all of those

years? You started drinking the Kool-Aid, right? What, you blocked what they did out of your mind because you thought you were helping people? Helping women? That's why you're so obsessed with helping *me*?" Emily reached into her pocket and pulled out the crumpled Post-it Note. "See, what you don't know is that I've started meeting the other five. I met Amanda, and I met a man named Max Smith who was once known as Jack Smith. And soon I'll meet the rest. I'll talk to them all. I'm sorry, Matilda, but you're going to jail. The question is not if. It's for how long."

She paused with the Post-it Note still outstretched as the woman in front of her stayed perfectly still.

"Your whole life has been a lie. You stayed behind to save those kids, and then you became a murderer. Saving me wasn't going to change that. Nothing would."

Emily took a step closer and put a hand on the woman's shoulder.

"Matilda?"

Matilda turned slowly and reached for the Post-it Note. She scanned it slowly before crumpling it and pushing it into her pocket.

And then she moved, whipping around fully, as she pulled her hunting knife out and raised it high above her head.

The fury, sadness, and pain in her eyes were the very last things Emily saw.

# CHAPTER FORTY-TWO

*Then*

The children bolted down the long hallway toward the exit. They didn't know what they'd find at the end of it, but it had to be better than what they were leaving behind.

Jack was at the front of the group, leading the way. He looked back over his shoulder as the others followed him, stumbling along. Brat and Gumball held on to each other while they ran. Perry was a few steps behind them. Lill was in the back, and she was moving more slowly than the rest, still seemingly in a daze.

When he reached the end of the hall and stood in front of the door, Jack turned back. He waited as the twins caught up to him. He frowned as he realized that Lill was slowing down.

"Lill, come on," Jack said as Perry reached his side, breathing heavily. "Come on, we have to go."

But Jack could see that something wasn't quite right.

Lill looked . . . different. Whereas the others looked scared and almost in a panic to get away, the expression on Lill's face was hard to define. She seemed to be moving in slow motion, jogging toward them. As they all stopped and watched her, Lill slowed down even more, and then she was walking toward them, not making eye contact.

"Lill," Jack said, taking a step away from the group and toward her. "Come on," he said, reaching out a hand to her. She'd always acted like a big sister to everyone, so to see her like this was disconcerting for Jack. She seemed to float slowly toward them, her gaze not focused on anything in particular.

"Come on!" Brat said. "They're heading downstairs. They're going to notice that we're missing any moment now, if they haven't already. We have to get out of here."

Suddenly, Lill stopped, and she stared straight ahead, her chest moving up and down.

Jack knew that he was going to have to help her the rest of the way. "Hey," he said softly as he walked up to her. "Are you ready to go? I know you're scared, but we have to get out of here. This is our only chance."

Lill's eyes had filled with tears, and she finally looked down at the younger boy. "Mother Deena," she said.

Jack swallowed. "Yeah, I know you'll miss her —"

"I have to say goodbye to her."

Jack didn't know what to say. He wanted to remind Lill that Deena had been in the auditorium, too. She'd seen what was happening, and she hadn't tried to stop it. But he didn't know if that was a good idea.

"You don't have time to say goodbye to her," Jack said, putting his hand on Lill's arm. "I'm sorry, but we can't go back down there. We have to go out that way."

"No," she said. "I'm sorry about Mother Breanna. I know how you feel. I get it. I just . . . I need to say goodbye to her. It will only take a second. She won't know I'm saying goodbye, but maybe I can meet her in the nursery."

"We don't have time!" Brat said as she gripped her sister's hand. Gumball didn't say anything, and Shy Perry looked down at his feet. "Come on, Lill. We have to go now."

"I'm sorry," she said. "I'll be right back. Please. It will only take a couple of minutes."

With that, she stepped away from Jack and

walked quickly toward the stairwell.

"Lill," Jack called out, but she opened the door and stepped inside.

"I can't believe she left!" Brat said. "What are we supposed to do? Go after her?"

"The more of us that go down, the more of us that might get caught," Gumball said.

"We have to wait for her," Shy Perry said, and everyone looked at him. "Right?"

"Right," Jack said. "We wait."

Lill ran down the stairs, skipping steps as she raced past the eighth floor.

She couldn't believe what they'd just seen. Frank had placed both hands over the sleeping infant's nose, and the entire room had watched as he held it there. The baby woke and fidgeted for a few minutes, and then stopped.

When they lifted him away and wrapped him in a sheet, it was clear that he was dead.

She felt sick, and she leaned forward and threw up in a corner of the stairwell. She took a few deep breaths and then straightened up and kept going.

She couldn't actually talk to Mother Deena; she knew that. But she had to say goodbye somehow. She stepped onto the third floor and headed back toward the nursery. She walked into the small room where she sometimes slept and grabbed her notebook off the night table. She picked up a pen and started to write.

Dear Mother Deena . . .

She told her what she'd seen and how she had to leave. She told her that she loved her and that she needed to get away. She told her that she was sorry and that this was the right thing for her to do. She didn't know what she would find outside, but she couldn't stay here any longer. And she needed Mother Deena to go, too.

*First chance you get, leave this place.*

She was folding the note when she heard a noise.

She looked up, and there was a figure standing there in the doorway.

Ellis.

"Hey," he whispered, looking around.

"What are you doing up here?" Lill asked, using one hand to wipe at the tears on her face.

"I just came to say hi," he said.

"You're not supposed to be up here."

"Kinda funny you saying that," he said. He pointed at the note in her hand. "What's that?"

Lill struggled with what to say. How to

convince him that she had to go, and he had to, too. Ellis always followed the rules; how could she get him to believe her?

She stepped forward.

"It's for Mother Deena," she said. "I . . . We have to leave this place."

"What?" he asked harshly. "What are you talking about?"

"A few of us are upstairs. We found a way out," she said. "Come with us. You don't know what they're doing here. We saw Frank . . ."

Ellis reached forward and grabbed the letter from her hands. Opening it, he scanned it quickly before folding it back. He shook his head. "Lill," he said. "What are you doing? What are you thinking?"

"I —"

"Do you know how much trouble you're in? All of you. How many are up there?"

"Four," she said.

"Who?"

He seemed angry, and Lill couldn't tell if it was at her or about what he'd just learned. Did he believe her?

"Jack, Perry, and the twins."

He seemed to mull it over for a moment, and then his expression changed. And the soft-spoken boy, the one who'd followed her in adoration, disappeared.

"You can't go, Lill."

"What?"

"You can't go. I need you. I . . . I love you."

"Ellis," she said, stepping forward and grabbing his arms. "Come with me. You'll never understand what I saw —"

"I was there," he said.

"What?"

"I was there. Frank asked me to come. He wanted me to see the ceremony. He explained to me why they have to do it. You don't understand, Lill. He's doing it to protect this place."

"What are you talking about?" she asked.

"You don't understand how we are," he said. "Boys. Men. We're responsible for so much of the pain and misery that takes place in our world. It's our nature. Women — you all are not like that. Don't you understand? He has to keep the balance. He has to limit the number of men in our community. It's the only way it works. Women are the key, and there can only be a few special men here to guide them. And I'm one of them."

He said this proudly, and Lill shivered where she stood, the look on his face haunting and sickening. For the first time in her life, Lill saw her home for what it really was, and she wanted to leave. Now.

"I'm going," she said. "If you don't want to come with me, you don't have to. But this is not okay."

She moved to step past him, and he grabbed her arm roughly.

"If you leave, I will wake every adult, and we will come after you. All five of you. There's no way you'll get out of here. They'll catch you. They always do. And you'll all be punished."

Lill could barely breathe, and she cried out as the grip on her arm tightened.

"Or you can stay with me, like you're supposed to. We are supposed to be together, Lill. You know it just as much as I do. If you stay, I won't say anything. The others will get away. Frank never liked Jack anyway, he told me. He just wanted his mom. So let them go, and stay with me. Please."

It wasn't an offer, but he made it sound like one, and Lill felt as if she were suffocating. The sobs escaped her lips, and she stared at him, unable to process what he was saying. But then he made it crystal clear.

"Either you stay and they go, or all of you stay," he said. "It's up to you, Lill."

Her shoulders slumped. She stepped near the door and looked across the hall at the dark nursery where the infants and toddlers were sleeping. She thought about one boy in particular — a one-year-old with dark eyes and a sweet giggle that sounded like a hiccup.

"If I say okay," she said, "you have to let me send up Steve. Please. Let him go."

Ellis didn't say anything for a moment. "Fine," he said, shrugging. "Anything else?"

"What if they send someone back for me? Jack isn't just going to leave me here. They'll go out, and they'll find someone to come back for me."

"You're right," Ellis said, nodding. "That's the other thing. You're going to tell them not to do that."

"What?"

He lifted the note that she'd written for Mother Deena and ripped it in half. "You're going to tell them *not* to," he repeated. "Time for you to write another note."

# CHAPTER FORTY-THREE

*Now*
When will you know that something is wrong?

*A51 . . .*

When will you get help?

When is enough truly enough?

*A51G . . .*

I was hurting, but I couldn't figure out why.

I was sitting at my kitchen table, Nell and Frank on either side of me, and I could see the love, frustration, sadness, and fear on their faces.

"It's time for you to get help," Nell said.

*There was a 3 in there.*

*A351G . . .*

"When will you stop ignoring what's right in front of your face?" Mike asked.

I was hurting — sad that I'd made them feel this way, that I'd disappointed them — and yet finally understanding that they were never going to leave me.

They were never going to send me back.

They'd sit beside me and hurt with me for the rest of my life, if that was what it took.

Mike and Nell were still watching me, but suddenly, their faces began to blur.

"Mom?" I said, but I couldn't see anymore, just a jumble of figures, numbers, and letters. Like the first time I'd had a vision in school, when the numbers on the test in front of me suddenly heaped into a pile. The figures danced in front of my eyes, blocking me from my parents, and I blinked to clear them.

*A351GH.*

I blinked again, and the world turned upside down. I was no longer in my kitchen but lying flat on my back on warm concrete, staring up at the sky, which was blocked by the faces of people looking down on me.

One of the faces got closer, and I recognized Gayla. She leaned close, putting a hand on my shoulder.

"Are you okay?" she asked, her voice a million miles away, too far to be coming out of her mouth, which was only a few inches from my face. "Steven, are you okay?"

I was lying in a pile of my own limbs at the bottom of the stairs, my chin wet from my own saliva, my arm bent beneath me, my legs on fire.

As I shifted my body and rolled over onto my side, the pain was overwhelming, and yet I knew instantly that nothing was broken. Physically, I was indeed okay.

But not in any other way.

"Steve?" Gayla said again.

"No," I finally croaked out, my eyes filling with tears, and for some reason, I think she knew what I meant immediately. "I'm not okay."

"Okay," she said quickly, nodding, her gaze on mine. She looked up at the people hovering around us. "Can you all give him some room, please? Do you need a bus?"

"No, just help me up."

She reached out a hand to pull me up.

I winced as I stood up. "I need to call Brick," I said. "I can't continue to put you in a position where my actions jeopardize your safety."

"You know anyone could have been pushed down those stairs, right?" she said.

"Maybe, maybe not —"

"But I get it. You have some things to work out. Can you at least do it after we catch these guys?"

I frowned. "They got away," I said. "I let them get away."

She nodded. "Yeah, they did. But not for long. We got the plate, and I called it in. Derrick and his team already traced it to an address about an hour away from here."

"Oh wow," I said. "Somebody actually got the plate?"

"Yeah," she said. "You. You were saying it over and over again while you were laid out there." She let out a small laugh when she saw my face. "Come on, let's go. I think we should talk to Brick. He might see things a little bit differently now."

Detective King and his team worked fast.

Ignoring my protests, Gayla took me by the hospital where they decided that a fractured wrist was the worst of my injuries.

"If you experience any headaches or other lasting pain, you need to come back in," the doctor said as I stood up. He put a hand on my arm. "I mean it."

I nodded, and we flew out the door.

By the time we made it to the station, Derrick's teams had already swept the three addresses linked to Ellis Davies, the man who owned the black sedan.

The first location was an empty apartment in the middle of town.

The second was a small county store.

But it was at the third — a four-bedroom

448

house about an hour from the square — that they found the car.

Five men, twelve women, and twenty-two minors. All living in the current Friends of Frank headquarters. The pictures were nauseating. Small cots sandwiched together in the junk-filled home. As we stood in the middle of the station, Derrick filled us in.

"Some of them are talking, and some aren't," he said. "But we've got enough to keep them here for a while. At least three women have already confirmed the ceremonies you told us about. They say they stopped years ago, but these sick mother-fuckers were killing male babies once a year to make sure they didn't 'ruin the community with their innate aggression.' In other words, Frank Davies, and now his son, wanted to make sure that there weren't too many men for them to compete with."

"Amanda said the ceremonies took place every year on June 2," I said. "Anyone give any clues as to why?"

"Yeah," Derrick said. "Apparently, the going story is that Frank Davies accidentally smothered a baby boy who wouldn't stop crying on that day, and something snapped in him. Maybe he realized how easy it was or how it could help him to have one fewer male in the complex. All I know is he was one sick bastard." He turned, rifled through the photos, and pulled a couple out.

"We found this symbol all over the house," he said.

My stomach clenched.

"That's the symbol we saw Emily — I mean, the woman from the hospital — that's what she drew on her body," Gayla said. "Know what it is?"

"Yeah, they say the cross symbolizes the female and the tornado her strength. Frank Davies promoted it as further justification for his sick practices of killing little boys."

I cleared my throat, staring at the photo. "So Ellis Davies is the man who was pretending to be Dan Lindsey."

"Yeah," Derrick said. "Speaking of Dan Lindsey, we finally found him. He took a road trip to Las Vegas with some friends. He and Emily got in a huge fight the week before his trip, and they hadn't been talking to each other or even sleeping in the same room. He thought she was just giving him the silent treatment while he was away."

"Poor guy," Gayla said. "To come back to this. What about the woman from the hospital?"

"Her name is Matilda. Ellis sure has some sort of hold over her. They're in rooms 3 and 4. Neither of them have said a word."

"What about the guy who pushed me down the stairs?" I said. "Did you get him?"

"Yeah. His name is Bill Boyd. He's in 7."

"I want to talk to him."

"I figured you would."

Derrick led me to the back of the station, and I walked inside room 7. The man sitting there looked up at me and narrowed his eyes.

"Why were you following me?" I asked. "Why were you in my wife's — my ex-wife's house?"

He balled his fists on the table but didn't say anything.

"Mr. Boyd?"

"I want a lawyer," he said.

"That's fine," I said. "And you can have one. But it might be a good idea for you to clear some of these things up for me first. It might actually help your case."

He took a deep breath. "I wanted you to let Matilda go. You were holding her hostage at the hospital, pretending like you were worried about her safety —"

"We were worried about *Emily Lindsey's* safety," I corrected him.

"Even so, she needed to get home," he said. "Matilda is an integral part of our community and a very . . . special woman. Ellis had me watching that Emily woman for a while. He always has me learn about the families, lifestyles, and backgrounds of the women who want to join our family. I saw through her right away."

"That's how Ellis knew so much about Emily," I said.

"She was going to destroy our family," Bill said angrily. "I only followed you because I wanted to get Matilda back. I wanted to talk to you, but I didn't really know what to say. 'You've got the wrong woman' didn't seem quite accurate."

"You got that right," I said. "Tell me about your home. I was told by a source that you lived in a much bigger commune. She said it was a building, eight floors or so."

He smiled softly. "We did, a long time ago. But after the children escaped, Frank had us move. We were getting noticed too much, too many people stopping by or trying to get in touch with Frank. We couldn't take the chance that one of those kids would say too much, endanger our family. We had to move."

"What about —"

"Detective," he said, raising a hand to stop me. "My lawyer?"

I sighed and stepped out to find Gayla waiting in the hallway.

"I got nothing from them," she said,

gesturing to rooms 3 and 4.

"Let me try," I said.

I opened the door to room 3 and stepped inside.

The woman, who I now knew was named Matilda, looked up at me, but she didn't say anything.

"Hi, Matilda," I said. "Do you remember me from the hospital?"

She didn't respond.

"Did you know a woman named Emily?" I asked, and I saw her flinch. "Emily Lindsey?"

She still didn't say anything.

"We're going to find out what happened," I said. "We're going to find out why you killed her." I scooted my chair closer to the table. "The man in the other room. Ellis Davies. Did he put you up to it? Did he make you do it?"

"No!" she said angrily. "Ellis would never do that. He's gentle. He ignores his nature. He's not like most men."

"Like most men?" I asked, but she cut me off.

"He protects me. He needed to get back, back to our family, but he stayed with me in that horrible hospital. He's always protected me."

"By killing innocent children?" I asked.

453

"By convincing you to kill Emily?"

"No!" she said. "That wasn't why I did it. I did it to protect our family. Don't you understand? I killed Emily because . . ."

"Because what?" I asked.

She blinked a few times and swallowed. "I loved her. I thought she understood me, that she needed my help. But she just wanted to ruin my family. Don't you understand? My family is all I have."

I heard a noise behind me, and I turned around to see Gayla standing in the doorway next to a woman.

Amanda Pearson. She was standing there, shaking, her eyes trained on the woman sitting in the chair next to me.

"Lill?" she said quietly, and I saw Matilda stare at the woman for a moment before pushing her chair back in shock.

"No . . ." Matilda said.

I stood up. "I'll give you two a moment."

"That's okay, Detective," Amanda said quietly, turning to me. "You can stay. I talked to Max Smith, the other person who Emily was planning on getting in touch with besides you. Turns out I knew Max, too. But not by that name. When I knew him, we called him Jack."

She turned to Matilda as she said this, and the woman's eyes widened.

"He's *okay,* Lill," she said. "He lives in California. He has a wife and a four-year-old. He told me that he talks to Perry, too, every now and then. They're okay."

I watched as Matilda slumped over the table, the sobs erupting from her body. I couldn't tell if she was happy or sad.

"Really," I said. "I'll give you two some time."

"*No,* Detective," Amanda said, turning to me, her eyes trained on mine. "Remember, I told you there were five of us who tried to escape that day. But Lill stayed behind. Instead, she sent up a baby from downstairs with a note that told us if we ever told anyone about Friends of Frank, they'd kill her. I know Ellis made you write that," she said, glaring at Matilda.

"No . . ." the woman said, wiping the tears from her face.

"Yes, he did," Amanda said. "But that little boy, I never knew what happened to him."

"What did?" I asked. "Did Max Smith — or Jack Smith, whatever his name is — tell you? Did he know?"

"He did," she said softly, looking back and forth between Matilda and me. "And, Detective, there's a reason Emily Lindsey had your name in her pocket. I think you should sit down for this part."

# CHAPTER FORTY-FOUR

Here's the thing about finding out you were born in a murderous cult and that the teenage girl who'd sacrificed herself for you more than thirty years ago had grown up to become a murderer herself:

*It changes shit.*

After I left Matilda and Amanda at the station that night, I went home and explained the whole thing to a horrified Mike and Nell. I didn't leave out a single detail, and we cried together over the phone. The next morning, I called Mary and Brick, and by the afternoon, I'd completed the paperwork for my official leave of absence.

"It's the right thing to do," Brick had said, and I saw the first ever crack in his stony demeanor. "We'll miss you, but we'll see you back here soon."

Gayla and I had gone out for lunch a couple of days later, and in typical Gayla fashion, she talked about everything else under the sun before getting down to the matter at hand.

"Whoever Brick assigns as my partner while you're out had better dream about something interesting. Otherwise, what are we going to have to talk about?" she asked, and then she paused, shaking her head. "Sorry. Bad joke. Um, so . . . are you okay?"

"Yeah," I said with a small smile. "It's different now that I know there's a reason for all of it, for the nightmares, the visions . . . It changes things, you know?"

"Yeah," she said. "I bet. So what are you going to do?"

"Well, I'm starting therapy again," I said. "I've tried it before but never really stuck with it. And I'm actually going to start going to Amanda Pearson's weekly sessions at the church."

"Oh, wow, really?"

"Yeah, I went last night. It wasn't so bad."

Amanda hadn't seemed at all surprised when I showed up the night before — in fact, she'd raced into my arms and given me a long hug before stepping back. "I'm glad you're here," she had said.

I had settled into a seat as she began to speak in front of the small group.

"Thank you all for coming," she had said. "This is an open forum, and I invite you all

458

to talk as little or as much as you want. I'll start by telling you a little about someone very close to me. My sister, Gloria. We called her Gumball, because she used to always chew gum as a kid," she said with a smile.

Amanda had cleared her throat and continued. "She was a wonderful woman and a wonderful sister. I lost her a couple of years ago, and trust me, I still have a lot of questions about what I could have done differently. I know that some of you in this room are caretakers, and you might be feeling the same way. The goal here for everyone is to make sure you understand that you're not alone and you don't have to hide anymore. Because believe me, hiding your pain is the hardest part."

She had paused for a moment, and our eyes connected before she looked away.

"So," she had said. "Who wants to start?"

I told Gayla about the session during our lunch, and she smiled. "So were you the one to start?" she asked.

"No," I said. "But maybe next time."

As we stood up to leave, Gayla put a hand on my arm. "Hey, if you ever want me to come with you to those sessions or to anything else, you'll let me know, right?"

"Yeah," I said, giving her a hug. "I will."

"What are you doing later tonight?" she asked suddenly, and I could tell that she was still worried. "Want to come over for dinner? Kevin is making his famous steak and potatoes, and we can eat out on the patio, have some wine —"

"Can we do it next week?" I asked. She frowned, and I followed up quickly. "I'm not putting you off," I said. "I just have something to do tonight."

"On a Sunday night?"

I nodded. "Next week, though, okay? I mean it."

She bit her bottom lip and nodded as we walked out of the restaurant.

Late that afternoon, I did have something to do. I stood outside of Kit's school and watched as families filtered in through the front door for the play.

It was already five thirty, and the play started at six. I knew that Kit and Lara were probably already inside somewhere. I waited near the bottom of the stairs. A few minutes later, just as I expected, I saw Greg hurrying across the street and heading in my direction. He stopped in his tracks when he saw me, a look of exhaustion on his face.

"Really, man —" he started.

But I cut him off. "I'm not here to cause any problems," I said. "I just want you to give something to Kit."

Greg frowned and stepped closer.

I reached into my pocket and pulled out the small black-and-white race car that I'd taken from my nightstand that morning. "He used to love this growing up," I said, shrugging. "He's really nervous about his performance today. I just thought it might calm him down a little."

He didn't move, and I reached out farther, pushing the car closer to him. "Please, man. Just say you found it in the house some-where. You don't have to tell him I was here."

"So you're not coming in?"

"No," I said. "And I'll lay off for a while. Lara doesn't want me around right now, and I have to respect that. And you're right: Kit will be okay, for now. He has her, and . . . he has you."

Greg's jaw tightened, and he took a deep breath. He reached out his hand and took the car. "I'll give it to him," he said. "Where's this sudden change of heart com-ing from?"

"Not a change of heart," I said. "Just figuring some things out."

"About the visions?"

I tensed up and took a step back. "That's not your place, man."

He raised both hands, the race car still in one of them. "You're right, it's not. But you do know that it's Lara's place, right?"

I narrowed my eyes but didn't say anything.

He sighed. "All I'm saying is that you should talk to her. I know you think she left you because of the nightmares and stuff, but it wasn't that."

I froze. "What are you talking about?" I asked. "Of course it was —"

"No," he said. "Lara left because you weren't willing to get help. You let her feel like you were letting her in by telling her about it right away — then you never wanted to talk about it again. Never wanted to actually address it. Every time she tried to talk about it, you'd either get upset or make a joke about it. You were scared and defensive, and she couldn't get through to you. You loved her because she made you feel like everything was okay, but everything *wasn't* okay. That's why she left. She could deal with the nightmares, Steve. She couldn't deal with the fact that *you* couldn't."

"How do you know all of this?" I whispered, and I cursed myself for being so weak in front of him.

"How do you think?" he asked. "Because

462

she's told me. She talks about it all the time. It eats her up, this thing with you and Kit. But if she knew that you were actually trying to get help, actually working on it, maybe she'd change her mind about you coming around."

I swallowed. "Would you . . . any chance you could talk —"

"Yeah, I'll talk to her. Just keep trying to figure out your shit. Nobody said it was easy." He lifted the car. "I'll go give this to him."

I nodded. "Thanks," I said before turning to head to my car.

I'd gotten halfway across the street when he stopped me.

"Hey," he said, and I turned back. He was spinning the car quickly in his hands. "Look, Lara likes to sit in the first or second row on the right side of the stage. I don't know why the right side. She thinks it's the better view."

"Okay," I said slowly. "So what?"

"I'm just saying, it's a pretty big auditorium."

I blinked, unsure I'd heard him correctly. "You mean —"

"I mean, I know how important this is to you." He stared me straight in the eye and stopped spinning the car. "If someone were sitting in the back on the same side . . . All I'm saying is, I doubt she'd see them." With that, he turned and walked up the steps into the school.

I stood there for a moment watching his back, and for some idiotic reason, tears welled up in my eyes. It wasn't the first time I'd almost cried in front of green thumb Greg, and it took me a few moments to pull myself together.

Finally, I took a deep breath.

*"Levisy tay-glees,"* I muttered to myself before darting up the steps behind him and slipping through the school's front door.

# READING GROUP GUIDE

1. Why does Steve try to hide the nightmares and visions from everyone he loves?

2. How does hiding them both help and hurt him?

3. What rhetoric did Frank use to justify the annual sacrifice to the other adults? What was his real reason for the sacrifices?

4. Jack, Brat, Gumball, Shy Perry, and Lill all have very different personalities. How do the children each show leadership in their own way?

5. What was each child's biggest weakness?

6. What role does *Carmen Street Confessions* play in Emily's life?

7. Why was Lill drawn to Emily? Why was

she so disappointed when she learned Emily's true intentions?

8. Why does Emily continue to pursue the story about Friends of Frank, even when it becomes dangerous?

9. Steve is finally working to address his nightmares. Do you think Lara will change her mind about his involvement in Kit's life?

# A CONVERSATION
# WITH THE AUTHOR

**How did you come up with the idea for**
*The Last Day of Emily Lindsey*?

It started with the idea of a woman who sits down on her couch and just completely shuts off. I had the idea one day when I was pretty much doing exactly that — I'd had a long day at work, I was tired, and I did the thing where you just sink down on the couch and shut down for the night. I started thinking about a story where that shut-down period lasts the entire night, and then the next day, and the one after that. Granted, when I did it, I wasn't covered in blood; that idea came later.

**Your first novel,** *Boy, 9, Missing,* **also contained two distinct story lines set during two different time periods. What's your process for creating stories with this structure? Do you write them**

**separately or together?**

Together. I generally know the arc for each story line in advance. But I still write the book in a linear fashion. I'll often scribble notes for later chapters if I'm writing one section and don't want to forget something. But I like to write these types of stories in the order and way that they'll be read; it just works better that way for me.

**What do you want readers to learn from Steve's journey?**

Steve thinks that he's protecting the people he loves — his parents, his wife, his partner — from himself by hiding his problems from them. But, of course, he's not doing as good of a job hiding them as he thinks he is, which only serves to hurt his family even more. By the end of the novel, he starts to learn that they're all with him for the long haul — even his ex-wife's new husband! — and that the best thing he can do is start to address his very serious issues with them by his side.

**Do you ever write characters based on real people?**

I haven't based a character completely on someone I know, but there are elements of friends and family in most of them. For example, Brat and Gumball definitely resemble myself and my older sister. Growing up, she was always the responsible one, while I was the type to run around with a bucket on my head until I toppled over.

**When deciding on an idea for your next novel, how do you filter the good ideas from the bad?**

I keep a running list of story ideas on my iPhone. I check it on a regular basis. The bad ones tend to linger there for months or even years until they get erased (either accidentally, or on purpose). The good ones keep bubbling to the top until I finally take a stab at outlining them or writing a first chapter. You never really know which ones are good ideas, only that some stay with you for a long time and at least deserve a shot at becoming something more.

**Do you write every day?**

Yes and no. When I get into a groove, I'll sit down to write every day — several times a day, if I can find the time. When I'm *not* in a groove, my writing habits are a lot more spotty.

**For your own reading, do you prefer**

**ebooks or traditional paper/hardback books?**

About a year ago, I would've said traditional printed books, for sure! But I've had to travel a lot in the past year and have gotten pretty close with my e-reader. So, I'd say it doesn't really matter at this point — I'll take a good story any way I can get it!

# ACKNOWLEDGMENTS

Thanks to the incredible Sourcebooks team for knowing books and lovers of books so well, to Shana Drehs and Lathea Williams for their incredible guidance and vision, and to my agent, Barbara Poelle, for being the very best of the best.

To my friends and family: there are not enough words to express my gratitude for all the love, texts, emails, squees, happy dances, and overall support you've shown throughout the past year. It has been nothing short of amazing. Seems most appropriate to just say thank you, thank you, thank you, *thank you.*

# ABOUT THE AUTHOR

**Nic Joseph** is the author of *Boy, 9, Missing*. She writes thrillers and suspense novels from her home in Chicago. As a trained journalist, Nic has written about everything from health care and business to aerospace and IT — but she feels most at home when there's a murder to be solved on the next page. Nic holds a bachelor's degree in journalism and a master's in communications, both from Northwestern University. For more information, visit NicJoseph.com or follow her on Twitter @nickeljoseph.

The employees of Thorndike Press hope you have enjoyed this Large Print book. All our Thorndike, Wheeler, and Kennebec Large Print titles are designed for easy reading, and all our books are made to last. Other Thorndike Press Large Print books are available at your library, through selected bookstores, or directly from us.

For information about titles, please call:
(800) 223-1244

or visit our website at:
gale.com/thorndike

To share your comments, please write:
Publisher
Thorndike Press
10 Water St., Suite 310
Waterville, ME 04901